Sorcery in Shad

TOR BOOKS BY BRIAN LUMLEY

TALES OF THE PRIMAL LAND
The House of Cthulhu
Tarra Khash: Hrossak!
Sorcery in Shad

THE NECROSCOPE® SERIES
Necroscope   *The Last Aerie*
Necroscope: Vamphyri!   *Bloodwars*
Necroscope: The Source   *Necroscope: The Lost Years*
Necroscope: Deadspeak   *Necroscope: Resurgence*
Necroscope: Deadspawn   *Necroscope: Invaders*
Blood Brothers   *Necroscope: Defilers*
Necroscope: Avengers

THE TITUS CROW SERIES
Titus Crow, Volume One: The Burrowers Beneath & The Transition of Titus Crow
Titus Crow, Volume Two: The Clock of Dreams & Spawn of the Winds
Titus Crow, Volume Three: In the Moons of Borea & Elysia

THE PSYCHOMECH TRILOGY
Psychomech
Psychosphere
Psychamok

OTHER NOVELS
Demogorgon   *Maze of Worlds*
The House of Doors   *Khai of Khem*

SHORT STORY COLLECTIONS
Fruiting Bodies and Other Fungi
The Whisperer and Other Voices
Beneath the Moors and Darker Places
Harry Keogh: Necroscope and Other Weird Heroes!

Sorcery in Shad

TALES OF THE PRIMAL LAND, VOLUME 3

BRIAN LUMLEY

TOR®

A TOM DOHERTY ASSOCIATES BOOK

NEW YORK

SORCERY IN SHAD: TALES OF THE PRIMAL LAND, VOLUME 3

Copyright © 1991 by Brian Lumley

Previously published in 1991 by Headline Book Publishing PLC, London, UK.

This book is printed on acid-free paper.

A Tor Book
Published by Tom Doherty Associates, LLC
175 Fifth Avenue
New York, NY 10010

www.tor.com

Tor® is a registered trademark of Tom Doherty Associates, LLC.

Library of Congress Cataloging-in-Publication Data

Lumley, Brian.
    Sorcery in Shad / Brian Lumley.—1st ed.
        p. cm.—(Tales of the primal land ; v. 3)
    "A Tom Doherty Associates book."
    ISBN-13: 978-0-765-31077-4 (acid-free paper)
    ISBN-10: 0-765-31077-5 (acid-free paper)
    I. Title. II. Series: Lumley, Brian. Tales of the primal land ; v. 3.

PS6062.U45S65 2006

                                            2006044549

First Tor Edition: September 2006

Printed in the United States of America

0 9 8 7 6 5 4 3 2 1

FOR ANYONE WHO EVER WISHED HE OR SHE HAD
A FLYING CARPET, AND ALSO FOR THE HECK OF IT!

CONTENTS

Prologue

ABSENT FROM HIS place in Klühn for five long years, at last Teh Atht had come home. But he'd returned empty-handed, his quest cut short by word of a strange curse befallen his beloved sophisticate city on Theem'hdra's eastern strand. And he'd returned angry in the knowledge of five years utterly wasted, which had been better spent in more pleasurable or at least profitable pursuits.

In many guises and by mazy, tortuous route, Teh Atht had crossed and recrossed Theem'hdra from the Paps of Mam to Tharamoon, from the Teeth of Yibb to Grypha on its swampy promontory overlooking the Bay of Monsters. He had wandered in the Nameless Desert, abided awhile upon a jewelled isle in the mighty Crater Sea, sojourned and studied with sorcerous colleagues throughout all the length and breadth of the Primal Land, but to no avail. That which he sought ever eluded his grasp, which for all his magicks large and small came no closer to solution.

In cold and lonely Tharamoon, bleak in the Chill Sea 'twixt Frostlands and the nameless Northern Peaks, he'd dwelled a year in the crumbling manse of that once mightiest of mages Mylakhrion, searching in the rubble and ruin of centuries for a clue and discovering naught; and in the Desert of Sheb he'd likewise lingered in lamia's castle, hoping to discover in Orbiquita's absence some small pointer to that which he pursued—in vain.

The demons and djinn of the deserts could not or would not assist; dryads and naiads alike deemed it unwise to dabble; even the weed-crowned Krakens called up from deeps of ocean turned away and submerged themselves when confronted with Teh Atht's quest and query. They said they did not know, and perhaps they spoke the truth, and anyway the wizard was loath to use threats and thaumaturgies upon them. For Teh Atht deemed himself a white as opposed to black magician, and his reputation was a kindly one.

Then, in the tropical forests of the coast east of Thinhla—beneath the vine-entwined ruins of some city unremembered of man, where Ahorra Izz, the scarlet scorpion-god, guarded his toppled temple, in conversation with that most ireful arachnid—there Teh Atht first heard of the encroaching DOOM which even now threatened Klühn and its people, and the home he had builded there on a bluff above the bay. And this information was delivered, in doleful clacking voice, by none other than Ahorra Izz himself, who said:

"Have you done with picking my brains, wizard? For if so there's that which you should know, concerning that hive of prideful men which is your home, that city on Theem'hdra's eastern strand called Klühn."

"Klühn?" Teh Atht at once looked up from where he sat, trickling a world's ransom in rubies (all worthless to him) through his fingers upon a roseate floor. He frowned. "And what of Klühn, pray? And if indeed there's aught of which I should be appraised, tell me also how come you're so farsighted, and all shut in down here beneath the sunless jungle floor?"

Ahorra Izz chuckled, a hideous rasping sound in Teh Atht's mind, but stirred not at all before his visitor. Indeed, how could he? For he was a statue of polished stone half as tall again as a man, all seemingly carved from a single block, like some great gleamy fossil! And his eyes were rubies big as fists; and his scythe-like stinger, poised on high, was sheathed in some silver metal whose fashioning was a secret lost in time and space. But by virtue of Teh Atht's magick he spoke, albeit in the mage's mind alone. And this is what he said:

" 'What' can wait, 'how' comes now. Myriad minion members have I; they scurry in the forests, thrive in the deserts and on the steppes, stay moist beneath the rim of rock and hunt under the moon. Now what say you, Teh Atht? How do you answer my riddle?"

The wizard uncrossed his legs, stood up and stretched. "Scorpions, of course. The green jungle scorpion, the rock scorpion of the uplands, the black desert scorpion and its grey cousin of Hrossa's steppes—but especially the scarlet scorpion of legend. And all make report to you, eh, here in immemorial vault?" But for all his yawn and careless shrug, still Teh Atht marvelled. With familiars far-flung and numerous as these, was any secret safe in all the Primal Land? Would that such an army worked for him! "And what have they told you, the scorpions of Klühn's alleys and secret temples?" he pressed.

"They have told me how in your long absence a strange sect is come into Klühn," Ahorra Izz answered, "and whisper of yellow-robed priests in a temple of terror! Their leader is one Gorgos—perhaps a man—but the 'gods' he worships are not of this world. Indeed, they are not gods!

Demons of the star-spaces, the Thromb wait on Gorgos to open up the gates for them!"

Gorgos! And now Teh Atht gasped aloud—even Teh Atht, descendant of Mylakhrion! He had heard of that most monstrous necromancer, of course, and had thought him long dead. But alive? In Klühn? Calling down the Thromb from the spaces between the stars? Life itself—*all* life—were forfeit, come to a terrible termination, should he succeed. Panic struck at Teh Atht's heart, but only for a moment. Then a thought occurred. He stood stock still, stared up at scorpion statue, peered into its scintillant ruby eyes.

"Could it be you've tired of my presence here and grown weary of my questions? This disclosure of yours could well be a clever ruse, by means of which you're rid of me; for of course you know that I must now hie me to my manse in Klühn, and there weave works against this Gorgos."

"Go in peace, Teh Atht," the horror clacked. "And by all means return one day . . . if any days are left! I have enjoyed your visit."

And then the wizard felt that indeed the cancer in Klühn was no mere figment of fancy, and he felt the bitter winds of space blowing on his soul. "I get me gone at once," he muttered, and made to climb stone stairs.

"Wait!" cried Ahorra Izz. "A further tidbit you should know. There are three who work against this High Priest, this Gorgos who some say *is* a man. And one of this brave trio *is* a man! What's more, I like him!" He chuckled in his weird way. "How's *that* for a riddle, O wizard?"

Teh Atht gathered up his rune-inscribed cloak, paused briefly at the foot of the stairs. "I'll answer it when next I visit," he said.

Ahorra Izz uttered his doleful chuckle. "Ah, ever the

optimist!" he said. "So be it." But Teh Atht was no longer
there to hear him . . .

IN HIS ONE hundredth and forty-third year, but sprightly for
all that, Teh Atht climbed the subterranean temple's stairs of
stone toward jungle's floor. Weighed down by dreads half-
formed and preoccupied with hasty planning, he forged
willy-nilly through curtains and ropes of smoking cobwebs
and stirred up dust of centuries unnumbered in his hurried
ascent. Across great landings where stood lesser likenesses
of Ahorra Izz, under vaulted ceilings all palpitant with myriad massed forms of the green-eyed pyramid bat, ever toward the tumbled ruins above he strove, and one thought
uppermost in his mind: that even now in Klühn a foulness
named Gorgos sought to rain Madness and Death upon an
unsuspecting Primal Land.

Finally he reached the surface, came out from the arched
entrance of a slumped ziggurat into bowels of foliage ram-
pant. And dizzy from his climb and fetor of the vaults both,
he paused awhile to breathe deep and blink in the emerald
light, what little of it filtered down through the high canopy
of vine and creeper and leprous orchid cluster. And he gazed
all about upon the jungle-hid ruins and considered his position: literally, his *location,* all these twenty hundreds of miles
from his beloved Klühn.

East of Thinhla, this place, tropical forest on the coast situ-
ated between unknown river morasses a-teem with leeches,
crocodiles and cannibal fishes; where even the vegetation—
some of it, anyway—was lethal, bearing spines and suckers
all charged with potent poisons. Barriers entirely natural
and wholly unnatural stood between Teh Atht and civilized

sophisticate city; and yet, where other men might at once give up the ghost, lie down and die, the wizard merely considered his options. And they were several.

He could set out at once, in the way of more nearly normal men, and simply trek the jungle—and die, most assuredly, in the space of one hundred yards. Hardly a feasible option, that! He could abide here until darkness descend, then call down a grim of night-gaunts to fly him home; except he'd never much trusted gaunts, which were known to have a certain affinity with Yibb-Tstll, a dark god of monstrous appetites.

If he'd brought his carpet of levitation with him, then that would bear him home; but jungle-spawned rots were ruinous to fabrics delicate as that, and so he'd left his flying carpet home. On solid ground, he might simply infuse his boots with powers of league-long striding; but alas the morass was treacherous, and sad thing to step down from stride of several leagues into gluey, bottomless bog! No, more subtle magicks were required here.

He reverted to that spell beloved of Sheb's desert djinn, by means of which he'd landed himself here in the first place; a magick requiring four entire days and a deal of concentration in its construction. And thus, last rune uttered and final pass performed—transforming himself to single tuft of thistledown, and simultaneously conjuring out of the clouds a dust-devil to bend down among the treetops—he contrived to have himself picked up and whirled in a trice back home to Klühn.

Journey of months and years accomplished in minutes, before he spiralled down and expanded once more into a man on the topmost balcony of his tower overlooking the Bay of Klühn, and there he reeled awhile under the first stars of night as nodding dust-devil raced away toward windy wastes of desert.

And so Teh Atht returned home.

Staggering there atop that high place, still dizzy from his flight, he leaned upon parapet wall and gazed toward Klühn—and immediately grew still, shocked rigid by what he saw. Which was this:

That all the people were at play in the streets where multi-hued lanterns bobbed, and apparently no DOOM befallen, and indeed an air of great merry-making and rejoicing abundantly displayed! What? And had that double-damned deity of an arachnid tricked him after all? If the only curse visited upon Klühn were merriment, then what the loss?

Raging, he swept inside, sought out his familiars three to question them—and only then remembered how, five years ago before taking his departure, because he could not trust them, he'd immobilized all three with the curse of Curious Concretion. In stony state, they'd know nothing of matters transpired in Klühn; but finding them in their places, certainly no worse for wear however dusty, he immediately unspelled them anyway. There was one who hopped, one who flitted, and one that flowed like a pool of oil and served mainly to lubricate the works of Teh Atht's astrologarium, wherein swam miniature stars and worlds and moons important in the wizard's forecasting.

"You, and you," said Teh Atht, wagging a finger at the former pair, hopper and flitter, "to work! What? Do spiders dwell here now? Has someone bequeathed me a desert in my absence, and delivered it to boot? Make all tidy, at once! And you!" he dabbled a finger in the liquid one. "Go oil something . . . no, wait! Float me my shewstone down to the kitchen, where doubtless affairs are likewise disordered!"

Grumbling in their way, the three set to work while Teh Atht stomped to kitchen and revitalized ancient foods, and fried up a pan of cheese and onions. And while he ate ravenously, so his crystal ball came drifting on a pool of sentient oil; and now past the food in his mouth the wizard mumbled a rune of recounting. Up the leg of his table crept viscous retainer, balancing the shewstone on tip of sticky pseudopod and finally slumping to rest beyond Teh Atht's plate, where he could observe and eat at one and the same time. The milky sphere had slowly cleared, and now Teh Atht commanded: "Tell me about Gorgos. Was he here; if so when, and why? Show me all, without delay!"

And bending to his will as always, the shewstone obeyed . . .

Pictures appeared in the clear crystal—sharp and real as life but fast-fleeting, so that they showed much in a short space of time—according to Teh Atht's instructions.

It had started five years ago, shortly after he set out upon his fruitless quest, when the first yellow-robed members of Gorgos' priesthood had commenced to arrive in Klühn from far-flung parts. From Thinhla, Eyphra, Thandopolis they had come, bearing the strange ikons and instruments of their faith. Close to Klühn's heart they'd bought land, built a temple of hemispheres with one massive central dome of copper, a task which had kept the city's artisans in work for all of four years. Ah, but long before the work was finished, then, too, had Gorgos installed himself within his Temple of Secret Gods. And rumour had it he'd brought a female creature with him: a girl-thing of rare beauty, however alien, combheaded and with shimmery silver skin. But only rumour, for she was never seen.

By means of an alleged "oracle," then the necromancer began to work blackmail upon the city's businessmen, its taverners, jewellers, merchants, using such ill-gotten gains to buy his priests, workmen, and finally soldiers! So that soon the entire city was in his grip, where none could escape the oracle's probing, the narrowed, penetrating eyes of the yellow-robes, the glaring and swaggering of armoured fighting men. But as if blackmail and other threats weren't enough, the master of that dire sect had a second trump card which no one could deny: magick, and a black and ominous magick at that!

For now the people found themselves levied of a tax, which they must pay in respect of the "protection" they received from Gorgos and his priesthood against . . . against what? Against dark forces which even now threatened to devour Klühn utterly, given shape and form in monthly manifestations of weird energies in the sky! Boiling clouds and strange lightnings, aye, and doomful luminous hell-webs on high, whose forces seemed mercifully (?) bled off by temple's copper dome, or deflected by the devotions of droning priests. For Klühn had sinned, apparently, and was now taken to task, which was why this Temple of Secret Gods had been builded here: to hold at bay a scourge and keep the city safe.

So said the priests; but common people wondered: what sin had they committed? And were the priests here to combat evil, or had it merely followed them, as fleas follow a dog?

"Hold!" cried Teh Atht, done with his food and impatient now. "I know most of this, and also that Gorgos would call down the Thromb, which were the end of everything! But quite obviously he was stopped. I know something of that, too. Three creatures put paid to his scheme for immortality as Lord of the Thromb, one of which was a man. Very well, now show me these three, for they interest me . . ."

And again the shewstone obeyed:

First there was the silver-skinned lass Gorgos brought with him to the temple in Klühn: his oracle, a Suhm-yi female gifted as all her race had been with the power of reading minds. Thus had Gorgos blackmailed Klühn. Stolen by the monster as a child and spirited away from her home in the jewelled isles of the Crater Sea, she had helped (however unwillingly) in the elevation of her master to great power. Ah, and also in his downfall! Teh Atht saw it all in his shewstone.

For now, come out of those same jewelled isles, a *male* Suhm-yi in search of a mate. Amyr Arn, his name, the last of his race other than Gorgos' she-creature—and his strange heart bent on vengeance! Not only would he take back Ulli Eys to where they both belonged, but if he could he'd put down her cruel master, too, and thus end forever the threat of the Thromb.

Recruiting to his cause a man—a common man, and yet extraordinary, too, in his way—the last Suhm-yi male had entered Gorgos' temple of terror to sabotage his plans. And none too soon! Just five nights ago, this had been, when the heavens were ablaze with eerie Thromb coruscations, and the temple's central dome gleamed orange and gold and colours all unknown in supernatural light from cauldron sky. Dressed in stolen or counterfeit robes of yellow, impersonating the temple's priests, Suhm-yi and colleague had smuggled themselves within, and—

But here the shewstone faltered; its picture faded and

merged into mist, and the very crystal seemed suddenly filled with a roiling motion. A thaumaturgical turbulence, of course! Such had been the forces at work that night in and around Gorgos' temple that lesser magicks simply could not function.

"Peace!" said the wizard, fearing his shewstone might shatter. "Enough—for now. Well done!" And the whirlpool mists grew calm and quickly congealed, and the crystal sat there in its pool of living oil like some great luminous pearl.

Teh Atht scratched his narrow chin. "Just three of them," he mused. "Suhm-yi man and maid, and a roughneck off the streets. Against Gorgos, priests, soldiers and Thromb energies? Remarkable! Indeed, incredible!" And out loud to the shewstone: "What remained when all was done? Show me that, if you can—but not if it's discomforting."

The crystal cleared, a picture appeared, and Teh Atht gazed upon a familiar scene. Klühn near its centre, where Gorgos' Temple of Secret Gods had reared its copper domes and received its dark tribute from beyond the stars: now a high-walled square of gaunt ruins, shunned, where not even the weeds would grow!

The wizard tapped his fingernail on table-top and the scene slowly faded. "Suhm-yi man, maid, and one other . . ." He frowned. "Where are the silver-skins now?"

The crystal showed him: they trekked the plains west in the dusk, heading for their homeland in the isles of the Crater Sea. And there was a joy in them where he led, and she sat upon their yak with her hand on his upon the beast's neck. Teh Atht felt glad and nodded.

"And one other," he mused again. "Is he in the city still, this other? If so, show him to me." He waited, but no picture formed. "Gone then, but gone where? I have to know, for there's more to this one than meets the eye—even the all-seeing eye of a shewstone!"

And so Teh Atht uttered the rune of Sustained Scrying, propping his pointed chin in cupped hands the better to see what he might see. And indeed he saw a great deal . . .

I

Chance Encounter

"YOUR GOLD OR your gizzard!" hoarse, desperate voice called out through sooty twilight, from bushes at the foot of the bottleneck up ahead, where the pass cut through a stony cleft. "I can slit either your purse or your throat, so take your pick—only quick now, 'cos my finger's itchy on the trigger of this crossbow!"

"Hold!" the lone camel rider sent back a shout, reined in his jittery beast. "Now hold there, friend!" He made a dusky silhouette against the indigo sky with its first fistful of stars. And he'd have made a fine target, too, *if* his ambusher had a crossbow! That wasn't the case, but no way the rider could know it.

"Put up your hands," the would-be thief now commanded, "so's I can see there's no weapon in 'em."

"What?" his intended victim replied. "And would you really take a man's life for nothing? Highwayman, you've picked a wrong 'un tonight, I'm afraid—where loot's concerned, anyway. Man, I'm broke! So stay your hand on that weapon. I've a loaf we can share, if you like, and a skin of passable wine. But that's all . . ."

The ambusher's ears pricked up: he was *starving!* And there was something in this lone wayfarer's voice, too. Memories stirred, of a time not too far past in Chlangi the Doomed . . ."Who are ye, sitting there so nice in my sights?" he hoarsely inquired.

Astride his camel, the Hrossak tried to locate the other; no good, he was a shadow in the darker shadows of the bushes. But where- and whoever he was, his voice had seemed strangely familiar. He could be any one of a dozen brigands the rider had tangled with along his mazy way.

The steppeman had put his hands up on the other's barked instructions; but behind the right one, hanging down along his wrist from a point trapped between index and next finger, a balanced knife poised for swift release. Only let him get a precise fix on his ambusher's whereabouts, and—

"What's your name, I said?" the furtive owner of the gruff voice once more demanded.

"I'm a Hrossak," the rider replied, shifting a little in his saddle. Was that a movement there in the bushes, by the bole of that gnarly tree? Aye, it was that—the outline of a crouching man! "Khash, by name, after my father, naturally," he continued, letting his throwing arm drift back a little, "—though the gods alone know why, for he never had any either!"

A gasp from the gloom. "Tarra Khash!"

Tarra threw himself forward and out of the saddle, threw his knife, too. Only at the last, hearing that gasp and the other speaking his name, had he managed to deflect knife's flight—else the lurker in the bushes were a goner. Then he was rolling in dust, hurling himself headlong into the blackest shadows, snarling his rage in the darkness even as he snaked the curved ceremonial sword from its scabbard strapped to his back.

In another moment he crashed through brittle bushes, found a boulder and slid himself over to its safe side, there came to a crouching halt . . . Close at hand, a wheezy, frightened panting. The Hrossak listened, grinned a humourless wolf's grin, called out: "And now it's your turn, friend. Seems you know me, which might or might not be a good thing. So in the dozen or so heartbeats you've left to live, best tell me who you are. That way I'll be able to say a few words over you, to let the gods know who I'm passing their way."

"Stumpy," the unseen other gasped at once. "Stumpy Adz, great lump! So called for a missing right hand—aye, and very nearly an ear, too! Come free me, quick! I daren't move my head for fear I slice my neck!"

Tarra took his first real breath in what felt like hours, lofted his scimitar and sheathed it unerringly in its scabbard, so that its jewelled hilt stood up behind his left shoulder where it curved into his neck. He put a hand on the boulder and vaulted it, glided soundlessly into the bushes and up to the twisted bole of the gnarly tree. And sure enough there stood Stumpy Adz, his head immobilized between a rough branch and the long, thin, razor-edged blade of Tarra's knife where it pinned his tatty collar to the bole.

"Old fool!" growled Tarra, snatching his knife free—but minding it didn't cut Stumpy's leathery flesh. "Some desperado you—*hah*! And what if it hadn't been me at all but some nighthawk, eh? And what if *he* really did have a crossbow? Indeed, a miracle of coincidence that it *is* me! Now what's this all about? What, you, a highwayman? At your age? And why the hell anyway? The last time I saw you, in Chlangi, I gave you gems to last a lifetime . . ." Eyes growing accustomed to the dusk, he glowered at the other, noticed his scrawny,

down-at-heel condition. Stumpy was thin and bent as old
Gleeth the crescent moon where he rode above the ridge.

"First you'd try to skewer me," the old man grumbled,
gingerly fingering his unmarked neck, then sighing his relief
when his fingers came away clean, "and now you'd have
me talk myself to death—if you don't beat me to it! Well, I'll
cut it short, Tarra Khash: hard times, my friend, hard times—
which called for harsh measures. I knew I took a chance,
but better dead than marooned out here, miles from anywhere, and slowly shrivelling to bones!"

Tarra noticed Stumpy's leanness, couldn't mistake his
trembling, which wasn't alone reaction to his narrow escape.
He whistled for his beast, which came at the trot. "Are you
hungry, Stumpy Adz?"

The other groaned. "Hungry? I could eat the saddle right
off your mount's back! Or you can keep the saddle and I'll
wrap my gums round the camel instead!"

Over his own shock now, Tarra grinned. "Well, you fed
and sheltered me once when I was in need." He grasped the
other's frail shoulder. "So I suppose it's only fair I return the
favour. Where can we make camp?"

Stumpy wearily led him to the face of the cliff, showed
him a shallow cave—more a scoop out of the rock—where a
great boulder had rolled free in ages past. Indeed the very
boulder lay shattered now, a broken wall of jagged rock
fronting the cave, which should shelter their fire and hide
its light. "I was going to sleep the night here," said Stumpy.
"With a little luck I'd wake with the morning, and with a
great deal of luck I wouldn't!"

Tarra tethered his camel, started to gather up dry sticks
and dead branches. But:

"Who needs a fire?" Stumpy muttered. "I've got my own, burning through the wall of my stomach! Stop torturing me and give me some food."

"Don't you want to see what you're eating?" Tarra frowned at him, struck hot sparks from his flint. The tinder caught at once.

"Just lead me to it and let me touch it," Stumpy grunted. "If it's edible I'll know it—and then stand well back!"

Yellow firelight flared as Tarra took down a saddle-bag. He opened it, produced apples, dried meat, a little cheese. Stumpy, hands shaking with hunger, seated himself upon a flat rock and fell to it. There were tears in his one good eye (the right one) as he got his few remaining teeth working on a piece of meat.

Tarra squatted down by the fire, warmed his hands, bit into an apple. He'd eaten earlier—a rabbit, taken on the plain with a well-aimed stone—and wasn't so hungry. But to watch Stumpy Adz going at it . . .

"How long?" Tarra asked.

"Four days," the grizzled oldster mumbled around mouthfuls, "maybe five. I've dreamed of this for so long, it's—umf!—hard to say if I was awake or—umf!—sleeping. Tarra, but this is *good!* Er, didn't you mention wine or some such?"

The Hrossak put on a surprised expression, shook his head. "No."

"Yes you—umf!—did!" Stumpy was indignant. "When you thought I had you in my sights, you offered me—umf!—half a loaf and some passable wine."

"But you didn't have a crossbow," said Tarra.

"What difference does that make?" Stumpy scowled.

Tarra shrugged. "Well, neither did I have the wine!"

But as Stumpy groaned his disappointment, so the Hrossak relented. He took out a small wineskin from the saddle-bag, uncorked it and took a swig, passed it over. Stumpy held up the skin, expertly squirted a quenching stream into his gaping maw. *"Ahhh!"* he said. And, *"Ahhh!"* again. Tarra reached out, neatly separated him from supply.

Now the Hrossak tossed his apple in the direction of the tethered beast, ate just a bite of cheese, took another pull at the skin's tube before plugging it. "Eat first," he told Stumpy, "and then I'll let you wash it down. But don't make such a pig of yourself that you get the cramps. There's water in the other pack for later." Then he said no more but let the old man get on with it.

While Stumpy wolfed his food, so he looked Tarra up and down. What he saw was this:

A big-hearted man, open as a book; an inveterate wanderer, with feet which wouldn't stop itching while yet there remained a hill unclimbed, or view unviewed; a great adventurer—the latter not so much by inclination as by accident. For troubles, trials and terrors, in forms numerous as the fingers on his hard hands, had seemed to dog the Hrossak's heels since the day he'd left his steppes. With one adventure leading into the next, sometimes it had seemed he'd been born under a cursed star. Or perhaps a lucky one? For here he was hale and hearty, come through it all with scarce a scratch.

Tarra Khash was young, maybe twenty-five or -six, and bronzed as the great idols of jungled Shad. They weren't much known for their guile, these steppemen, which meant he'd most likely be trustworthy; indeed in Chlangi, Stumpy had discovered that to be a fact. And it was of old repute that once a Hrossak befriends a man, then that he's his friend for life. But on the other hand, best not to cross one; their memories were long and they didn't much care for scores unsettled.

As for the physical man himself: he was a tall one, this Tarra, and for all that he was lean and narrow in the hip, still his muscles rippled under the clinging silk of a dark shirt and the coarse weave of his tight, calf-length trousers. Hair a dusty, tousled brown, and eyes of a brown so deep they verged on black; long in the limbs, with shoulders broad as a gate; strong white teeth in a mouth never far from a grin . . . aye, he was a likely lad, the steppeman. But in no wise a fool, and ever growing wiser in the ways of the world.

Tough? Oh, he was that all right! That curved wand of death he wore across his back, for example: the merest silly sliver of a sword when Stumpy saw it last. For all the hilt's pretty jewels, it hadn't been much to mention as a weapon. Ah! But didn't it hold fond fighting memories for the Hrossak? It must, for he'd risked his life for it! King Fregg Unst the 1st of Chlangi had stolen that from him in Shunned City; and Tarra, against all odds, had taken it back! And what of Fregg now? Best not ask . . .

No rings adorned Tarra's fingers, nor the lobes of his ears. There were thieves in Theem'hdra who'd take a man's entire arm just for a gemstone in a ring on his smallest finger! Stumpy's eyes went lower, to Tarra's soft leather boots where they came up almost to his knees—and the sheath stitched into the outside of the right-hand boot, which housed his throwing knife. Aye, and with that he'd be *deadly* accurate! *Too true*, thought Stumpy, fingering his neck again.

For his part, Tarra had likewise been looking Stumpy over. The old lad was a failed thief, as witness his stump for right hand. They were hard on light-fingered types in certain parts, and even harder in others. This had probably happened in Klühn, fairly sophisticate city. In Thinhla they'd have hanged him, and in Khrissa pegged him out on the frozen mud-flats at the mouth of the Marl with the tide rising.

Stumpy was tiny, old, gnarly as the tree Tarra's knife had pinned him to; but he'd been a fighter, too, in his time. Now he wore a patch over his left eye; or rather, he wore it over the empty socket. Grizzled and brown from all weathers, white-whiskered and with a couple of snaggy yellow fangs for teeth, he looked like some sort of dwarfy pirate! But Tarra knew that despite his telltale stump, eye-patch and all, still the oldster had a good heart. And a far too-healthy appetite!

"What are you gawping at?" Stumpy growled now, wincing a little and holding his belly.

"Cramps?" Tarra inquired.

"Likely," Stumpy grimaced again. "I suppose I ate too fast."

"Warned you," the Hrossak nodded. "All right, sit still and I'll see what I can do." He brought a blanket from his beast's back, spread it over Stumpy and tucked him to his chin, then picked him up gentle as a child and put him in a spot close to the fire, with his back to a warm sloping rock. Then he brought him a sip of water.

"But no more wine," he said, "for that'll only make it worse. It's your guts complaining about neglect and ill-treatment, that's all. So just rest easy for now and tomorrow you'll be all right."

It was night now and the sky aglow with stars, and old Gleeth riding high like the blade of a silver scythe. Tarra sipped wine, chewed on a morsel of meat, waited until the fire's warmth worked through to Stumpy's bones and softened them up a little. Finally the old lad stopped grimacing and groaning, vented a ringing fart and a somewhat gentler sigh, and:

"I suppose you'll want to know how come I'm here, penniless and all, after you left me rich just a four-month gone in Chlangi?"

"In your own time, Stumpy," said Tarra. "Tomorrow will do, if you're not up to it now."

"Oh, I'm up to it," the other growled. And in a moment: "Well, it was mainly the fault of that lass Gulla!"

Gulla was Stumpy's daughter, whom Tarra had met in Chlangi—but only "met" there, and that was all. He remembered her now and winced a little, but not so much that Stumpy would notice. She'd been a big girl, right enough: comely about the face but built like a fortress. It had bruised Tarra's ribs just looking at her! He'd considered himself lucky to escape unscathed.

"So," Stumpy continued, "she reckoned it was coming up to her marrying time, and she didn't much fancy the local stuff. Couldn't blame her, really. Pickings weren't much in Chlangi, unless she'd settle for a pockmarked pirate or warty son of mountain scum out of Lohmi; Fregg's lot were a right old riff-raff, as you'll doubtless recall. Anyway, I'd waited around until then—you know?—to let it be seen that I was still just poor old Stumpy, who never had two buttons to rub together. For if that gang of yeggs and sharpers had suspected for one minute that I'd been with you against Fregg that night—that I'd helped you, and been well paid for it— well . . ." He shrugged and let it tail off.

"Oh, they wouldn't give a toss for Fregg, but gemstones are something else again! And me with a king's ransom buried under my dirt floor, eh?" He chuckled, then asked:

"Incidentally, what *did* happen to Fregg? They never found him—not that anyone looked too far! But unlike him to run off and leave his long-accumulated treasure-trove bursting at the seams like that, all for the taking. And his old runecaster, too, Arenith Han: they reckon *he* was less than mincemeat!"

Tarra nodded. "Lamia got 'em," he said, but very quietly, and glanced narrow-eyed all about in the shadows beyond the fire's light. "Orbiquita! She had a grudge against both. Settled it there and then. But for Orbiquita, I'd likely be there now—broken bones in a shallow grave . . ."

"She took scum like them and not you?" Stumpy wriggled bushy white eyebrows in undisguised inquiry. "Funny! I thought she was supposed to lust after hot young bloods like you?" He shrugged again. "Anyway, I'd heard as much: that it was Orbiquita got 'em. And she didn't just take them two, neither. The way I heard it she killed a dozen that night, tore 'em to bits with her bare hands!"

"Not bare." Tarra shook his head, shuddered. "Scythes! Hands like scythes, and feet to match. Don't ask about her teeth . . ."

"Seems you've your own tale to tell," said Stumpy, wide-eyed now and mouth agape.

"Some other time," Tarra answered, "but not tonight. Night's the wrong time to be talking of lamias and such. And anyway, I'm more interested in what you've got to say."

"Well, then—" Stumpy continued, "—so there I was with a lass who wanted a man, and only a handful of cut-throats to choose from. So I bided my time until the whole town was drunk one night, then stole a camel and got while the getting was good. It wouldn't have done to buy a beast, for then they'd wonder where I got the money and come after me. But we were clean away, and we headed for the pass through the Great Eastern Peaks."

"On your way to Klühn," Tarra nodded.

Stumpy shook his grizzled head. "On the *route* to Klühn," he said, "but I've something of a rep there," (he waved his stump) "so that wasn't our destination. I'd set my heart on a little house in one of those white-walled villages at the foot of the Eastern Range, where sweet water comes down off the mountains and there are lots of green things to grow. That was all I wanted: peace and quiet, a house and garden, and a place to watch my grandchildren grow up fat and happy."

Tarra picked a scrap of meat from between his strong teeth. "Sounds about right," he opinioned. "So what went wrong?"

"Nothing, not right then. Got through the pass and cut south, eventually found us a village halfway down the Eastern Range, snuggled between twin spurs a mile across. A place with a stream and good, loamy soil in its gardens. An old boy had recently died there, and so we bought his home where it sat right at the edge of the water. I could fish right out of the window, if I wanted to! Women were scarce there and Gulla got courted for the first time in her life—by three of 'em! After a week she knew which one she wanted: the only one of 'em who was bigger than she was!" He grinned a gummy grin, Tarra smiling with him.

"So the both of you were well fixed up," the Hrossak nodded. "Now tell me the worst."

Stumpy's grin turned sour. "It was a queer thing, that," he said. "So queer I'm still not sure about it! But this is the way I remember it:

"Gulla and Robos—her lad—had gone off on touch-and-taunt. That's the local term for it, anyway: when just before marriage a young couple try it out, as it were, to see if all will fit properly and who's to wear the apron, etcetera. A week spent high up in the hills with only the goats and the clouds for company, where they'd build a shelter for two and do all their fingering and fighting, their *ooh*ing! and *aah*ing! and . . . you know? All of that stuff.

"They'd been gone, oh, a day or two. I woke up early one fine morning and thought: 'fish!' It was the sort of morning when you can feel 'em rising—the fish, I mean. So I took line and hooks, a blanket to stretch out on, a slice of stale bread to chew and roll into little balls for bait, and headed upstream. I climbed through the foothills and time lost all meaning to me, climbed till I found a pool in a rocky basin, with the water filling it and trickling over the rim. Perfect! I took a dozen small fish inside an hour, determined to have three for lunch turned on a spit, the rest to take home and smoke for later.

"Now, in that high place I could see for miles. Oh, I've only one eye, but it's a sharp 'un! And the air so clear and all.

"I fancied I could even see the Eastern Ocean, more than two hundred miles away, but that was probably just the flat, shiny horizon, or maybe a mirage. But I *was* sure I could see the ruins of old Humquass on the plain, which was once a vast fortress city so big its walls had roads built on top of 'em! Now the ruins lie to the south-east, and as I'm looking at 'em—at that far smudge of ancient jumble—I notice a cloud of drifting dust. Coming from that general direction but much closer. I watch and wait, and I keep fishing; though in all truth I've started to lose interest in the fish, for this new thing has trapped my attention. Dust, aye, rising up from a long straggly line that inches its way like a troop of ants along the eastern borders of Hrossa."

"A caravan?" said Tarra. "From Hrossa? Unlikely! Not much on commerce, my lot, and when they do trade it's usually by sea. No, they keep to themselves, mainly—er, with the odd exception, of course."

Stumpy raised an eyebrow, glanced at the other with old-fashioned expression on his leathery face. "The *very* odd exception, aye . . ."

And at last he continued. "Anyway, from Grypha or Yhemnis I can't say, but caravan certainly. At first sight, anyway. I fix a fire, cook my fish and maintain a watch. As I eat, the dust cloud gets bigger and closer all the time; and now, because the wind's in my direction, I can even hear the distant tinkling of bells, the snorting of beasts, the creaking of leather and clatter of wooden wheels striking pebbles. And I think: why, they're heading straight for Haven's Hollow!—that being the name of the village.

"And me perched half-a-mile up, so to speak, I get a bird's-eye view of it: I can even make out the beasts and their several burdens, and something of the masters who prod 'em along. Ah, but damned strange caravan this, Tarra Khash! Decked out to look like one, aye—but a ship under false colours for all that, be certain! Indeed, a pirate!"

"Not a caravan?" Tarra gawped. "Then what?"

"Raiders!" Stumpy spat the word out. "Slavers!"

Tarra felt the hairs come erect back of his neck. "Blacks?" he growled. "From Yhemni jungles, or Shad across the straits, d'you think? Scourge of Grypha and the southern coast all the way to Thinhla, those lads—but busy with their miserable, bloody work so far north? Unheard of!"

"Blacks there were." Stumpy nodded curtly. "And their leader a curlyhead, too—but others among 'em more bronze than black . . ." He looked accusingly at Tarra.

"Well *I* wasn't there!" the Hrossak protested. "I was in Klühn, and beset by problems of my own, believe me!"

"Oh, I do," said Stumpy. "No, not you, Tarra, but Hrossaks certain for I saw them with my own eye."

Steppemen, slavers? It was hard to swallow. But no reason why Stumpy should lie, so Tarra would have to accept it. And anyway, he'd met outcast Hrossaks before, however small a handful: outlaws, banished for their evil ways.

"Get on with it," he growled, somewhat surly now.

"It was their wagons and beasts that sent me scrambling back down the rocks and scree slides," said Stumpy. "They were no more than a mile or two away by then, and suddenly I was sore afraid—not for myself, but for all the new friends I'd made in that pretty little village down there. Friends and neighbours, farmers most of 'em, whose only iron implements were scythes and ploughshares. And hope against hope, even as I clambered down that too long way, still I prayed I was wrong."

"Something about their wagons, their beasts? Make sense!" said Tarra, but he felt something of the sick terror glimpsed in the old lad's fire-dappled mien.

Finally Stumpy blinked, scowled and got on with it:

"Well, they had a few ponies, rare enough in these parts," he said, "and a string of camels and yaks—but their real beasts of burden were great lizards! Hrossak lizards, Tarra Khash, which only steppemen have ever been able to control or master. But even so, the lizards and the camels weren't the only poor beasts toiling in that caravan. For chained to the long—the *too* long—wagons were slaves galore, taken, I imagine, from all the villages farther down the foot of the range. I could hear their moaning and crying now, and the clanking of their chains.

"I was halfway down from the pool by then, and that was when it happened." He paused, perhaps for breath.

"Well?" said Tarra, impatient now.

Stumpy hung his head. "Lad, it was a horrible sight. And nothing I could do about it. The raiders had come in sight of the village, and no longer any need for subterfuge. Now they could stop being a caravan. Slow-moving to this point, as soon as they saw the village and smelled blood the mask fell away. And then they were like hounds unleashed!

"The long wagons—five of 'em, the longest things on four pairs of wheels each I've ever seen—were left behind with a handful of overseers, who worked on the chained slaves with whips to keep 'em quiet. The ponies set off at a gallop, kicking up the dust, throwing a wide half-circle around the village. Camels took on two armed raiders apiece, went trotting into town where their riders quickly dismounted. This much I'll say: there were no Hrossaks in on the raping and blood-letting. No, for they'd mainly stayed behind to tend the big hauling lizards. But the blacks and a handful of coarse-maned Northmen . . ." He broke off, shook his head.

"Northern barbarians, too?" Tarra could see it all in his mind's eye, and he knew from personal experience that the reputation of the Northman wasn't just idle gossip.

Stumpy nodded. "Blacks and Northmen, aye," he answered grimly. "There were maybe two dozen families in that village. Lots of burly lads, all completely untried in combat, and a few pretty wives and daughters. But mainly the women were old—thank all that's good! As for heads of families: farmers and greypates, like myself.

"Now I'm three-quarters down from the heights and shouting myself hoarse, and people out in the fields looking up to see what all the commotion's about. The ponies and riders tightening their net and closing in on the village, and in the main street itself—butchery!"

"But why?" Tarra was aghast at visions conjured. "I thought you said slavers? What good are dead slaves?"

"Young 'uns, they wanted," Stumpy told him with a groan. "Young lads and only the prettiest maids—and of the last there were only two or three in Haven's Hollow, be sure. As for the rest: death for the aged of both sexes, rape and yet more rape for the girls, until the dogs had had their fill and put an end to it with their swords. Aye, damned few lasses and young wives, Tarra, and two dozen or more blacks and maned barbarians. I'll not draw you any pictures . . ."

The Hrossak ground his teeth, drove a balled fist into the palm of his hand. "Slave-taking's bad enough," he finally growled, "but what you describe is—"

"Devil's work!" Stumpy cut him off. "And that's what they were, those butchers: spawn of the pit!" And after a moment: "Do you want to know the rest?"

Tarra shook his head at first, then nodded, however reluctantly. "Aye, best tell me all and get it out of your system."

"My house was burning when I got down," said Stumpy. "The whole village was burning, and blood everywhere! The blacks and barbarians were in the alehouse, smashing barrels and pouring it down. I saw it all: the bodies in the fields, the naked, raped, gutted lasses, the lads bludgeoned senseless and shackled, and the blood and the fire—and I think I went a little daft. I came across a Northman in the shadow of a burning house, still having his way with some poor girl. She was dead—of terror, I suppose, with her eyes all starting out of her head—but he didn't seem to mind that. I minded it. I picked up his great sword and sliced the dog right down his sweaty, hairy spine!

"And that was it, what I needed! Killing him had given me pleasure, an amazing relief! I was transformed—into a berserker! Me, old Stumpy Adz, roaring in a blood frenzy! I rushed into the alehouse with my bloody sword, and cursed them all in their own heathen tongue—then skewered a frizzy through his gizzard. They'd laughed at me at first, but that stopped 'em. Then someone got up behind me and clonked me hard on the head. For me, that was the end of it. Everything went black and I knew I was going to die, and it didn't bother me much . . ."

"And yet they didn't kill you!" Tarra shook his head.

"Oh, they did," said Stumpy, "but only on the inside. Why didn't they kill me? But I was mad, wasn't I? A crazy man! The Yhemnis have a thing about madmen: they won't kill a loony, for if they do they have to care for his needs and carry him on their back for eternity in the afterlife. That's their belief. No, safer far to maroon him somewhere to die all on his own—which is what they did to me."

Tarra marvelled at the old lad's hardiness. "So they dumped you here, where for four or five days you've just wandered, eh?"

Stumpy shrugged. "I found a few berries, the wrong sort, and they made me sick. I got a little water from a spiky cactus, and that made me sick, too! Until at last I was sick of everything, not least life. Then I heard your beast coming clip-clop up the pass, and I thought: Stumpy, one way or the other, this misery ends right here."

Tarra nodded. "Fortunate for you it wasn't the other!" he said. He moved about in the glow of dying embers, found more branches and tossed them on the fire. And finally, turning again to Stumpy, he said: "Aren't you tired yet?"

For answer Stumpy buzzed like a nest of wasps. Tarra saw that his chin was on his chest, noted the steady rise and fall of the blanket. Out like a candle snuffed! That was good . . .

Or was it? The night had come in chilly and Stumpy had Tarra's blanket. He sighed, went to where his beast had gone to its knees, lay down along its flank. And using saddle-bags for a pillow, he quickly fell asleep—

II

Black Caravan, White Gold!

—AND AS QUICKLY came awake!

Much too quickly, so that his mind was almost left behind as his body sat itself up.

"On your feet, great lump!" Stumpy shouted again. "Come on, man, get a move on!"

Stumpy? A move on?

What the hell . . . ?

Tarra brushed sleep from his eyes, remembered where he was and who with, and Stumpy's story of—how many hours past? Quite a few, for Gleeth was gone from the sky, and the stars fast-fading—and he scrambled stiffly, stumblingly to his feet even as his beast snorted and spat and reared aloft on spindly legs.

"Here, my hand," yelled Stumpy from camel's back, his voice shrill with urgency. "Quick man, take hold!"

"Take hold?" Tarra stumbled this way and that. Yesterday he'd come many, many miles, and he'd been very deep asleep. And now all of this motion and commotion; shadows moving in the dusk of pre-dawn; camel hissing and rearing, and the old idiot on its back screaming and beckoning. A nightmare, maybe?

No maybe about it! A crossbow bolt zipped past Tarra's ear, sliced a groove in beast's rump. Now the Hrossak was wide awake, and now, too, he leaped for Stumpy's out-stretched hand—too late!

The camel was off like a shot from a sling, impelled by the pain in its rear. It toppled Tarra aside in its panic flight, threw him down in dead embers from last night's fire. Then camel and Stumpy, too, a single wild silhouette against the grey of dawn, sinking out of sight over the brow of the hill.

Spitting curses and ashes both, Tarra came upright—and a pony ploughed right into him. But he saw its rider, a Northman wild and woolly, and he felt a hand grip the hilt of the sword on his back even as he fell. With a whisper of steel the weapon was taken from him, and now all he had was his knife. He crashed through brittle bushes, rolled in dust, yanked out the knife from its sheath on his calf—and froze right there.

A frizzy stood over him, loaded crossbow pointed straight at his heart. *Goodbye, everything,* thought Tarra. Then—

"Don't kill him!" a low voice growled. "He's a live one, this buck steppeman, and a good thing for all of us if he stays that way. Aye, for Yoppaloth will be pleased to have him in his arena of death. What? Just look at those eyes: black as night and no flicker of fear in 'em, just fury. I'd say he's probably the meanest buck we've taken!"

Close by, a pony whinnied and there came sounds of a rider dismounting. Then a snorting and clattering of camels, and their humped outlines and smoulder-eyed riders hem-ming the grounded Hrossak in. Finally that low voice of au-thority again, but closer, saying: "You, Gys Ankh, outcast of your race no less than this one, get after that old madman. It was you urged me to let you kill him, so there'd be no witnesses. Well, now he's riding like the wind! So get after him and finish it. But by your hand, not mine. I'm not having that old bag of bones riding my back in the afterlife!"

There came a curse and the sound of hooves drumming, and the fading, "Yee, yee, *yee*-hiii!" of a Hrossak hot in pursuit. Hrossak, aye: Stumpy Adz hadn't been mistaken about the make-up of these polyglot raiders. And at last the owner of that doomful voice stepped into view: a tall, wiry Yhemni in rich red robe, his skull-like head topped with cockscomb of stiff-lacquered hair, painted red along its crest. Of mixed blood, Tarra could see, he was thin-lipped, slant-eyed, gaunt and hollow-faced. And black as any black man Tarra had ever seen. The Hrossak guessed it wasn't just the colour of his skin but also that of his life.

Away in the east the rim of the world grew milky with soft light as the sun escaped Cthon's nets and strove to rise again for the new day. Misty light glinted on Tarra's knife; and still the black underling stood over him, his deadly weapon steady on his heart.

"Well?" said the tall Yhemni chief of these cut-throats. "If you're going to throw that knife, throw it. Likely you'll nick Um-bunda, there, and maybe even kill him—but even dying he'll be sure to put his bolt in you."

Tarra found his voice. "So maybe I should toss the knife your way instead?" he growled.

Before he could redirect his aim, the spindly half-breed stepped quickly back into shadows. And now his voice came brittle as thin ice. "I'll count just five, Hrossak," he said, "and that's your—"

"Save your numbers," said Tarra, letting the knife fall with a clatter. "I can't beat all of you. One at a time, maybe, but not in a bunch."

With that he would have climbed to his feet, but half-a-dozen blacks fell on him at once, binding him securely. While this was happening their leader came close again and stood watching, his skull-face split in a grin. "So you're a fighter, eh? Well, you'll get your share of that, steppeman—in Shad!"

Fighting . . . in Shad . . . in a certain "arena of death"? And now Tarra had just about all of it. As his captors bundled him down to the stalled "caravan" (best think of it as a caravan, he supposed) so he cast his mind back on tidbits of information gleaned here and there in his wanderings. About certain wizards, for instance, with names like Mylakhrion—and Black Yoppaloth!

Aye, and it was rumoured that Shad had seen a long line of Yoppaloths. The current sorcerer bearing that name would be the ninth. Black Yoppaloth the 9th, of the Yhemnis. *Huh!* But Tarra supposed it had a certain ring to it. Blacker rumours still had it that in fact this was that same foul necromancer who'd lived in Mylakhrion's time more than a thousand years ago, though it was past Tarra's fathoming how that could possibly be. As for Shad across the Straits of Yhem: that might well be caravan's destination, but a certain grim-faced Hrossak wouldn't be with it when it got there, be certain!

Shad . . .

Now what, if anything, did Tarra know about Shad? Nothing for sure, except that it was the twin of Yhemnis, which it faced squarely across seventy-five miles of windy straits. As for rumour: Shad was legended to be splendidly barbaric—a city of gold, bronze, ivory, ironwood—jungle-girt hive of pirates and slavers. But merely legend? No longer; it seemed the latter was now indisputable fact! And yet many a year, indeed more than a century, since last

Shad raided against whites and so far from jungled coast. Normally the blacks took other blacks, Yhemnis like themselves, from the coastal villages north and south of Yhemnis the city on the mainland's steamy coast. And vice versa, when mainland blacks would raid on Shadarabar. So what was different now? Had the two sides got together at last? Unlikely, for their rivalry was historic.

Dragged unceremoniously down to the winding, narrow trail through the pass, Tarra was manacled to the side of one of Stumpy's "too long wagons," where a dozen desperate youths and young men hung in their chains and their rags in various stages of exhaustion. A like number was chained on the other side. Then he was left alone, and as dawn turned to day along came a bronzed, greasy, scar-faced man on a lathered pony, jerking his mount viciously to a halt alongside Tarra. He took a cruel whip from his belt and shook down its coils to the earth, looked down at Tarra from under bushy black eyebrows, Hrossak on Hrossak. "That old fool who was with you," he grunted. "It seems he's got away."

Tarra shrugged. "Just an old loony," he said. "But not so daft he didn't know a good camel when he stole one!"

"Oh?" the other pulled in his chin, cocked his head a little on one side, seemed surprised by Tarra's answer. "Chatty, are we? Aren't you sort of overlooking the fact that you're now a slave?"

"It was you who spoke to me, friend," Tarra quietly reminded him, "and I supposed you required an answer. Also, we're two of a sort, and it seems to me both a bit out of place here. Me, I was on my way back to the steppes, when—"

The slaver's whip sang, and Tarra gasped his pain and shock and turned his face away. And again the angry snapping of the whip—again, and again—as his silky shirt was reduced to ribbons on his back. Aye, and his back a little, too. When it was over, he also hung in his chains. But he'd not once cried out. And:

"There!" said his tormentor with something of satisfaction, coiling up his whip again.

Tarra found voice. "Seems I—*uh!*—must have angered you somehow . . ."

"No," the other shook his matted head of hair and grinned down at him—a sneering grin Tarra would never forget. He spat into the dust at Tarra's feet. "You didn't anger me, and not much likely to. That beating was for nothing, 'friend,' so mind you don't go doing something, right?" And he spurred his pony away, kicking up dust to sting Tarra's raw red stripes.

The chained steppeman gazed after him and thought dark red thoughts; and with much creaking, shuddering and jolting, finally the big lizards began to haul and wheels to turn, and the caravan got under way again . . .

BY NOON THEY were down out of the pass and heading south for ancient, ruined Humquass. The way was dry, dusty, a near-desert. With the sun at its zenith, the horizon shimmered white, and slavers and captives alike were feeling the heat. But at least the prisoners, trudging along in their chains, could stick to the shade of the big wagons.

If at first Tarra had wondered what they hauled, wondered about the cargo of those strange, long vehicles, he wondered no longer. At first opportunity, unobserved, he'd lifted up a flap of canvas and gazed beneath. Boats, great Yhemni canoes, but massive-built! And there'd be one to each of the five long wagons. They had sails, too, all folded down now, and chains that ran along the gunnels, and manacles on the oars. No need to wonder how these slavers would return to Shad: they'd go home in triumph, with their captives sculling them speedy across the straits. Why, there'd be room in vessels big as these even for the monster lizards!

Humquass was just in sight—a rim of jagged black edges on the scrubland's horizon, like low broken hills—when they came on an oasis. The great lizards smelled water and sent up a hissing like a vast pit of snakes, and their Hrossak riders let them build up to something of a lumbering trot as blue waters opened under spindly green palms. The long wagons were drawn in a circle round the oasis; huge wooden buckets of water were fetched for the beasts; the overseer blacks prowled up and down and inspected their captives, ensuring that all was well with them. Little need to worry about that, for they were burly lads all: white gold in Shad's slave-markets, or gladiators in a wizard's necromantic arena.

Tarra frowned and wondered: burly *lads*, aye, but hadn't Stumpy Adz also said something about lasses? He had indeed! The canvas on the first wagon was thrown back; blacks jumped up onto its platform, gestured with whips and gave guttural commands; frightened female faces appeared, and a dozen gorgeous girls were made to climb down. They paraded there by the wheels of the long wagon, chained together, trying their best to cover their modesty with what scraps of clothing had been left to them.

By now all of the beasts had been watered, the slavers had filled skins from the oasis, last ripples were dying on the surface of the blue pool under the palms. Along came red-robed frizzy boss on a pony, idling his mount where he gazed down on his lovely captives. Only a wagon away, Tarra could hear his raised voice:

"Go, bathe yourselves, wash off grime and grit. Swim, if

you will, and take your ease for an hour. But hurry, before I change my mind!" And off they went, stumbling a little, soft-skinned under a harsh sun, to bathe themselves at pool's margin. And:

Oh-ho! But you're asking for trouble now, my gleamy black slavemaster friend! thought Tarra Khash. What? And hadn't he seen half-a-dozen Northmen during course of trek so far? And was it likely that those coarse-maned barbarians of northern fjords and mammoth plains would endure this fla-grant flaunting of delicate female flesh? Tarra doubted it.

He was chained to that side of the wagon facing the pool. The others strung there with him hauled themselves wearily up onto platform, sat legs adangle, leaned back against giant canoe's curving strakes and in its shade. They hung their heads, slumped there and groaned of their aching bones; but Tarra merely stood watching the girls where they bathed themselves not one hundred feet away. A slaver passed down the line with chunks of bread, ladling water from a bucket. Tarra took a crust, sipped a little water, and the black passed on. Tarra munched on dry, tasteless bread, stopped munching, felt the corner of his mouth begin to twitch in warning spasm. It was too quiet; a certain tension was in the air; it was going to happen now!

Three huge Northmen tethered their ponies to a palm far-thest from the pool, wiped sweaty palms down their leather-clad legs and grinned at each other, and as on some silent command began to shamble toward the pool in the tracks left by the girls. Involuntarily, Tarra strained in his chains, glared at the huge single iron staple hammered home in hardwood, which held him there immobile. A shadow fell on him.

He looked up, eyes half-shuttered against the glare of

sun. It was the caravan's master, still astride his pony; and now Tarra recognized the weapon in its scabbard at his hip. There could be no mistaking that jewelled hilt or the curve of the blade's sheath. The gangly black slaver had taken Tarra's sword for his own.

"They call me Cush Gemal," the Yhemni half-breed made belated introduction. "And you?"

"Tarra Khash, a Hrossak," said Tarra. No need to name his race, but he did so for pride's sake. Gemal saw that his eyes had gone back to the Northmen, halfway now to the pool. One of them was peeling off his shirt, displaying the bristly mane that ran down his back to base of spine. Another's belt hung loose, swaying with his lurching gait. The caravan's master followed Tarra's nervous gaze.

"No Hrossak females there," he said, curiously. "And yet you fear for them."

"You'd do well to follow my example," said Tarra, "if you'd carry them back to Shad intact!"

"Oh?" the slaver seemed half-amused.

In his agony of apprehension, Tarra had grown unmindful of his tongue. "You've obviously little knowledge of Northmen," he groaned, licking his suddenly dry lips. "No Hrossak women, you say? Man, you couldn't trust those hairies with your pony!"

The other gave a guttural chuckle. "Ah, but I *do* know Northmen, Tarra Khash! And I agree with you entirely. But the leader of that trio has crossed me once too often, and this is my way of drawing him out."

"You'll do that right enough," Tarra gave a jerky nod, strained again at his chain, "with periodic parade of female flesh before the eyes of scum like that. But it won't do the girls much good . . ."

"I believe you'd actually interfere!" Cush Gemal marvelled. "Even though they'd kill you for it."

"Just let me out of these chains and I'll show you how right you are," Tarra grated.

The Northmen were at pool's rim, and as they came through the palms and rushes the girls saw them, saw their intention. They quickly crushed themselves together in a knot, used their hands to cover their nakedness. The barbarians stood ankle deep in the water and leered at them.

Gemal touched the hilt of Tarra's ex-sword. "Is it a good weapon?" he murmured.

"Depends who's using it," Tarra growled through clenched teeth. He couldn't turn his eyes from the frozen tableau at the pool, which wouldn't stay frozen much longer, he knew.

"Then let's see how well it does in the hands of Cush Gemal!" the other snapped, and suddenly animated, he spurred his pony toward the pool. As he rode he called ahead:

"*Hold!* You there, Gorlis Thad. What's this? Don't you know those girls are virgins? Indeed you do! Also why they were taken and who they belong to. Only bruise one of those fruits and Black Yoppaloth will flay you alive. Break one and he'll make drums of your hide and a fine fly-switch of your sweaty mane!"

Gorlis Thad! Top dog of northern pack a Thad, eh? Tarra had heard of this barbarous family, so huge it was almost a tribe in itself. Indeed he'd killed one, during a brief and vengeful visit to the isles of the Crater Sea. Thad: the name itself made his nostrils wrinkle, as if it carried a stench. The most ingrown, degenerate, murderous Northmen of them all, the Thads, and never a one born that a man—or any woman—could trust.

Gorlis must be the one who'd taken off his shirt, who'd waded into pool and was even now dragging a girl out by her hair. All chained together, where she went the rest must follow; and so they trooped along behind, all moaning and covering themselves with soaking rags, the water streaming from their lovely bodies.

At the edge of the pool Gorlis turned, saw the rider Cush Gemal bearing down on him. He'd heard his shouting, scowled at his threats. "What?" he shouted at the man on the pony where he reined to a halt close by. "You're worried about that stinking shaman six hundred miles away in Shad? Well, it's my skin, Gemal, so let me do the worrying, right?"

"Fool!" Gemal hissed. "Dolt! He could be watching you right now, at this very moment. Shaman? Aye, he is that, and his eyes are everywhere!"

Gorlis' sidekicks had also laid hands on a pair of girls, but at first mention of magick they turned them loose, stumbled up out of the water, stood glaring at their ringleader. Like most Northmen, they were cowed by merest mention of wizardry or witchcraft. But not, apparently, the Thad himself.

He scowled his scorn at them, looked up at Cush Gemal. "I've promised this fine pair of lads a bit of sweet meat," he said. "They're not much for going without—not while it's standing around just waiting to be taken—no, and neither am I. So I say unchain just three of 'em, for half an hour, and no harm done. I'll promise you that much: no harm done, not permanent anyway. We'll use one of the boats, so's not to get the other bucks worked up. Out of sight, out of *mind*, eh?" And now he grinned through his beard at the caravan's master.

Gemal sneered cynically, nodded his red-crested comb of hair. "Out of sight, out of mind? I'll say you are, Gorlis

Thad!" The half-breed slaver slitted his eyes, swung easily down from his mount. "Why, Black Yoppaloth would know if you'd even breathed on one of his brides! What? You risk your eyes just *looking* at them! So I'll say it one more time, Gorlis Thad: let go that girl's hair and get back to your place, or there's trouble here and now . . ."

"Then let it be trouble!" Thad's hand snaked toward the throwing knife in his belt.

Watching all of this, Tarra Khash winced, or blinked, it makes no difference; but in any case he shuttered his eyes for a moment, the merest moment, before opening them on unbelievable scene. Prior to that, however, during the course of conversation between black slavemaster and northern barbarian, he had taken the opportunity to glance all about. Apart from the three Northmen central to this affair, at least five others looked on from where they sat or stood by the wagons. All were armed to the teeth, where with sidelong glances they measured up Gemal's superior numbers. In a fight it would be a close thing, for the four or five rogue steppemen would probably join with the Northmen against the blacks; even in steppes outcasts such as these, instinct to side with the underdog would be a powerful force. Outnumbered more than two to one, still they'd make a damn good go of it, Tarra knew. The Yhemnis must know it, too, and yet a curious thing: not a man of the frizzies seemed remotely concerned! They merely looked on, as if the outcome were already decided. Which perhaps it was.

But in any case Tarra had winced, or blinked, and now unblinked—then gaped at what he saw!

Gorlis Thad's knife was airborne, a silver streak speeding close to gleaming black breast—but Tarra's jewelled scimitar had somehow managed to sprout from Gemal's hand!

Drawn from scabbard? What? In the blink of an eye? Even in two blinks? And yet there it was, deflecting hurtling knife like tossed apple; and Gemal thin-faced, nostrils flaring where he advanced on the stunned Northman. Fascinated, Tarra continued to watch.

Even in the water, one of Gorlis' colleagues had retained a great broadsword; now in a squeal of steel he unsheathed it, tossed it down on the sand at Gorlis' feet. One crashing blow of that great sword, and the slender scimitar would shiver to shards. And now the barbarian knew that he had Gemal's measure. He bent to retrieve the broadsword— and Gemal leaped forward, edge of scimitar resting lightly on Gorlis' neck. The Northman froze, drew back his hand from hilt of broadsword where it lay.

His eyes went this way and that, and colour drained from his face. "And how's this for a fair fight?" he suddenly shouted.

Gemal, too, raised his voice: "*Now* he wants a fair fight, who without warning hurled his knife! What say you—do I give him one?"

The entire caravan, barring only slaves themselves, answered with one voice: "*Aye!*" And Tarra noted that the Yhemnis shouted loudest of all. He wondered: is Gemal *that* good? And got his answer in the space of a double heartbeat.

As Gorlis Thad straightened up, tall as Cush Gemal himself but blocky as a bull, so his half-breed opponent tossed down his scimitar alongside broadsword. "Now we're equal—" he started to say, but already the treacherous barbarian had uttered a *whoop* of savage glee, gone to one knee, grasped his weapon's hilt—which was exactly what Gemal had known he would do.

As Northman's hand closed on weapon's hilt, Gemal

slammed his sandalled foot down on the other's wrist, stooped and retrieved the scimitar. It came alive in his hand as he straightened, slicing Gorlis through his trousers from groin to rib-cage.

Blood drenched the sand as Gemal lithely turned to face Gorlis' henchmen. "You?" he offered. "Or you?" They skulked away. And still Gorlis kneeling in the sand, holding in his unfettered guts. Then he looked up, through eyes already glazing over, to where Gemal sheathed his weapon and mounted his pony; and finally he fell face-down, mouth gaping, on the sand.

"Make ready!" cried Gemal, guiding his mount back toward Tarra Khash where the Hrossak openly admired him. "Load up! Tonight we make camp in yonder ruins." And not a man of the barbarians offering the slightest resistance, but all averting their eyes and carrying on with their duties as if nothing whatever had occurred. Which was perhaps to say a lot for commonsense, and an equal amount for Gorlis Thad's popularity.

Gemal rode close to chained Hrossak, briefly reined in. "It's a good weapon right enough, Tarra Khash," he said. "I thank you for gifting it to me."

As he spurred away Tarra looked after him and nodded. But to himself: "Best consider it a loan," he said, "for which repayment later . . ."

"PEACE!" SAID TEH Atht, holding up long-fingered hand to stay his crystal's activity. "Let it be for now—but continue to watch and remember all. I shall doubtless desire to scry it later . . ."

His bones creaked as he stood up from his viewing, and as

the shewstone reverted once more to opaque and milky sphere he groaned and stretched his cramped limbs a little. Since the Hrossak's moonlight meeting with Stumpy Adz in the pass, the wizard had slept when they slept, observed when they were up and about, and apart from that he'd done precious little else. There was much to fascinate him here, and also several mysteries to unravel.

Tarra Khash, for instance: he was a strange one, this Hrossak. Not often that a common man comes to the attention of lofty mage, whose thoughts and schemes would normally dwell on higher plane; and yet Teh Atht was interested—intensely so. Aye, for this wasn't the first time he'd heard of this brawny Hrossak, nor merely through any mundane or common gossip.

A certain lamia in her sulphurous lair knew of him, thinking strange, fond thoughts for a lamia! (This was Orbiquita, Teh Atht's "cousin," with whom by virtue of their blood bond he had the power to converse over vast distances. For Mylakhrion, that most fecund of all wizards, had been her progenitor, too; indeed, and according to legend, he was both "father" and "brother" to the entire sisterhood!) While Teh Atht had sojourned in her castle in Sheb, he'd tried to contact Orbiquita in the great subterranean cavern beneath the Nameless Desert where she slumped asleep, cocooned in lava, serving a sentence of five years solitude for some sin against lamia laws. He had *tried* to contact her, but all he got were dreams and fancies: dreams of Tarra Khash, in fact, whom she seemed to fancy more than somewhat!

Now, it were certainly not strange for lamias to lust after iron-thewed, handsome steppemen; but to *long* for a man? And with such affection? At the time Teh Atht had merely thought it odd, no more than that: it was her dream, after all, and dreams are curious things at best, which do not always tell the truth. And so, being no voyeur (shewstone to the contrary), he'd not lingered but left her to her dreaming.

That had been the first instance. But then:

Ahorra Izz, scarlet scorpion god in his jungle temple, had also known of Tarra Khash; or if not his name, certainly he'd known of the man. "Three who work against Gorgos," he'd riddled, "and one of them a man!" A man called Tarra Khash, aye. Moreover, that singular arachnid deity had owned to "liking" him! First most loathsome lamia, and now ireful insect intelligence? Oh, he was a charmer for sure, this Hrossak, and perhaps much more than that. Worthy of further investigation, anyway.

Teh Atht's fruitless five year quest had left him weary, and he'd vowed that when he got home he would take his ease; yet now, sensing that his and a certain Hrossak's destinies were fast intertwined, he felt full of a strange urgency. It were imprudent (indeed, nigh impossible) to go direct to Tarra Khash and make his interest known: interest in the Hrossak himself, in his curved sword with its curiously fashioned and gem-studded hilt—ah, and *great* interest in Black Yoppaloth's current slavemaster, the cryptogenic Cush Gemal! For the steppeman hadn't yet settled to captivity and would be doubly nervy; he might well react to magick in much the same way as a superstitious Northman, who would avoid it if he could, or fight it to the death if he couldn't! And so Teh Atht's eventual approach would need to be well considered and crafty in its execution. Wherefore, better to leave it until later, when the Hrossak had lost something of hope and might be ready to grasp at straws. Or whatever else the wizard had to offer.

And meanwhile?

Teh Atht sighed. One quest ended, however disappointingly, and another about to begin. Genuine, healing rest, of the sort he'd looked forward to—with his slippers, books, and perhaps a succubus or two to keep him warm nights—were now out of the question. A wizard's work was never done. He'd know no peace of mind until certain riddles were resolved. And who could say, perhaps it might mean the resolution of that earlier quest, too.

Where to start was easy, but first—

He went to his bedchamber, stretched himself out and uttered the rune of Rapid Repose, at once began to snore. Ten dreamless hours sped by in a like number of seconds, and refreshed Teh Atht sprang up. It wasn't as good as the real thing, of course, but better than nothing.

Now he must hie him to Nameless Desert, find a blowhole and descend to planet's fiery bowels, there seek audience with Orbiquita. Only this time in person, and not just mind to mind. Aye, he'd wake her up from sulphurous slumbers, and at last attempt to fathom her fondness for this mere man, this Tarra Khash. And *that*, too, would be a neat trick, if he could turn it. For a mortal, even a wizard, to commune face to fearsome visage with a lamia were nothing less than fraught!

But alas, no way round it. Not that he could see . . .

III

A Mage Immortal!

TARRA KHASH LAY under the moon and stars, a coarse blanket
for his cover, with his stomach growling and his thighs on fire
from forced march to ruined Humquass. He'd trekked a fair
bit in his time, however, and knew that pain alone wouldn't
kill him; not the natural pain of tired muscles, anyway.

Chains had been lengthened, allowing for a little mobility,
but only one blanket to each pair of captives, so that he must
needs share it with one other: a blond-haired, blue-eyed
youth of some fifteen summers. A farm lad, Tarra guessed—
with muscles a-plenty but little fortitude of mind—who'd
snivelled a bit and then gone to sleep; but the Hrossak
remained wide awake, only biding his time.

The moon had put on a little weight since last night, but
not much; three weeks yet before it would swell into an orb;
and where would a steppeman find himself then, and what
would he be doing there? Fighting in some nightmare arena
of magick? Best not to seek to know, he supposed.

Tarra turned carefully in the shallow, sandy depres-
sion he'd dug for himself and gazed all about. Outwards:
Humquass' once-massive, now broken walls formed a black,
fanged horizon, with the stars floating on jet above its rim.

Inwards: the wagons were ranged in a wide circle around central fires already burning low, where a few black slavers squatted and conversed in lowered tones, while a handful of barbarians and Hrossaks gambled with dice. And close to the lead wagon with its precious cargo of pure maidens, there stood a silken tent, black, with black tassels at the four corners of its scalloped canopy. Cush Gemal's tent, where doubtless he slept on plump cushions even now.

The Hrossak's glittery eyes swept the area of the central fires. Many Yhemnis were bedded down there, wrapped in their blankets. The last three or four gamblers finished gaming, cursed their luck or collected up their winnings, slowly ambled off into the shadows. Two drunken Northmen remained, guzzling a wineskin dry, then leaning together and burping into firelight's glow. Tarra watched them, waiting until they, too, took their staggering departure.

There would be a watch out, of course—frizzies doing three-hour shifts through the night, perched high up in the broken walls—but they'd be looking outwards, watching for wandering nomads or possible pursuers. They'd not be much interested in what went on down here. Not that a lot would be going on, for Tarra was still chained. This was the problem to which he'd now apply himself.

He'd already studied his chains well enough: scrutinized each link, run them through his hard but sensitive fingers, looked for rust and signs of wear—all to no avail. Well forged, those chains—damn their makers to every hell! As for the manacles (manacles in name only, for they left one hand free): they were short, single sleeves of iron "worn" on a captive's right wrist, where they fitted too snug to be slid down over crafty fingers. Tarra's manacle, like those of all the rest, had two large rings or staples in its flange, through which the chain passed before returning to the wagon, where it further passed through a single large staple whose prongs were driven deep in ironwood frame. Then the chain passed down the flank of the wagon a double pace, to another staple which anchored the next captive, and so on. Even if a slave were strong enough to tear iron from ironwood, he'd still remain manacled between two more slaves. No, *all* of the staples would need to be wrenched out together, and even so the slave band would remain chained in a bunch.

Slaves, aye, and Tarra Khash starting to get used to the word. And him one of 'em . . .

He began to feel a mite sorry for himself, checked the feeling at once. What? Why, he'd be grovelling next, or whining in his sleep like this farmer's pup at his side! He gave the lad a gentle pat on his back anyway, then slipped out from under the blanket and crawled into the shadow of the wagon. It wouldn't hurt to have another feel at those staples; the more you study a problem, the surer its resolution—usually. Coming upright beside the long wagon, he held his chains taut so they wouldn't jangle against his wrist manacle.

Manacle . . . *hmmm!* And again he considered the iron sleeve on his wrist. They were locked with curious keys, these vile bracelets—or one curious key, at least. Tarra had only seen the one, when it had been used to shackle him; and of course he'd consigned to memory the face of the Yhemni who'd used and then pocketed it. All possibilities must be considered, including that there *might* come a moment of confusion, when it *might* be possible to clout a certain frizzy on the head and go through his pockets.

But now he put that thought aside for the moment; it would be a desperate measure at best, only to be considered if things got totally out of hand. Now he found his staple and tugged at it, then gritted his teeth and tugged harder, finally scowled and punched at it with his fist, which only served to bruise his knuckles. Solid as a rock, that iron loop, with just enough clearance for the chains to slide. A man would need to be superhuman to break these chains or wrench these staples loose!

Beginning to feel frustrated, Tarra turned to the nearest wagon wheel and fingered its wide rim. Ironwood, yes, but still only wood: even rolling over rock it wouldn't cut iron or snap chains, merely crush the rock!

There came a *hiss* and a *honk* from close by and Tarra started, then glanced quickly all about. The great lizard that hauled the wagon had sensed him standing there and queried his presence, but no one seemed to have noticed. The lizards were known to voice complaints like this periodically, usually warning of nothing whatsoever.

"*Tss! Tss!*" Tarra hissed low, in the way of Hrossaks cautioning their beasts. He stepped light round the front of the wagon and stroked the clammy hindquarters of the huge creature squatting there between massive shafts. The lizard turned its long neck and gloomed on him slit-eyed. "Quiet, old scaly," he husked, "or you'll wake the whole camp!"

Not very likely, for most would be well asleep by now, but still it were time Tarra returned to his own gritty bed. He turned from where he gazed at lizard's ridgy rump, went to all fours in the dark and crept back round to the side of the long wagon—then jerked to a halt where his chains were caught on something. Or where they were trapped *under* something.

. . . Like booted feet, for instance! Tarra stared at leather-clad feet where they stood square on his chains, then slowly lifted his gaze to see who it was who'd caught him creeping around. His heart sank. It was Gys Ankh, who'd chased and lost Stumpy Adz in the foothills, then taken his spite out on Tarra's back. Outcast Hrossak, no doubt for damned good reasons.

"Going somewhere, 'friend'?" Ankh made quiet inquiry, his scar a band of livid white over his right eyebrow and square down his face to his chin. "But I distinctly remember telling you to be good . . ." The coils of his whip snaked down onto the sand. Tarra's thoughts ran wild, in every direction, but all came back bloodied. He'd suffered once at the hands of this bully, and this time it was bound to be worse.

"Well?" Gys Ankh stood over him.

Tarra slowly came to his feet, wiped his hands down his pants as Ankh backed off to striking distance. The crack of the whip would be heard, of course, but what odds? What, someone chastising a stubborn slave in the night? Little cause for concern there. "I . . . I was restless," said Tarra lamely, with a shrug.

"Much more so in a moment," Ankh grinned lopsidedly. "Aye, damned restless! And how'll you sleep with sand in your grooves, 'friend'? Face-down, maybe? Not much good, that, for it's my intention to cut you there, too! Restless? I'll say you'll be." He drew back his arm sharply and the coils straightened out, slithering along the sand to his rear.

Things twanged in Tarra's head, then snapped: twin threads of hope and patience. He'd just run out of both. He fell to a crouch, leaned with a silent snarl toward his tormentor. Gys Ankh chuckled, backed off a pace. "Aye, come and get it, 'friend,' " he said. "Discover for yourself why they kicked me out of Hrossa!"

Tarra needed no more urging: he leaped, and Ankh snapped his whip—or tried to and almost jerked himself from his feet! He turned, saw the youth under the blanket where he'd taken firm hold on the end of his whip, went to kick him in the face. But silently raging Hrossak was on him, dropping chains over his head in a loop, shutting off air and sudden shriek of terror both. They crashed down together on the sand, Ankh groping for his knife, Tarra butting him, kneeing him in the groin, choking his life out, generally allowing him no space for thought or movement; and the youth holding the blanket over both struggling forms until the scarface stopped moving. Ankh managed to choke out one last word—a curse, Tarra suspected—twitched several times and went slack as a eunuch's foreskin. But for several moments longer, just to be absolutely sure, Tarra drew the chains even tighter about the bully's throat.

Now came lad's whisper, by no means cowed, even jubilant: "Is he—?"

Tarra nodded. "Stone dead, aye," he whispered, "or I'm not Tarra Khash. But quiet now, or you'll soon be able to ask him man to man!" They stuck their heads out from under the blanket, listened for long moments, breathed deep and grinned at each other in the dark.

"What?" said Tarra then, his voice low. "No tears? But I had you figured for a mother's boy. Whimpering and whining one minute, and helping me kill a man the next! So what's your story, eh?"

The lad hung his head. "Did you hear me crying?"

"Aye, though I suspect you were asleep."

"I wasn't sleeping," the other denied. "I think I've forgotten how to sleep! But I swear my tears were for someone else, not me." He ground his teeth in suppressed fury.

"For who then?"

The lad looked at Tarra, his young face white as chalk in

the thin moonlight. "My sister. She's only a year older than me—but she sleeps with the other girls in that lead wagon!"

Tarra drew a sharp breath. This explained a great deal. He nodded. "Well, I can understand your misery," he said, "but not your interference on my behalf. You risked your neck to help me. Indeed, it's still very much at risk!"

The youth's turn to nod. "This dog Gys Ankh whipped me, too, when I was taken. If I was going to die a slave in Shad, knowing my sister for a naked whore in some black wizard's palace . . ." He shrugged. "I might as well die here and now, helping you to kill Ankh. At least I'd have my pride."

"Keeping your pride's one thing," Tarra grunted, "and keeping your head is another. Now we've to deal with this one before he stiffens up on us." The dead rogue Hrossak lay between them, his body still warm.

The youth shuddered. "Can't we dump him in the boat on the wagon there?"

"We could," said Tarra, "except it might be a noisy bit of work. So far we've not woken anyone up—and lucky for us these lads are knackered from walking all day and many a day. They're captives like us, I know, but by now some of 'em'll be desperate. They'd likely turn us in hoping to save their own skins. Anyway, wagon's the first place they'll look for him, just wait and see. Come morning, Gys Ankh gone and his mount still here? Sleeping off a skin too many in a nice warm wagon, obviously. Then they'd find him, and you and me closest to him. Hot irons applied in the right places, and be sure we'd talk . . ."

"So what do we do with him?"

"What's your name?" Tarra briefly changed the subject.

"Loomar," said the other. "Loomar Nindiss. My father took Jezza and me out of Grypha two years ago when our mother died. We built a little farm down south on the Eastern Range, close to Hrossa's borders—but not too close. There was the makings of a village there. Then, maybe three weeks ago—" Again he ground his teeth, hung his head.

"That's a familiar story," Tarra growled. "Can you dig, Loomar?"

"Dig?" Loomar looked up.

Tarra nodded. "Right here, right now. With your hands. Like this."

He started to scoop out sand, shoving it with his forearm out under the edge of the blanket. They took sand from under Gys Ankh's body, which slowly settled into the hole. An hour later it was done: a shallow grave, true, but no trace of the bully remaining on the surface.

Then Loomar showed Tarra the dead man's knife, nine inches of sudden death, its blade gleaming in starlight. "I took it from him when you were choking him," he explained, "else he might have stabbed you. I'm going to keep it."

"The hell you are!" said Tarra. "If they find that on you, they'll use it to skin you alive!"

"It's my skin," Loomar protested. "And anyway, why should they search me?"

"Because we're together," said Tarra, "and they'll most certainly search me! So you see, it's my skin, too. Now be reasonable." He gently took the knife, worked it point first, deep down out of sight into the sand. "And now—goodnight."

Loomar couldn't believe it. "You . . . you're going to sleep? On top of . . ."

Tarra cut him short. "Tomorrow's another day, son," he said. "A hard day, which can bring almost anything. We're not in the clear yet. Me, if I'm riding the rapids to hell, I want good strong arms for my paddle! So sleep. Believe me,

you'll feel better for it. How'll you be any good to your sister, skinny as a runt and weary to death from lack of sleep?"

That last did the trick. Loomar rolled over, curled himself
up. Tarra felt something of the tension go out of his body.

He gave Loomar's back a gentle punch, settled himself
down, and in his usual way made overture to Shoosh, god-
dess of the still slumbers. *Lady, if you're out there, come and get
me. I'm all yours.*

And eventually she came.

MORNING WAS A confusion, until Tarra remembered where
and what. During the night a wind had raced around the ruins, piling up the sand a bit on his side. When he yawned
and opened his eyes, what breeze remained blew dust in his
face and brought him spitting awake. It was just past dawn,
last star a fading gleam, sun free of Cthon's nets and already
pushing up his rim over the edge of the world.

The wind had made a good job of removing all traces of
last night's digging; the sand had been greatly levelled out,
except where it lay banked against obstacles—like Tarra's
face and form. Big lizards coughed and honked to greet the
dawn; camels snorted and spat; there was movement round
the extinct fires and among the wagons. A Yhemni slaver
came striding, his baggy silken breeches flattening to the
fronts of his muscular thighs.

Tarra expelled dry crusts from his nostrils, poked his
tongue about carefully in a mouth that tasted like a Northman's sandal, blinked his eyes as the black slaver grabbed
blanket, yanked it from his and Loomar's huddled forms.
"Up!" the black grunted. "Dig holes, take bread, water. Then
we go."

Tarra squinted after him as he moved among the rest of the slaves. He glanced at Loomar. "Dig holes?"

"To answer nature's calls," the youth replied, spitting out sand. "Or maybe Hrossak's don't?"

For answer Tarra carefully scraped a small hole where he'd slept, dropped his trousers and squatted. "Oh, we do," he said. "And what's more, I know just the right place for it!"

Loomar sprang to his feet and moved away; but he'd seen Tarra's meaning at once, nodded his admiration of the Hrossak's scheme. Now he waited for him to get done and tidy up the job with scuffed sand, then went and finished it off in like manner.

They weren't given water for washing and so made do with the clean white sand, which sandpapered grime from flesh clean as a whistle. Then chains shortened to draw slaves in close to the wagons, a ladle of water to sip from (all too briefly, before passing on down the line) and a crust of bread each. Tarra managed to snatch a big lump, which this time he wolfed without pause. Lots of activity now: loading completed and frizzies starting to mount up on their camels, Northmen clambering bareback aboard tough, shaggy, half-wild ponies, and Hrossak wagoners sitting bronze in the broad wooden saddles of their mighty lizard beasts—all except one. Five beast-masters yesterday, and this morning only four . . .

The last lizard in the circle sprawled all unconcerned between its shafts, honking disdainfully at its leathery brothers where they tried to call it up onto vast, waddling legs. Heads began to turn; slavers scratched their necks impatiently; Cush Gemal appeared on a pony near the lead wagon, pointed, waved, shouted, gave orders. Tarra Khash, trying to look puzzled, stood tethered to the side of his wagon, raised an eyebrow at Loomar Nindiss. Give the lad his due, he managed to look gauntly innocent.

Blacks began clambering over wagons, under canvas, into and out of boats; but no sign of Gys Ankh, and puzzlement rapidly turning to rage. A frizzy came down the line, clouting slaves about their heads, shouting: "Gys Ankh? Hrossak? You see? Where Gys Ankh?" He reached Loomar, who cowered back, then stepped past him and collared Tarra by the ear. "Gys Ankh? You see?"

"*Ow!*" said Tarra. And: "What did you say?"

"Hrossak!" the other shouted at him. "Where Hrossak?"

Tarra looked nervously all about, licked his lips, shrugged. "Er, I'm a Hrossak," he said, ingenuously.

"Not you!" the frizzy shouted, drawing back his fist. Tarra's left hand was free. He knew that if the black hit him he probably wouldn't be able to control that hand. It would simply lift the other's knife from his belt and plunge it up under his chin. Which in turn would write *finis* on all this.

Cush Gemal's voice intervened at the last moment, and all black heads turned in his direction. From close to the lead wagon, Gemal shouted: "Ankh's pony is here, and certain of his belongings. But if *he's* here it can only be under the sand! We can't linger over it, for a rider was seen last night circling the ruins. He was just a lone rider, and he kept a safe distance, but he could be the first of many. We're not the only raiders in the Primal Land, and not too far from Hrossa, either. Anyway, if there are pursuers they'll be fast and we're slow. So time's not for wasting. Therefore, make a quick search—then we go."

Tarra's frizzy turned from him, narrowed his eyes against the sun's glare where it struck on white sand. He spied the dappled, scuffed area where Tarra and Loomar had lain, the ridge of sand where it had banked against the sleeping Hrossak. He glanced sideways at the pair. "You, and you— you sleep?" He pointed at the patch of suspect sand.

"Er, yes, but—" said Tarra.

The black stepped half-a-dozen paces, probed with the toe of his sandal. His foot came out wet and stinking. "What? *What?!*" He turned on the pair in a fury.

"Me!" Loomar called out, shaking like a leaf in a gale. "I . . . I dig hole there . . ."

"Why—you—not—*say?*" the frizzy came stamping, his fists knots at his sides. And finally Tarra recognized him: the slaver with the key! He reached for Loomar, and Tarra reached for him—and Cush Gemal's voice reached all three. He leaned from his pony, snapped:

"Leave them be!" The black slaver scowled at them, nod- ded respectfully at Gemal, made off dragging his tainted foot in the sand to cleanse it.

"Tarra Khash," said Gemal. "You're a Hrossak. What do you know about these hauling lizards?"

Tarra looked up at him. "I know there's nothing I *don't* know about them!" he said. Gemal nodded, called stink-foot back, ordered Tarra's release.

"Hrossak," said Gemal, "you can walk or ride, it's your choice. Riding you'll save your feet and perhaps earn yourself a semi-permanent employment, maybe even a reward. From slave to beast-master by stroke of fate, or slave until death from some other sort of stroke. Make up your mind . . ."

Tarra looked at his freed right hand, clenched it tight, then looked again at Cush Gemal. "Seems the decision's made," he said.

Gemal nodded his crest of lacquered hair. "We'll see how trustworthy you are—if at all! Except we'll not trust you too much, not just yet. There'll be a man behind you in the wagon, with a bolt aimed at your back. So just do what's expected of you and . . . I'll talk to you again, when we break at noon."

That was that. Tarra was led to Gys Ankh's beast where he used its knee as a step up to its broad back, and so into his saddle. A good many years since he'd last driven a big hauler like this one, but he didn't think he'd forgotten how. And anyway he'd soon find out. He looked about.

At the back of the saddle was a basket of greenstuff, tidbits for well-behaved beast; and hanging by the saddle a coiled whip, long and thin. This was also for the lizard, if he should turn awkward. Tarra could use the whip expertly—once upon a time, anyway. Back on the steppes, he'd often used the whip as a threat, never as an actual weapon. Kindness would normally get the job done far quicker. But of course this lizard was new to him, and Tarra himself strange to the lizard. That was something else he'd soon be finding out about.

"*Tsss! Tsss!*" he hissed. "Up, old scaly, and all's well." The great beast turned back its head, blinked slitted eyes, honked a disinterested inquiry.

"*Tsss!*" Tarra repeated, with some urgency now, aware of his back where it made a target broad as a tavern door. "Up, my leathery lad, or Tarra's in trouble!"

Out of the corner of his eye he saw Cush Gemal, standing in his pony's saddle and watching all. Tarra gulped, shook down the whip. The lizard's slitted green eyes turned a little red and his scales came down flat upon his hide. Then Tarra reached behind and took a fistful of greenstuff, wrapped it round with the tip of the whip and made a small knot. Without pause he flicked his arm and sent bundle of cabbage leaves snaking forward. Into one side of crusty mouth flew that morsel, and drawn back out in a flash without touching tender flesh. But greenstuff gone and lizard chomping happily! Of course, for Gys Ankh hadn't been here to feed him this morning.

"Double rations at noon, old scaly," Tarra urged. "Only let's be up now and moving, eh?" And again: *"Tsss! Tsss!"*

And at last response. Up came the rear legs, tilting Tarra forward, and up at the front one at a time, tilting him sideways and then straightening him out. He cracked his whip over the beast's snout, but well clear of delicate nostrils and horn-hooded eyes; and with a single snort the creature got going. The wheels of the wagon behind creaked as they started turning, and the slaves ranked on both sides began their accustomed shuffle. And now they were mobile.

"Good!" cried Cush Gemal from the side. "Take meat with me at noon, Tarra Khash, for there are things I'd like to know about you . . ." He cantered forward to the head of the caravan, which now wound out of ruined Humquass and headed just south of east.

The feeling's entirely mutual, thought Tarra, his bronze body swaying easily to the gait of his strange and massive mount. *There are things I'd like to know about you, too . . .*

IN IMMEMORIALLY ORDAINED cycles of an hundred years duration, the wizards of Theem'hdra were wont to pursue with increased vitality and inspiration their search for immortality. All save one, for apparently Black Yoppaloth of the Yhemnis had already found it. Or perhaps not. Mylakhrion, in his day, had seemed similarly interminable— and what was he now but dust and bones?

Now, there are men and there are men, and there are wizards and wizards. There *were* ways by which a man might aspire to aeons of existence; but black, inimical magick had never been Teh Atht's chosen route. White magick, or at worst grey, had always sufficed; though truth to tell, at various desperate times he'd been tempted. But to his knowledge black sorcery benefited no one, and least of all its users. Not in the long run.

Mylakhrion, perhaps the mightiest mage ever, had called on Great Cthulhu for means of infinitely elongating life, only to discover it shortened to nothing. Loxzor of the Hrossaks— a steppes-bred singularity among sorcerers, powerful necromancer in his life but dead now some six or seven hundred years—had likewise sought to control the uncontrollable . . . and for all his foul formulae had been eaten by a slime. Exior K'mool, Mylakhrion's one-time apprentice . . . well, his termination remained conjectural. Several times, tracing Exior's pattern in the spheres of his astrologarium, Teh Atht had discovered no sure surceasement; it could be that Exior had achieved that longed-for longevity, but not in this world. Essence-sniffing spells had failed to detect tiniest trace . . .

Ardatha Ell, who had wandered the worlds and universes and studied the secrets of spheres within spheres, was said to sojourn in Elysia; but since he was not of this world in the first place, his case should hardly be counted. And of other wizards, black and white, who had searched for life everlasting, only to discover that the search outlasted the life: their names were legion.

Azatta Leet had died in Chlangi early in his twelfth decade, ten of which had been spent deciphering a certain Rune of Revitalization. In the hour of his triumph, upon speaking the words of power, he had become a mindless pre-historic liquid which evaporated in a stray beam of sunlight, from which it had not the sense to crawl! "Revitalized," aye, but too far: for instead of returning to his youth he had become as his most remote ancestor, a denizen of oceans primal even to Primal Theem'hdra, and mortal to a fault.

Phaithor Ulm, doubtless hot on the trail of personal perpetuity, had necromantically examined exanimate intelligences which, disgruntled, had given him false information—by use of which he'd rendered himself as a handful of green dust. The pitfalls were many.

And yet at its peak the cycle sent sorcerers of all persuasions into frenzies of heightened activity, invariably reducing their numbers and rewarding none at all. As to the why of it: wizards are generally a prideful lot, and to achieve immortality would be to assume the most coveted mantle of all, the fame of Mylakhrion himself. Indeed it would be to surpass him, and in so doing become Wizard of Wizards! What? Why, lesser mages would crawl to the feet of one so mighty, imploring his very tutelage!

Hatr-ad of Thinhla (suspect sorcerer at best) might assume the duties of Teh Atht's hall porter; Khrissa's All-High Ice-Priest would be his potwatcher; Moormish of the Wastes would find employment translating tedious and meaningless glyphs . . . and so on. Sweet dreams! But if some other should stumble on the secret first: then picture Teh Atht as decoder, or porter, or potwatcher, and so on. Tasteless inversion at best.

Five years ago he'd sensed the onset of the cycle, set out upon his quest, only to have it end in the Temple of the Scarlet Scorpion, with a warning of DOOM about to befall all Theem'hdra, whose heart was his own beloved Klühn.

Since then he'd returned home, discovered said DOOM diminished to extinction, and observed the antics of a man—a mere man—in his crystal shewstone. Ah, but perhaps not a "mere" man, and certainly a most interesting one.

And now Tarra Khash seemed bound for Shad in Shadarabar across the Straits of Yhem, to be used in certain ceremonies of Black Yoppaloth's devise. Him and likewise the many slaves and maidens taken there with him. And an entire century fled since last the Yhemnis of Shadarabar raided on mainland whites, and the cycle of immortality-lust fast approaching its peak among Theem'hdra's thaumaturges. Oh, a very definite connection here, aye, and a state of affairs in which Teh Atht perceived a rare opportunity.

Now, it is seen how the Primal Land's wizards were rivals all; none more aware of that fact than Teh Atht himself, who knew well enow the difficulties to be encountered in attempting to breach any fellow wizard's protections—the spells each sorcerer employed to maintain and ensure absolute privacy—*especially* at the onset of the looming hour of propitiation. To dare even the most covert surveillance of Black Yoppaloth's machinations at this time would result in dire rebuke, be sure! If indeed this were that same Yoppaloth of histories a thousand years old, retribution were surely swift and most certainly mordant!

Teh Atht had read somewhere how, as a result of just such imprudent prying, Exior K'mool of Humquass had invoked a certain Yoppaloth's wrath: the Yhemni mage had conjured against him a squad of onyx automatons, with quicksilver blood and unbreakable crystal scythes for arms. Not even the curse of Curious Concretion would work on them, because they were stone already! And how might one freeze or poison quicksilver blood? Only by extreme good fortune, and at the very last moment, had Exior recalled a laconic Rune of Liquescence (with which in less perilous times he'd reshaped poorly constructed shewstones), melted the scythe arms of the robots and so rendered them comparatively harmless. But still and all they'd clumped around Humquass for a week before the last of them stamped himself to cryptocrystalline shards.

Dangerous then to send any familiar creature spying on him, lest Yoppaloth discover it and send back something much worse; but what if Yoppaloth *himself* took to his own bosom just such a spy? Aha! Different story then, for sure— especially if that spy should be kept in ignorance of his role!

And wherefore Teh Atht's desire to spy on the Yhemni mage in the first place? Simply to discover if indeed he *was* that same Yoppaloth come down the centuries—and if so, how! Perhaps there was that in his methods which Klühn's resident sorcerer could use to his own ends. He doubted it, for the Yoppaloth of legend wasn't much known for white or even grey magicks, but it were surely worth the shot.

All of these thoughts had been in Teh Atht's mind while he drifted high over Theem'hdra to Nameless Desert. It was a journey he might have accomplished in minutes, but that would mean suffering the debilitating nausea of great speed; and also, he'd desired to spend time merely thinking things out. And so he'd flown a circuitous route and slowly, which were just as well; for as evening came down so he'd found himself nodding where he sat cross-legged, in contemplative attitude, in the softly indented centre of his levitator. Already the false vitality gained from magickally accelerated sleep was wearing off, his mind succumbing to weariness and dull sloth; and in any case it were never a good idea to go lamia-visiting by night.

Even now he spied a red-glowing blowhole reeking of sulphur and setting the sands a-shimmer with its heat, and knew that down there somewhere in a lava cavern where red imps leaped and cavorted, "cousin" Orbiquita kept her stony vigil, all cased in a sort of Curious Concretion of her own. He suspected she'd know very little of Black Yoppaloth, but probably a good deal about a certain Hrossak.

Still and all, however much or little she knew, it would all keep until morning. And so Teh Atht formed a Warm Web about himself and flying carpet both, and lay him down to sleep a genuine sleep. And his carpet circling safely on high, through all the long night . . .

IV

Orbiquita—Cush Gemal —Weird Magick!

ORBIQUITA SLEPT AND nightmared. Nothing strange in a human being tossing in the throes of fever-dreams, conjuring monsters from subconscious mind—but weird indeed for a monster to conjure human beings! She dreamed of Tarra Khash (as she'd been wont to do a great deal recently), a Hrossak in trouble. And now he was brought back fresh to mind by Teh Atht's urgent, whispered inquiry:

"Orbiquita, are you awake? Wake up, cousin, for I wish to speak with you about a man called Tarra Khash."

The wizard had slept late, almost till noon. Then, starting awake, he'd remembered his reason for being here and mouthed a simple spell of Self-Contained Coolness. And all enveloped in a bubble of sweet air, he'd flown his carpet almost vertically into volcanic vent and descended to lamia lair.

"Oh, Tarra, Tarra!" Orbiquita moaned her brimstone passion. And she writhed somewhat in her cocoon of lava.

Teh Atht drew back a little, looked nervously all about. This was after all a forbidden place, and he risked much in coming here. He had his spells, his various protections, of course; but so did lamias, along with awesome armaments, and few as powerful as the Lamia Orbiquita. Forbidden and forbidding, this lava cavern, aye, for it was the inner sanctum of the entire Sisterhood: their secret Place of Places, their "holy" place, if that word had meaning at all to such as them. Teh Atht's eyes scanned what to him was a veritable scene from hell:

The great cave, one of many in a cavern honeycomb, was red with heat; from its bubbling lake of lava, grotesquely carved "islands" stuck up here and there like fungi of some alien moon. Keeping their distance, red imps like great glowing insects danced nimbly from island to island; they somehow managed to avoid the reek and splash of liquid rock, while glowering at Teh Atht most menacingly. Then one of them tossed a mass of burning sulphur (which bounced of course from the surface of his cool, encompassing, invisible sphere) and made vilely threatening gestures.

Annoyed, the wizard scowled and began to draw a pattern in the air with his forefinger, but when the thing was only half-shaped the imps took fright and raced off to safety, leaving him to his own devices. He grinned then, for his "spell" had been a bluff, an intricate nonsense, by no means inimical. No, for he needed all of his sorcerous strength and most of his concentration just to maintain a cool, clean biosphere in this furnace place.

And aware that his time was limited, again he turned to Orbiquita.

Her island stood central and smouldering in the oozy, gurgling, flowing red rock of the place, and upon it she sat all hunched up, cradled or enthroned in ash of tephra, like a stalagmite of lava aglow with its own fiery internal light. Externally she was layered with rock-splash, which had hardened on her warty, leathery hide, so that an ignorant person might mistake her for the veriest fossil; but her blowhole nostrils smoked and her loathsome bosom rose and fell in ponderous measure, and when her hands twitched in her dreaming, then scythe-like fingers clashed and grated together.

She was here as a penance, and here would stay for a five-year spell, at which time some similarly foolhardy sister would take her place. Thus the Sisterhood chose its guardians of this lair; but since there was little likelihood of anyone finding his way here—or even caring to—the Lamia in Residence usually weathered out her stay in stony slumbers.

"Tarra Khash," Teh Atht repeated. "I must speak with you, Orbiquita! If you know this man, which I verily believe you do—if you *have* known him—now wake you up and tell me about him. It's likely to his benefit as well as mine, I assure you . . ." And he drifted closer, carpet and life-sustaining bubble and all. Perhaps she heard his voice, or felt the cold like a draft upon her, or merely sensed the presence of an outsider; whichever, now she came awake.

Her face twitched, eyes cracked open and blinked, then glared sulphurously; great jaws gaped and lava layers scaled off in clattering scabs of stone; and finally, from a sudden eruption of steam and tainted reek came her rumbling, doomful voice:

"Who is it disturbs my sleep? Who *dares* come here to seek me out? Who speaks to me of . . . of Tarra Khash?" And here a strange, strange thing: for on speaking his name her voice broke and became more nearly human, more surely female, and now at last Teh Atht began to understand. He'd scarce deemed it possible before, but now he guessed the truth: Orbiquita, devourer of men, had finally found one to love!

Now she stood up and stretched, bloating to the full form and monstrous mass of true lamia. As the smoke cleared, so

Teh Atht floated face to face with his "cousin," and wondered as he'd oft wondered aforetime how even the mighty Mylakhrion had cohabited with such as this. She sensed the thought, knew its author at once. And she nodded what were possibly a greeting, at least a sign of her recognition.

"Teh Atht," she said then, her voice descending to sibilant, perhaps sarcastic whisper. "Most wondrous mage of Klühn, come a-visiting his cousin in her shame." More fully awake now, she shook her head in a seeming puzzlement, so that lava shards splintered and went clattering. "And did I hear you mention a certain name? And if so what is it to you? Or is it that you're here simply to insult me?"

"Insult?" He peaked his thin grey eyebrows in a frown. "I uttered no—"

"Uttered, no—" she cut him off, "—but you *thought* an insult!" And she stretched back her leathery wings, leaned forward, hunched to the rim of her island. Her scythe feet gouged the rock as lesser knives gouge clay, and her breath was a sulphurous musk. "How could Mylakhrion bring himself to mate with lamias, indeed!"

"*Ah!*" Teh Atht held up a finger, backed off a little. "But I meant no offence, Orbiquita. One might similarly ponder the fact that lamias *consented* to such immemorial, er, unions! And then there's the sheer how of it, which were—"

"Paint me no pictures, wizard!" again she cut him off, her voice hissing like steam. Then she cocked her head on one side a little. "Oh, and are you so naive? Do you imagine he took my mother's mothers to bed clad in their true forms? Never! As women, he took them, and under some foul spell so that they could not revert and devour him! And who are you that you should find this so unnatural?" Here she smiled slyly, or at least did that with her face which Teh Atht supposed was a smile. "Why, haven't I heard it rumoured that you yourself bed succubi?"

Teh Atht grew warm despite his unbreakable bubble of cool, sweet air. "It is the *nature* of the succubus to come to men in the night!" he quickly protested.

"*Huh!*" she snorted from flaring nostrils. "And is it also the nature of men to *call* them to their beds? Make no denials, cousin, for I have read it in your mind. Mylakhrion's blood runs in your veins. He was an artful necromancer, aye, but he was also a lustful man—and all the men in his line after him . . ."

Teh Atht must break the deadlock, and would definitely prefer to change the subject. "You're in argumentative mood, Orbiquita," he said, "and time's a-wasting. I've so much air in here, and then no more. And so I say again: I meant no insult or injury. And I implore you: what can you tell me of a certain Hrossak, a man called Tarra Khash?"

Her turn to draw back, as if suddenly splashed in her eyes with acid. "I . . . I had forgotten," she said then, "how you have the power to read my mind as easily as I read yours. And so you're a peeping Tom, too, eh, Teh Atht? How much have you read?"

He shook his head and waved his arm placatingly. "Only that you've known him. And that by accident. I stayed a while in your castle and would have spoken to you from there, but you were dreaming. And your dreams were filled with this Tarra Khash . . ." And more hastily: "But I wasn't prying, as you see for yourself. Oh, I *might* have stolen your dreams, Orbiquita, but instead I came to you openly. Of course I did, for as you yourself have pointed out, we're of one blood."

She dwelled on that a moment. "And you want to know

about . . . about Tarra Khash?" Abruptly she turned away. "Then I can't help you. I know nothing of him, except that he's a man. In every sense, a man . . ."

Teh Atht said nothing but waited, and eventually she turned his way again. "Well?"

He shrugged, casually played his ace: "Then he's likely done for, and my quest for immortality gone with him."

"Done for?" she hissed, alarm plain in the rippling of her warty flesh. "I had dreamed he was in danger, and are you saying it were no dream but reality?"

The wizard nodded. "Your lamia precognition, Orbiquita. There's a bond between you and him, no matter how you may deny it. And so, wherever he wanders, when he faces danger you'll sense it here in your lava cavern. Aye, and he faces it right now!"

She was all ears now, her breathing erratic, claws clashing willy-nilly. "How done for?" she demanded. "What, Tarra Khash, my Tarra, in danger most grave? You fear for his life? Even you, a mighty mage? Now tell me where he is, and the nature of this threat. Tell me at once, or flee this place while yet you may!" She went to probe his mind, on which Teh Atht at once drew shutters.

"We trade," he said. "A tale for a tale. You tell me what you know of him, and I'll return the favour—though little good it will do, with you pledged to guard this place for a five-year!"

She glared at him then and ground together teeth that could crunch granite. But eventually, and grudgingly, "So *be* it!" she said. "Now listen and I'll tell you all—or most . . .

"It was some months agone, the time of lamia renewal—of sisterhood vows and powers both. I was on my way here, to the Great Meeting of all my sisters, but I'd left it late and my magick had waned somewhat. Also, the moon approached its full, and as you're doubtless aware, lamias are not at their best in Gleeth's full glare. For my own reasons I travelled in human guise, a young girl mounted on a white yak, with a parasol to keep the moon from burning me. Then—skirting the Mountains of Lohmi *en route* for Nameless Desert—trouble!

"Villains out of Chlangi ambushed me, made off with my beasts, my book of runes, a ring come down to me from our ancestor Mylakhrion. Aye, and they took much more than that. They . . . they made vile sport with me under the leering moon, of a sort I'll not describe. Then they pegged me out naked in Gleeth's glare and rode off laughing.

"Tarra Khash found me, else I were not telling you this now. Injured, he was, for the same bunch of bandits had fallen on him, too. He'd taken an arrow in his back and seemed near all in. But I didn't know that when first I saw him. He was just another man come to molest me; what with moon's deadly ray and his ravishing, I'd surely be a goner come morning.

"But I was wrong. When by right he should be caring for himself, instead he cared for me. I fancy he even suspected my true nature, but still he cared for me.

"He cut me loose, covered me, put me on his camel and hurried me to a safe place. He sheltered me from the moon, built a fire, offered me food and drink. Indeed, he offered me whatever I needed for my comfort, all of what little he had. But that was how *he* viewed himself, not as *I* viewed him. Indeed, he had *much* to offer a moon-weakened, sorely depleted lamia. And so trusting was he that he put himself at my mercy, completely in my power.

"I could have taken all, slaked my thirst in a moment, but . . . I chose merely to sip. I kissed his neck," (Teh Atht shuddered), "tasted his blood—only a taste, no more. And good blood it was: rich and strong, a trifle wild, even heady! "Twere a battle with myself not to gorge on him there and then and be done with it. Aye, and better for me if I had.

"But instead I balmed his wound, left him sleeping, used the strength he had given me to call up desert djinni who bore me here. I was late, without excuse, and so bound to do my stint in this brimstony place. Ah, but first I asked a boon of previous lava lamia: that she give me only sufficient time in which to avenge myself, regain my ring and rune-book! To which she agreed.

"My powers were returned to me in full and I sped me to Chlangi the Doomed, where once again Tarra Khash was of service. He knew the where of my ring and book; what's more, he planned his own retribution on a certain Fregg, so-called 'king' of that city of dogs and thieves. Fregg had stolen his sword—the merest stump of a blade, however ornate and scintillant its hilt—but no man steals from Tarra Khash. Not with impunity. Against all odds he'd take it back, and with my assist he did! And I got my revenge, my ring, my book. More than this, lava lamia got her breakfast, grilled alive on these searing rocks. And so Fregg's no more . . ."

Again the wizard shuddered. "And is that all?"

She glared at him. "No, not the half of it!" She glared again, then sighed, and her voice became a groan, almost a whimper. "For since then . . . he's in my mind, in my dreams, in the very air I breathe. Even in this place, over sulphur reek and roar of vented steam, I smell his breath, hear his voice. I care for nothing save memories, all too brief, of him." She looked at Teh Atht almost in desperation. "The iron has gone out of me, my will deserted me. What say you, has he spelled me, cousin?"

He nodded. "So it would seem, Orbiquita, aye. And a spell rarely broken, called the Lethargy of Love. More, I'd say the dosage were lethal!"

His words sank home and she started up. "Love? *Love?* You are mad! I am a lamia, and Tarra Khash a man. Does a spider love a fly? Does a browsing beast in a field love the grass? Does a roaring fire love a log? Only to consume it!"

"The symptoms of what ails you don't lie, Orbiquita," he answered. "You were in the guise of a woman when you met him, and women have their weaknesses. Ten thousand other men might have found you that night, and done what Tarra Khash did, and died for their pains. But they didn't find you, he did—and something stirred in your blood. The world itself is a cauldron, the mighty vat of some sorcerer god, and we are all ingredient to his works. That is all it was with you and Tarra Khash, that was all it took: chemistry!"

"Begone!" she groaned. "Go now, Teh Atht. Leave me to my thoughts, my miseries. For I think you may be right, and so I've a deal to ponder."

But as he caused his carpet to retreat from her and made to turn away: "No, wait!" she cried. "First tell me where he is and the nature of his plight. We made a pact, remember?"

Teh Atht turned back, told her all he knew as quickly as possible, for the air in his bubble was almost expended. "And now I must go," he breathlessly concluded, "or else stay here for good!"

"Will you not help him?" she cried as he turned away and made for furnace flue to the surface.

"Methinks it may be in my interest so to do," he answered over a distance, ascending through smoke, steam and bellows' belch. "But alas, it's hard to find the means. A hazardous business, Orbiquita, interference in the schemes of a fellow sorcerer. This much I'll promise you: I'll follow his course as best I can. And if aught of evil befalls him, at least I'll make report of it."

And bursting from the blowhole, dissolving his bubble and breathing clean air again, he heard in his mind her furious threat: "You'll make report? Of harm befalling Tarra Khash? To me? Think well before you do, Teh Atht. For if he dies you'll not need return here. I'll hound you to hell, 'cousin,' and gnaw on your ribs there!"

And, because lamias aren't much for idle threats, for a third time Teh Atht shuddered . . .

TARRA'S BACKSIDE AND hips were bruised black and blue from his jolting ride; but they'd quickly harden to it, he knew. He was well out of practice, that was all; and anyway, better a few bruises than the torment of the slaves, now that they rested and their trembly limbs began protesting. Still and all, noon had come soon enough, when the slaver caravan groaned to a halt in its accustomed defensive circle. Then Tarra had climbed stiffly down, fed his beast the promised double ration, watered it, too, all the while casting cautiously about to see what he might see. Like perhaps a pony going spare, with saddle-bags, water and what all. But no such luck.

What he did see was the sly grin on a certain frizzy's face, and the way he kept his crossbow nocked and ever pointed just a little too close to Tarra Khash. Then came his summons to attend Cush Gemal in hastily erected, tasselled tent.

He went, with his Yhemni guard close behind, and found a fire already prepared, meat steaming on a spit, and Gemal inside on heaped cushions, taking his ease with a weird wooden smoke-pipe and a silver jug of wine. "Come in out of the sun," said Gemal. "Sit down, take wine, and in a little while eat. And meanwhile tell me your thoughts."

The half-breed slaver's voice was not unpleasant, Tarra decided. It was low, dark, should be warm but came out cold as snow on a mountain's peak. And strange for a Yhemni (or at least for a man of Shad and the jungles around), it was not without culture; with echoes doubtless of Gemal's mixed ancestry, and a hint of study and learning far above the accustomed level of lands beyond the Straits of Yhem. All of this from a few spoken words? Not entirely. Gemal's bearing and the respect he mustered in the other blacks, aye, and the light in his black eyes, all of these things were contributary to Tarra's analysis.

His ancestry . . . The steppeman wondered about that. Black as ebony, Cush Gemal, and yet thin-lipped, slant-eyed like certain tribes of Northmen, tall and cold as a Khrissan, ornately crested as any sophisticate of Klühn or Thandopolis. Of polyglot parts, this slaver, but in no way mongrel; exuding power, it was almost as if he came from a tribe or even a land apart, from worlds unknown. Either that, or there were elements of all the Primal Land in him, with jungle predominant.

Tarra looked at him again, openly, even admiringly; he hadn't forgotten how swift had come Gorlis Thad's uppance. Why, that burly bellowing Northman hadn't stood snowflake in hell's chance against this cold, black, hollow-cheeked, close to cadaverous chieftain! Now *there* was a thought! A tribal chieftain! Even a Chief of Chiefs—and why not? For certainly the way he commanded respect, not only from his own people but also Hrossaks and Northmen alike, would seem to place him in some such station.

All of this but a moment's thought, and Gemal's eyes dark

on Tarra where the steppeman sat cross-legged on a large green cushion, with a small silver jug cool in his hand. And the sweet smoke of Gemal's pipe circulating in tent and Hrossak lungs both; and his low, knowing voice offering no threat but yet quietly urging as he now repeated: "Your thoughts, Tarra?"

The Hrossak's thoughts, especially in respect of someone who could have his head in a moment, would normally be private, unspoken. And yet now: "I'm thinking you're a strange one," said Tarra Khash, his tongue astonishing him with its frankness.

Gemal hardly seemed offended. He gave a laugh. "My thoughts about you are much the same!" he said. "I captured you, may kill you even now, and yet you don't hold me in awe. You spoke of *my* strangeness, not of your own fear."

"I hold you in something of wonder, perhaps, and a deal of curiosity. But awe?" Tarra shook his head. "I *know* you're not ordinary, not in any way—that's obvious to me as water's wet! But I'm not awed by your power over me; for here and now that power's a fact, and I can't change it—not here and now. If you do kill me, *then* I'll likely be awed, but only in the last second. Or perhaps in the second after that?"

Gemal puffed more smoke in Tarra's direction, smiled in his skull-like fashion, said: "More of your thoughts, Hrossak, for they're refreshing and they interest me greatly."

Tarra paused a moment before answering, sniffed the smoke and thought: *That's Zha-weed he's puffing on, which wizards use in their magicks, and less able addicts to lighten their burdens. It brings pleasing illusions and loosens the tongue . . .* And he also thought: *Perhaps I'll feed my big lizard a little of your Zha-weed, Cush Gemal, then set him free to create a diversion, and finally—*

"Well?" Gemal frowned, however slightly. His eyes had fastened on Tarra, and now their concentration grew intense.

"I intend—" Tarra began, automatically and out loud this time—at which moment the tent's flap was drawn back, pungent smoke blown aside and fresh air wafted in. It brought mouth-watering smells with it, and the Hrossak's mind cleared in a moment. "—to enjoy this good food you've offered me, Cush Gemal!"

Gemal scowled at the black who stood there with silver platter, sizzling meat, razor sharp carver, and scowled not a little at Tarra, too; but then, in another moment, he laughed out loud. The frizzy departed and for a little while they ate in silence. Then Gemal said:

"And have you no questions for me? Don't you even care about your fate? Surely you're curious about your destination, and what's to become of you there?"

Tarra shrugged. "I've always been a wanderer," he said, "an adventurer—though as you see for yourself, not so much from choice as by accident. Indeed in this respect it seems I'm accident prone! But it has to be said that this is something of an adventure, and entirely in keeping, even if it's not in accordance with my plans. What's more I'm on the move again, albeit in a direction which could be improved upon! So all in all, p'raps I'm not so badly off." He shrugged again. "As for my fate: the fates of all men are wont to change from day to day. I was a slave; now I drive a lizard and eat with a Chief of Chiefs; who can say what's waiting for me tomorrow? You mentioned our destination, which I believe to be Shad. Ah, but Shad's still a long way off . . ."

"What?" Cush Gemal raised thin, slanting eyebrows. He smiled, but warningly. "That sounds close to a threat, Tarra Khash, however veiled! Should I put you in chains again, or do you choose to serve me well and faithfully for another day or two—and then go free?"

"My freedom?" Tarra stopped eating. "That's tempting. And all I must do is drive the big lizard?"

Gemal watched his face. The steppeman's eyes flickered briefly—perhaps longingly?—over the glittering, serrated edge of the carver where it lay on the silver platter between him and his host. Try as Tarra might, he couldn't keep from glancing at it. Gemal noticed but made no comment. Instead he answered the other's question:

"We're heading for the shallow salt lochs where they wash in from the Eastern Ocean. We came in by that route and it's how we'll go out. Another day and a half, two days at worst speed, and we'll be there. But it's important that there's no delay. These are momentous, world shattering times. Soon, in Shad . . ." He paused abruptly, blinked, flared his nostrils. And Tarra thought:

'Ware, Cush Gemal! It's the Zha-weed, my friend!

"Let it suffice to say," Gemal continued, "that I can brook no delay—and that the loss of a good Hrossak drover would inconvenience me. Of course, I could simply abandon one wagon and boat. But that would also mean abandoning a fifth of the slaves I've taken. Indeed it would mean slaughtering them! Black Yoppaloth has no plans at present for war with the mainland, and so there can be no survivors from this little trek, no wagging tongues carrying tales to mainland cities. We want no armadas sailing out of Klühn and Thandopolis on missions of red revenge against Shad!

"So you see I've a neat and tidy mind, Tarra Khash, the very opposite of yours in that I demand that things go *exactly* according to plan! I planned to take a certain number of male slaves and female beauties back across the water to Shad, and

I'll do my utmost to make that plan work. Also, I planned to ship at least four Hrossak lizards, which are unknown in Shad and will make for magnificent parades in the arena. And so, if you'll continue as you've started and drive your beast to the water—and give me no problems along the way—there I'll pay you off and let you and beast both go free. That will leave me with a vessel to carry myself and Black Yoppaloth's brides, and four more for slaves and lizards."

"Why turn me loose?" asked Tarra, ingenuously. "That hardly seems the way of a slaver to me. Why take only four lizards when you could take five? Why attempt to strike a bargain with me when I'm in your power? And as for *paying* me . . . ! Why even bother to explain anything to me when there's nothing I can do to change a thing, what- and whichever you decide?"

Gemal looked at him, nodded, smiled a wry smile. "You called me a Chief of Chiefs," he said. "But even a Chief of Chiefs can be lonely; aye, and especially he can grow sick of power. With these men you see around you: my every word is their command—which bores me utterly! It *pleases* me to have someone I can bargain with! Do you see? These men look on me as their master, and others see me as a monster, but I'm rarely seen simply as another man. You look on me with some curiosity, but with little or nothing of fear. However different you sense me to be, however strange, you *know* I am just another man. And I suspect you acknowledge no mere man as your master. But at the same time, I don't think you're incapable of humility. Perhaps in this we have something in common, perhaps not . . .

"Anyway, I like you for what I've seen in you—so much indeed that I might easily have taken you back to Shad simply to keep you with me, eventually to become my companion and friend. Aye, and I might still do it, so don't force my hand! Accept what I offer and leave it at that."

Tarra glanced at the knife again, then let his eyes linger there and deliberately drew Gemal's eyes to that same spot. The slavemaster looked at the shining blade, looked at Tarra, raised an inquiring eyebrow and waited.

"Why have you tempted me, Cush Gemal?" said Tarra. "Oh, only a fool would attempt to kill you here, I know . . . but still I *might* have tried. Or was this a test of some sort?"

Gemal smiled a thin, knowing smile and returned his gaze once more to the razor-honed carver. "Not so much a test as a trial," he eventually answered. "Or perhaps a lesson?—but only *if* you had taken the bait. If you had . . . then I would know we could never be friends, and by now you'd be dead." It wasn't a threat but a statement of fact, as Cush Gemal saw it.

"A trial? A lesson?" Tarra looked bemused. "What sort of lesson?"

"A lesson in trust. I was showing you how much I'd be willing to trust you. Or maybe I wasn't."

"I don't understand," Tarra shook his head.

"Reach for the knife, Tarra Khash," Gemal invited. "Do it swiftly. Take it up as if . . . as if to kill me!"

"What?"

"Do it!" the slaver insisted.

"But I have no desire to—"

"I know that, now," said Gemal, "but do it anyway. Go *on!* Test your mettle against mine—if you dare."

Tarra's father had used to say: "Never dare a madman or a fool, and never accept one from either!" His hand blurred into action, came to rest atop Cush Gemal's where it was there first!

"Yibb!" said Tarra, merely breathing the word. "And I thought *I* was fast!"

"You are," said the other, "and if your joints weren't quite so stiff you'd be faster still." He turned his hand on its back to clasp Tarra's in strong, slender fingers. "So now you see there's no subterfuge. I'd merely caution you against making trouble for yourself. For if you do I'll be obliged to chain you again, and kill you where the land meets the water. Or take you to Shad as a slave, which I've no wish to do. I'd have you as a friend, Tarra Khash, but never as a slave; for as a slave I'd need four others just to watch you! And anyway, I've read it in your eyes that Shad's not the way you wish to go, not in any event."

He stood up, drew the steppeman up with him. "So be it," he nodded. "When we reach the water I'll give you gold, enough to repay your costs, and turn you loose. For I have to agree: Shad's not the place for you. It's in my bones that there'd be trouble for you in Shad, perhaps for both of us."

They stepped from the tent. Outside, across a sky so blue it seared the eyes, faint wisps of cloud were drifting from the east. In that same direction but as yet far away, the sky was patterned like the scales of a fish; also, at the very edge of vision, it seemed that nodding dust-devils cavorted and careened, astir on the horizon's rim.

"Bad weather ahead," Tarra pulled a wry face. "It'll make the big lizards unruly."

Gemal nodded. "The season of storms approaches," he replied, frowning. "All the more reason to make haste." Suddenly he staggered, drew a sharp breath, grasped Tarra's shoulder with shaking claw, purely to steady himself. All his limbs were at once atremble. Close by, a pair of blacks saw, took fright and would have hurried away. Tarra wondered at their terror; but Gemal saw them, beckoned them to attend him. Trembling more than he, they crept close.

"Go," Gemal croaked in Tarra's ear as the frizzies took hold and gave him their support. "Get away from me. Back to your lizard and safety."

Safety? thought Tarra. *From what?*

The two shivering Yhemnis, eyes bugging and obviously mortally afraid, helped Gemal back to his tent. He went like an old man, seeming strangely shrivelled and drawn down into himself. But at the flap of the tent he caught his blacks by their wrists and drew them in after him.

Tarra wondered: *A contagious fever? Is that what's wrong with him?* . . . Or was it something else? "Cush Gemal!" he called out. "I'll drive the big lizard to the ocean lochs, never fear."

"I know it well enow, Tarra," came back the answer from inside the black tent. But it was a harsh, gasping croak, in no wise Gemal's previous voice, and there was more of pain than strength in it . . .

BY THE TIME Tarra got back to his monstrous beast and drew its hoods up over ridgy eyes, a wind had sprung up that drove the sand with stinging force. It would be a short blow, Tarra guessed, but a bitter one. The clouds were scudding now and beginning to pile one into the next; behind them, the sun a fading orange blob, growing ever more dim.

Tarra spoke words of reason to his beast and it huddled down. Then he crept under the big wagon, found Loomar Nindiss cowering with the rest of the slaves. The sand flurries weren't so bad under here. He called the lad to him and Loomar came crawling and clanking, shouted: "What's up?"

"Eh?" said Tarra. "The storm, d'you mean?"

Loomar shook his head. "I saw you go to Gemal's tent. Is all well?"

"Maybe better than that," said Tarra. And he began to relate all that had happened. But—

"*Ahhh!*" a concerted sigh went up from all the slaves crouched under the wagon. They all stared wide-eyed and slack-jawed toward Cush Gemal's black tent. Tarra and Loomar peeped out from under wagon's rim, followed the massed gaze of the others.

A dust-devil—but a giant, almost a tornado—picked its way through a gap between two wagons and closed with Cush Gemal's tent. For a moment the tent belled out a little like an inflated lung, then fell slack as the wall of the twister enveloped it; but the tent was not drawn aloft, nor even caused to strain at its guys. And where the wind gusted all about, and smaller dust-devils raced here and there, in and about the ring of wagons—and where canvasses flapped in the spiteful wind, and beasts and men cowered from the sting of whirling sand—Gemal's tent stood as before, unflustered, becalmed, black tassels hanging slack! The tent was in no wise affected, for indeed it stood central in the silent "eye" of the twister! And there the great funnel of whirling sand remained, with Gemal's tent untroubled at its centre, while all about was a chaos of wind and rushing, circling sand.

But the frenzied rush of sand-laden air had seemed to create electrical energies, trapping them in the core of the twister; for while Gemal's tent remained untroubled, it was not unaffected. No, for ephemeral green fires shivered and danced in its silken, scalloped eaves and dripped like phosphorescent rain from its tassels—but only for a little while longer. Then—

In a matter of moments the uproar lessened and the swaying column that reached from dunes to sky broke up, hurling its tons of sand afar to fall like stinging rain; the clouds began to break up and beams of sunlight blazed through; lesser dust-devils dwindled and departed, racing off to extinction somewhere across the desert. Finally, blacks, Hrossaks, Northmen began to move again, emerging from various boltholes, mostly under canvas. But all eyes remained glued to Gemal's tent, from which the dancing green fires had now departed, where at last the flap was thrown back and tall, crested slavemaster emerged, began shouting orders. All appeared to be back to normal.

Tarra Khash marvelled. Five minutes ago the half-caste had seemed all in, gripped in the spasms of some mortal illness. Now he looked and sounded stronger than ever! What's more, he even seemed less emaciated, if that were at all possible.

The drive resumed almost at once, with Cush Gemal riding beside the lead wagon, but this time his tent was left standing till last. Tarra made a great show of removing sand from his lizard's eyes and nostrils, sat upon the beast's feet and cleaned its claws, generally made hard work of getting under way; and thus he contrived to be at the very end of the line when the caravan stretched itself out toward the east. And in this way, too, he could look back a little way to where shuddering frizzies decamped Gemal's tent and packed it away on a camel.

Then they scooped a shallow hole in the sand, in which they dumped a couple of former colleagues, covering them quickly before mounting up. This could only be the pair Gemal had drawn into the tent with him. So Tarra surmised.

Difficult to say for sure, for from the one or two glimpses he'd managed to get they now seemed little more than bags of bones, shrivelled and sere as mummies.

And Tarra Khash knew he'd made a queer, queer friend indeed . . .

V

A Wizard's Quest— In Gemal's Camp

IN ONE CORNER of the Primal Land, Cush Gemal's caravan of slaves lumbering for the salt water lochs now only forty miles away; and in another . . .

Teh Atht arrived at Orbiquita's castle in the mainly shunned Desert of Sheb and flew in through a high window. His flying carpet bore him down a vast, winding stone stairwell which opened into a great hall on the ground floor; and here he stepped down into dust and cobwebs, small drifts of sand blown in through various cracks, and the long accumulated litter of myriad mice and bats. He sighed and wrinkled his nose, carefully lifted the hem of his rune-embellished robe, looked all about in the gloom.

He sighed again. Lamias were less than fastidious, he knew, but Orbiquita must be slattern of all slatterns. Aye, and the slovenly creature his cousin, at that! But this wouldn't do; he could hardly entertain guests with the place in this condition.

"Go," he told the carpet in a tongue only it understood. "Fly fast to Klühn, return at once with the one who hops and the one who flits—but leave the one who seeps there, for he'll only slow you down."

The carpet rippled itself gracefully in acknowledgement of its master's command, backed swiftly away, spiralled up the corkscrew stairwell and disappeared.

And now the great white mage of Klühn thought back a little on how he came to be here . . .

Leaving Orbiquita in her lava lair, he'd first thought to pay a visit to the Suhm-yi man and maid who'd known Tarra Khash in Klühn and with him destroyed Gorgos' temple there. But that were easier thought than acted upon. Suhm-yi means "rarely seen," and if Amyr Arn and his love did not desire to be found, then it would prove singularly difficult so to do.

When last seen, Amyr and his Ulli were heading west toward the Desert of Sheb, first leg of their long trek home to Inner Isles. Very well, and Teh Atht had set off in that same direction. But as time crept on and the tired sun began to sink toward ever watchful Cthon beyond the rim of the world, where he waits out the day with his nets, so the wizard had wearied of hit-and-miss aerial surveillance. Then, too, in a small oasis far below, at the edge of Sheb's rolling dune expanse, he'd spied the tiny camp of some lone traveller.

Descending in a tight circle, Teh Atht had then made out a five-pointed Star of Power footprinted into the sand, with shimmery pool and shady palms nestled at its centre; at which he'd wagered with himself who this must be. None other but Moormish of the Wastes, whose simple protective device had backfired on him. At ground level it would scarce be noticed, but from up here it was a dead giveaway!

At first delighted, now Teh Atht soured a little as he circled lower. His mood was governed by what he knew of the man in the flat, nomad-styled tent below.

There were two such hermit sorcerers among Theem'h-dra's fraternity (?) of wizards: Moormish was one and Tarth Soquallin the other, but the latter was off somewhere far to the west and hadn't been heard of for many a year. So this must be Moormish of the Wastes, who'd been named after his predilection for forlorn and perilous wastelands. It *could* be a common man, of course, but that seemed unlikely. First there was the protective star tramped meticulously in the sand, and second the location of the camp itself. Common men weren't much given to wandering here, where lamias were wont to dwell, and Chlangi the Doomed swollen like a ripe boil scant fifteen miles away, full of the scum of the land.

Naturally (for reasons which will be seen), if Teh Atht had a choice, it would have been Tarth Soquallin he'd choose to find here; old hermit Tarth had always been his close friend and confidant, ever since the time they'd served together under tutelage of Imhlat the Teacher. Moormish, on the other hand, was sour as a green lemon and much given to grumbling; he'd hardly welcome the unannounced arrival of *any* wizard here in his private place, not even one white as Teh Atht. But . . . beggars can't be choosers; a wizard is a wizard, even if he's a notorious grouch; and right now Teh Atht was sore in need of a reliable shewstone. Moormish, habitual wanderer that he was, would doubtless have his with him.

"Hail, Moormish!" cried Teh Atht, settling his carpet to the sand and stepping down before the gaping flap of the squat, dun coloured tent.

"Begone!" came back harsh cry from within. "Hop back on your carpet and scarper. You're an intruder here, Klühn-ite, whose presence will muddle my meditations!"

Ah, well, thought Teh Atht, *so much for a welcome! And no use beating about the bush here!* "Permit me a glimpse—the merest peep—into your shewstone, Moormish," he called out loud, "and I'll bother you no more but be off at once."

Moormish appeared shufflingly from the gloom within. Thin as mountain air, dry as a husk, tattered and grimy, he scowled blackly through deep-sunken eyes and prodded Teh Atht's chest with a knobbed walking stick. "Do you know why I live out here in the wilderness?" he snapped. "No, obviously you don't or you'd know better than to come. It's to avoid the 'company'—the peeping, prying, overbearing presence—of people like you. And not only people like you, but people like anybody! It's called the freedom of solitary existence, privacy, a lone retirement. I have *chosen* to seclude myself. And you have chosen to disturb me. Worse, you'd casually probe about amongst my most precious possessions: a 'peep' into my shewstone, a 'bite' of my bread, a 'sip' of my water. And all of these things left tainted by your touch!"

Now Teh Atht was offended. He'd asked for neither food nor drink and certainly had no intention of tainting Moormish's supplies. And as for spending a few moments in private with the old claustrophobe's crystal: be sure Moormish would deny him *that* privilege to the bitter end! Except Teh Atht had no time to spare, and so was driven to extremes.

The shrivelled sorcerer's stick was still touching his chest, fending him off. *Good!* And he sent a dose of Undiluted Deafness down it on the spot, which all unseen, unfelt, and especially unheard, at once blocked Moormish's eardrums.

"You're a crazed old recluse!" Teh Atht shouted then, at the same time smiling and nodding agreeably, testing his spell's efficacy.

"Eh?" said Moormish, squinting curiously. He put a finger in his ear and wiggled it violently.

Excellent! thought Teh Atht with a grin; and without further ado he uttered the curse of Curious Concretion, so that in a moment Moormish was marbled. Then, leaving the fossilized mage with finger in ear and stick jabbing at nothing—as grotesque a pose as one could wish—he moved past him into the gloomy, smelly tent and sought out Moormish's crystal.

The shewstone stood alone upon a low, circular wooden table, with several ancient, well-patched cushions piled close by. Teh Atht preferred to remain standing, straightway made himself known. The sphere answered in a simple code which the wizard at once deciphered, making it out to say: "Ah, Teh Atht! I've heard of you. And is old Moormish dead, then? He must be, or else you've stolen me!"

"No, not dead," Teh Atht chuckled. "Merely dumbfounded. Or perhaps deaf-founded? Or maybe even stone deaf-founded!" And he told the shewstone all.

"He'll be mad as hell!" the agitated sphere groaned, its milky screen all astir. "And he'll doubtless take it out on me."

Teh Atht shook his head. "He won't know," he said, "unless you yourself tell him. I certainly won't, not if we can come to some—arrangement?"

"Scry all you will," said the sphere at once. "I'm at your mercy."

After that it was the simplest thing to find Amyr Arn and Ulli Eys, and pinpoint their precise location and direction of travel. And so convenient their bearing and rate of travel that Teh Atht was given to utter a small cry of delight. Perhaps things were falling in order at last.

He thanked Moormish's crystal and began to turn away . . . then checked himself to ask: "Incidentally, does your master use you as an oracle, too? As diary, calendar, *aide-memoire*, and so on?"

"Aye, and other things to boot," the shewstone waxed bitter. "For when things go amiss with him, it's me who takes the blame. Only peruse my several bruises!"

Teh Atht had already noted the battered condition of the crystal, the dents and gouges where its picture was wont to blur and go out of focus. He offered his commiserations, said: "But of course he's sworn you to secrecy—that is, in respect of his most private and personal pursuits?"

"Vows I may not break," the shewstone replied, "on penalty of being myself broken!"

"A pity," said Teh Atht. "I had wondered if perhaps Moormish sought immortality, and if so how close he'd come to finding it . . ."

"But don't you all seek it?" the crystal seemed surprised. "Small secret that, Teh Atht! And how close are you?"

For answer the wizard merely sighed.

"Then go in peace, happy at least in the knowledge that Moormish is no closer. More I dare not say."

Teh Atht went. Outside the tent, shadows leaned more slantingly and the air was cool. A kite sat upon Moormish's shoulder, observing him curiously, perhaps hungrily. It pecked at his ear and squawked abrupt complaint, then soared aloft in search of softer fare.

Eradicating his footprints in the sand where they led from mortified magician in and out of tent, Teh Atht placed himself before Moormish and reversed the runic restrictions. Moormish blinked, withdrew his finger from his ear, said, "That's better! . . . Or is it?" He blinked again, gazed all about, suddenly staggered and let fall his stick where Teh Atht leaned his weight against it. He frantically rubbed at his eyes.

"What's this?" said Teh Atht in feigned concern. "Are you ill?" He took a pace forward but Moormish backed hurriedly away.

"My ears," said the other. "And then my eyes. You seemed to flicker just then, and suddenly it's grown quite dim!" He shivered.

"Dim?" said Teh Atht. "It's merely the sun slipped behind a cloud there in the west." He tut-tutted. "But don't your symptoms bother you, my friend?"

"Symptoms? What symptoms?" snapped the other. "And don't call me your friend. As for my shewstone: I'll show you the knob of my stick!" He stooped to snatch it up. "Now begone!"

Teh Atht shrugged. "So be it," he said, moving his mouth with vigour but merely whispering the words. And returning to his carpet he added, again in a whisper: "But if I were you I'd have it seen to."

"Eh?"

"There you go again!" Teh Atht now shouted. "Deaf as a post, eyesight playing tricks with you, and shivering as in some alien ague! Aye, and apparently loss of orientation, too. It's all this sand and solitude, Moormish. You need the company of men—a closer proximity of persons, anyway—and you could do with seeing a physician. I'd head for Klühn if I were you. And now, while you still may." He tut-tutted again, bade his carpet rise and proceed north by north-west.

Below and behind him, Moormish of the Wastes cocked his head on one side and glowered this way and that, rubbed his eyes again, finally stumbled uncertainly back inside his tent and lowered its flap. He might guess the truth eventually, but little he'd be able to do about it. It was sad, but Moormish really was failing, and his magick with him. The wizard when he flew away considered that in the circumstances he'd given the hermit best possible advice.

After that . . .

. . . There had been other matters Teh Atht must attend to—the first of which being to place himself in the path of silver-skinned man and maid. No great difficulty there, for he'd known the region through which they travelled well enough. Aye, and he'd also known that Orbiquita's castle lay directly in their way!

EVENING WAS SETTLING when the five long wagons formed their accustomed circle in the timeless sand. Tarra fed his beast; he played "work and reward" games with the huge creature, using greenstuff tidbits as prizes when the lizard "understood" his gestures and whistles and answered promptly to his instructions; he finally climbed up on its head and oiled behind the eye-flaps and the delicate scales which protected vestigial gills. The monster accepted him now as its master, possibly even as a friend, and made no complaint when he stood upon its lower lip to knock crusts of sand from the rims of its blowhole nostrils. The other Hrossak drivers made much the same ado of their own huge mounts, but Tarra's care was that much more special. He didn't merely desire a beast who'd work for him, but one who'd die for him if necessary. For it might just possibly come to that.

Meanwhile the slaves were fed, and Tarra noticed that their portions were bigger tonight and their water measures more nearly adequate; what's more, there were even small,

sweet apples on the menu! He scratched his chin and nodded to himself: the trek was coming to its close, and supplies
being balanced accordingly. Things must have worked out
well, that food was still so much in evidence.

As the frizzy with the basket of bread and fruit finished
distributing to the slaves of Tarra's wagon, so the Hrossak
approached him for his share; but the slaver shoved him
away, grunted something unintelligible, pointed to where
fires were being lit and spits set up in the centre of the circle.
Tarra got the message at once; after all, it seemed hardly
right that a man who had broken bread with Cush Gemal
should continue to eat with slaves . . .

He wandered to the rim of the inner circle of fires and
stood looking on, his mouth fairly watering. Then a young
Hrossak driver spied him standing apart, called out for him
to come and join the mongrel crew gathered there. Apparently he'd been accepted. He went, watched small joints of
meat go onto the spits and start sizzling, noticed out the corner of his eye a pair of Northmen riding in from the east
leading a spare pony all laden down with baskets. He'd seen
them ride on ahead some hours earlier, at which time the
baskets had been empty. Now they were full, and the pony
who carried them feeling the strain a bit; and as the dusty,
bearded, broadly grinning pair reined in by the fires, so Tarra
guessed what was the beast's load. Fruits of the sea, yes!—
that great Eastern Ocean whose salt tang he now realized
he'd been smelling all day long, which suddenly was quite
unmistakeable—the baskets were full of large gleamy fish!

Expert fishermen, the Northmen hardly needed to brag
how they'd netted this lot in a single cast: by simply walking
into the loch, spreading a long net between them, and then
walking out again! But they did anyway. True or false, Tarra

cared not at all. Not while he knew he'd have a fine bit of fish for his supper tonight.

Then the wineskins came out, sour stuff but palatable enough after the first swig, and the joking, tall storytelling and gambling commenced. Tarra staying just a little apart and speaking when spoken to, and Hrossaks and Northmen alike all seeming in much lighter mood tonight, though for a fact the frizzies were as doleful and "black in the face" (Tarra kept both thought and word to himself) as ever. Ah, yes: trek's end in sight, and this lot plainly glad of it.

Tarra found himself a stone to sit on, listened to various tall tales from the Northmen, whose range and wit were astonishing. In gay mood they made for sparkling companions, these bristle-manes. A pity they were so untrustworthy, so volatile and, when roused, so notoriously bloodthirsty. Hrossaks, too, a humorous bunch, if a little dry and thoughtful about it. The steppemen were ever careful not to insult, because they themselves rarely forgave the insults of others.

Eventually the last rays of a setting sun stuck up like the spokes of a golden fan in the west; indigo spread across the sky from the east, darkening a blue in which the stars gleamed so much brighter; and Gleeth, the old moon-god, probed with his waxing horns from behind the far distant silhouette of the Eastern Range. A gentle evening breeze sprang up, not so much a trouble as a relief, and settled westward toward the lochs and the sea; and at last the meat was ready. Tarra settled for fish, lobbed a beauty expertly from spit onto his stone, stood fanning his hot fingers and listening to his belly rumble while it cooled a little. Then, with a warm place to sit, he broke open the crisped scaly skin to let out the fish's steam in splendid gusts. And as the slave-takers ate and relaxed from the day's drive, so silence descended. This was partly because mouths now found work chomping, mainly because Cush Gemal had put in an appearance, tall, spindly and gleamy red and black in the firelight.

Most of Gemal's Yhemnis kept to a fire of their own some little distance away; those who deigned to eat with the white- (and bronze-) skins stood up to show Gemal their respect— their fear? Hrossaks and, reluctantly, barbarians followed suit.

"Sit," said Cush Gemal with a wave of his hand. "You've done well, all of you, so be at your ease. The salt lochs are only hours away—an early start tomorrow and we'll be there 'twixt dawn and noon, and well under sail by the time the sun slips from zenith. See how the breeze favours us? It's off the land, blows for the Eastern Ocean. Only let it keep this up and we'll sail all the way to Shad, and never an oar dipped! Now I'll walk alone with my thoughts awhile."

He strode away, then paused and turned. "Watchkeepers, don't drink too much. I fancy we're followed, however discreetly. So far our mission's a success—let's keep it that way. We want no problems so close to ocean's margin." Finally he glanced at Tarra. "Hrossak, someone should find you a jacket, to keep the sand out of your cuts. Aye, and there'll be flies to lay their eggs in you, by the time we reach the ocean's rim."

Tarra shrugged. "I'm quick to heal," he said, "but for a fact it does grow chilly nights."

Gemal nodded and walked away.

The young Hrossak who'd called Tarra over to the fire came and sat beside him. "Oho!" he said. "And it seems you've made yourself a fine friend! Aye, and chatting with him like a brother! There aren't many men that skinny black cockscomb will pass the time of day with—or night, as 'twere. I'm Narqui Ghenz. You're a Khash, aren't you? A name to be reckoned with on the steppes, once upon a time."

"Tarra," said that worthy, nodding. "I'm a wanderer. By now I'd have wandered home if I hadn't bumped into this little packet. What's your excuse?" And he continued to eat his fish.

"*Huh!*" said Ghenz. "You're fortunate in that you can still go home. Me, I took a wife too many. It's my head—or a couple of even worse bits—if I go back! Depends how you look at it, and who gets to me first. Me? I think I'd rather they took my head . . ."

Tarra stared at him. "You hardly seem old enough to have taken one wife, let alone two! A bit daft, wasn't it?"

"It was." The other grinned. "But not in the way you're thinking. They were other men's wives I took, not mine!"

For the first time in days, Tarra laughed. "Say no more," he said, "for I've been a bit of a ladies' man myself in my time." Then his grin turned to a frown. Yes he had, but that was before a certain female kissed his neck one night in the badlands near Chlangi the Doomed. A rare and fearsome female, that one, called Orbiquita; and yet . . . Tarra hadn't given much thought to women since then. A man seared by the sun doesn't stand greatly in awe of a hearth-fire. He fingered twin blemishes on his neck, white specks against the bronze, and his blood tingled in a strange, even a morbid fever. Then he saw Ghenz watching him wonderingly and came back down to earth.

"That explains why you're not in Hrossa," he said, "but not why you're here with this lot."

Ghenz shrugged. "Have you ever been to Grypha?"

"In my time," said Tarra, nodding. "When I was maybe your age. A Hrossak youth runs away from home, he heads for Grypha. A man gets himself banished, and his first stop's Grypha. It's been a refuge, of sorts, for exiled steppemen ever since they builded it there. Grypha the Fortress, it was once called, for its peoples warred a lot with us Hrossaks in those days. Also, it had something of strategic value: it stands on the Luhr and so guards the west, and looks across the Bay of Monsters on Yhemni jungles and Shadarabar. Many of its olden fortifications are still standing, however battered; ah, but not so much warriors as wharf rats have inherited it now! A cesspool built on a swamp, whose stink is washed by the Luhr out into the Southern Sea. But even a river can't clear it all away. What, Grypha? Why, it's a byword for shady deals and shadier dealers—like some kind of steaming, sophisticated Chlangi, but not all *that* sophisticated!"

"That's what I meant," said Narqui Ghenz. "Chased out, I headed for Grypha—and discovered it to be the sinkhole of Theem'hdra, with villains black, white, brown and bronze all intermingled there like . . . like lumpy soup! Oh, there's money to be made there, for those who don't much care, but I'm a Hrossak and I like clean air. Except . . . where to go next? I'd thought of Thinhla, or Thandopolis way across the world, but they were such a long way off. It costs money to join a caravan west, and even more to take a ship. Work my passage? Out of Grypha? Likely I'd end up chained to an oar forever, or until I could no longer row—and then marooned on a rock somewhere to live out my life on crabs and seaweeds. So there I was in a bit of a quandary.

"Then, when I was all spent up, I heard of a fellow Hrossak recruiting lizard-handlers for some sort of trek. That was Gys Ankh, by the way—though devil only knows what's become of him! He *seemed* a decent sort at first, turned out to be a black-hearted bully. I'm glad he's gone.

"Anyway, there was to be a small down-payment—for services to be rendered, you know?—and a big lump of cash when the job was done. But all hush-hush and no questions asked. So I signed up. By the time I found out something of what it was all about we were meeting Cush Gemal and his Yhemnis at the inlet of a salt loch north of the Straits of Yhem, fifty miles or so south of where we are right now. Gemal and his blacks had brought their long wagons with them, in pieces in the boats, which all of us joined in to put together again. We Hrossaks had taken our lizards with us (Ankh had somehow stolen them out of Hrossa), they were soon hitched up, and then we headed for the villages along the east-facing side of the Great Eastern Peaks. Then, too, we discovered for sure what we'd become—slavers!"

"And that offended you?" Tarra stared straight into the other's eyes.

"Some," said Ghenz, uncomfortably.

"But not so much you'd risk running off and trying your luck on your lonesome, eh?"

"*How* run off?" Ghenz suddenly snapped. "What, and end up with a Yhemni bolt in my back? You've seen how Cush Gemal deals with troublemakers! But I'll tell you something: me and the other three Hrossaks, we've tended our lizards and that's it. No murder, no rape, no brutality of any sort toward the slaves or the girls. Gys Ankh was the only really rotten apple, and he's gone now. Anyway, what makes *you* so holy?"

"Calm down," said Tarra evenly. He looked casually all about, made sure no one would overhear their conversation. "How'm I to know these things until someone tells me, eh? So where do the Northmen come into all of this?"

"They were recruited in Grypha, too," Ghenz replied. "—for their riding skills. With those ponies of theirs they could ride down runaways, act as scouts, form a fast-moving rearguard if necessary. Aye, and they were paid well for their labours, half in advance—enough to ensure they'd stay on right to the end, anyway. Moreover, they were promised equal shares of all plunder taken, like the rest of us, and women galore along the way. Any woman they wanted—*except* Black Yoppaloth's brides. Those were to be the pick of the crop, taboo, strictly untouchable. As Gorlis Thad discovered the hard way!"

Tarra was silent for a while, then: "Did you understand when you started out how you'd be finishing up in Shad?"

"No," Ghenz shook his head, "nor will we. We see the big lizards safely across the water to Shad, get paid off there, and Gemal lends us a crew of blacks and one ship to sail us back to the mainland. That's Hrossaks and barbarians alike."

Tarra slowly nodded, picked a while on the bones of his fish. And quietly he said: "And you believe he'll do that, do you?"

"Eh?" Ghenz raised his eyebrows. "But that's our agreement! I mean, what else would he do with us?"

"Oh, nothing much," Tarra shrugged. "Except maybe butcher you, take back whatever he's given and whatever else you've got—including the gold out of your teeth—and feed your carcasses to certain little jungle-bred friends of his! Did you know there are supposed to be cannibals in Shadarabar's jungles?"

Ghenz went a little white. "You mean you think he'll pay us off with black treachery?" he hissed.

"It was just a thought, that's all," said Tarra, standing up and stretching his joints. "Me, I'm not much bothered, since I get off at ocean's rim." He made to walk away but Ghenz followed, caught at his arm.

"Listen," he said, "I've a jacket for you. Since Gemal

seems to think highly of you, that might stand me in his favour."

"That's kind of you," said Tarra. "But best to take all I've said with a pinch of salt. I was just thinking out loud, that's all." He walked with Ghenz to the youth's wagon, accepted a warm, fur-lined jacket and tried it on. It was a good fit. Ghenz was meanwhile silent, his brows black where they formed a scowl in the middle. Finally he asked:

"How can we be sure he'll not deal with us badly?"

"Dunno," said Tarra. "But if I were you I'd first observe how he deals with me."

"Eh? How do you mean?"

"Well, he's promised to make good my losses and my time, let me keep my big honker and turn us both loose when we reach the loch. I figure if he sticks to that, then that he'll probably play fair by you lads, too. We can only wait and see. But as you've seen for yourself, life's pretty much easy-come, easy-go to him. I'm talking about the butchery in the villages, to which he must have agreed; about Gorlis Thad, who he cut down like a blade of grass, without a backward glance; and about these blacks of his, who fear him mightily—and who I've noticed are wont to shrivel and drop dead if they spend too much time in his company . . ." And Tarra watched the youth's reaction to that last.

He wasn't quite sure just what he expected, but he was sure that what he got wasn't it. "Disease," said Narqui Ghenz, shrugging. And his expression didn't change at all.

"Eh?" Tarra's jaw fell open. "What's that you say? Disease?"

"Why, yes," Ghenz added matter-of-factly. "What else? It's something out of the jungles, which only takes the blacks. They collapse, dry up, die very quickly and without pain. When did you see it?"

"Back at our last stop," said Tarra. "In the storm? And as for that storm—did you ever see weather like *that* before? That weird green glow round Gemal's tent? Two frizzies went in there with him, just before that 'storm' broke. Gemal himself went in looking fit to die, and came out full of fight! But when we moved out of there I was last in line, and I saw the other two. They weren't fit for anything but a shallow grave."

Still Ghenz was unconvinced. "That makes eight of 'em, then," he said. "Two where we met their ships out of Shad, at the salt loch; two more on the fourth night, after we'd done our first village; another two on the seventh night, just before we picked you up; and now—"

"—They're falling faster, then?" Tarra cut him off.

"Eh?"

"This 'disease' is gaining ground, picking up speed, burning through 'em ever faster. And always taking them in pairs . . ."

Ghenz thought about it. "So it seems. But why concern yourself, since it's only the blacks?"

Tarra almost answered: *And what happens when Gemal runs out of blacks?*—but he thought better of it. What he did say was: "Me, I took one look at that freakish storm, that cold green fire in the heart of the twister around Gemal's tent, and I thought: magick! And when I saw those corpses, well, that sort of confirmed it."

Ghenz laughed. "Then you'd be better off speaking to the Northmen," he said. "They're the ones for the spook stories!"

Tarra partly understood the other's point of view. Ghenz was a young man, open as a book and straight off the steppes (where wizards were given short shrift, and had been ever since the days of ill-legended Loxzar of the Hrossaks) and he wouldn't have come across much in the way of the Dark Arts. Not yet, anyway. But Tarra's own far-flung adventures

had bent his beliefs to the contrary—very much so. And as
for that peculiar storm and the green fires accompanying
it . . . well, Tarra had been witness to much the same sort of
thing once before. And not so very long ago.

That had been in Klühn, at Gorgos' Temple of Secret
Gods, and it had heralded the very Blackest Magick imagi-
nable! Tarra remembered it well, would never forget it:
those weird energies building over Klühn, patterned like the
webs of giant, lightning-spawned spiders, with strands of
fire spun down like alien silk to the dome of that temple of
horror. Thromb energies, they'd been, which opened gates
in space and time to let in Forces from beyond the stars—or
would have, if Tarra Khash and Amyr Arn hadn't cut them
off at source. That source had been Gorgos, gone now back
where he belonged—or what remained of him, anyway.

"Are you all right?" Ghenz had taken his arm. "Staring at
the stars like that, with your eyes all vacant . . ."

"Was I?" said Tarra. He sniffed the air, said: "I was gauging
the weather, that's all."

"Oh?" Ghenz was interested, doubtless in respect of forth-
coming voyage to Shad. "Well, what's it to be? Fair or foul?"

"A bit of both, I think," said Tarra. And to himself: *change-
able, at best.* Then he excused himself and headed back to the
fires.

"Fancy a game, Hrossak?" called out one of three Northmen where they tossed coins in the firelight.

"Gambling's for them who can afford it," Tarra ruefully
replied. "Me, I've only the jacket I wear on my back, and
that's where it's going to stay. But I'll watch awhile, if it
doesn't bother you." It didn't, and Tarra stood watching. In
just a few more minutes one of the three pulled a wry face
and turned out his pockets, signifying that for him the game

was over. Never good losers, Northmen, he stooped and snatched up the square Khrissan gaming coins, bent them one at a time between thumb and fingers and tossed them down. Undaunted, the two remaining players took out new coins and began a two-sided game of pitch-and-toss all over again. One of the two would end up lucky, or unlucky depending how the other took it. Meanwhile Tarra and the sulking, hulking loser went off to sit together and stare into a fire.

"Gambling's a damned fool's game," growled the Northman in a little while. "And I'm a fool born!"

Tarra nodded his agreement. "I've lost my shirt on occasion, too," he admitted.

"Oh?" the barbarian hardly seemed interested. "And what's your poison?"

"Dice," said Tarra.

"*Hah!* Not likely!" The other was vehement. "What, dice? Too easily loaded, for my liking."

"As I discovered," said Tarra, scowling into the dying embers.

"But what the hell," said the Northman, shrugging. "All life's a gamble."

"True, very true." Tarra nodded again. "And Yibb only knows that the stakes are high enough, this time around."

"Eh?"

"This trek, I mean," said wily Hrossak. "What? And here's you and your lot—aye, and my lot, too—all sailing off to Shad with Cush Gemal, and not a lad of you knowing a single thought that's in his head. And how's that for playing with loaded dice?"

"Eh?" said the other again, frowning.

"I mean," Tarra was patient, "what if he's playing you

false? D'you think you can bend him like a thin Khrissan
gaming piece? Not on your life! And once you're in Shad,
why, then you're at his mercy."

The Northman scowled in his beard, slitted his eyes and
stared hard at Tarra, finally shook his head. "I don't follow
you," he said, and Tarra could see that he really didn't. And
for the first time he began to understand something of Cush
Gemal's power.

"You're not worried," he said, but more slowly and carefully, "that you might end up marooned, or worse, in Shad?"

"You know," the other replied, "Gorlis Thad used to
sound much the same as you; used to say much the same
sort of things. Likewise Gys Ankh. Trouble-makers, both of
'em. Well, you saw what happened to the Thad, and as for
Ankh—who knows? But when that bronze bastard went
missing, you didn't see Cush Gemal making much of a fuss
over it, did you? 'Ware, steppeman! That tongue of yours
could do for you."

"Do you take his word, then," Tarra pressed, "that he'll
see you safe home again once he's shipped you to Shad?"

The other thought about it, finally nodded. "Aye," he
said, simply as that. "Oh, he's a queer 'un, be sure: black as
squid-slop and cold as ice on the moon. And yet somehow
warm, too, at times. But . . . I think I trust him. Indeed, I
think we *all* trust him; and it seems there's a sticky end for
them that don't. So if I were you I'd give it a little time,
steppeman, and see how he grows on you."

"I think I know what you mean," said Tarra, slapping his
knees and driving himself to his feet. "He *is* growing on
me!"—*like a wart, and you know how hard they are to get rid of.*

Moving back toward his big lizard and its wagon, where
already the slaves were bedded down, he almost stumbled

over a heap of cooked fish, untouched, still smoking in the night. He took up an armful, some meat, too, and distributed the food to the chained unfortunates. Then he sat beside Loomar Nindiss and watched that ever-hungry lad wolf his portion. Done at last, Loomar asked him:

"Well, what have you found out?"

"Nothing much," Tarra shrugged. "Except that tomorrow you sail for Shadarabar over the Straits of Yhem. I've tried to sway this lot against it, but—" And he shrugged again.

"And you?" Loomar's eyes shone soft in moon- and starlight.

"Not me," Tarra shook his head. "Cush Gemal's warned me against it. And when someone like that utters a warning, I reckon men should heed him . . ."

VI

Amyr and Ulli

AMYR ARN AND Ulli Eys were Suhm-yi (indeed, they were the last members of that never numerous, especially insular race) and therefore mentalists; they had their own tongue and were natural linguists, but they were equally at home with telepathy. The latter mode required a certain familiarity; it improved with use and proximity; in the old days, it had never been used without mutual consent. It need hardly be said that in two such as Amyr and Ulli, all codes and conditions were well satisfied.

Now, travelling by the light of the stars in the Desert of Sheb—where only the wind gave voice, and then low and moaning—the Suhm-yi man and maid found themselves unwilling to break the silence, and so conversed by mind alone and sparingly.

"A light ahead," said Amyr voicelessly, "in that jut of deeper darkness there."

From the back of their single beast, where Ulli had the better view: "I had noted it, husband," she likewise replied.

"These are strange lands," he said, "and often threatening. We'd best be prepared for whatever lies in wait."

Ulli smiled down on him where he loped ahead, leading

their plodding yak, and he felt her smile on the back of his neck, which gleamed something less than its customary silver under the stars. "I know you will be prepared, Amyr," she answered. "And while I am with you, I know no harm will befall. Or if it should, then that it will be a greater thing than our two hearts together, which is a size beyond my imagining."

"Ulli," he said, "I have forgotten the old ways. No, I have forsaken them. For survival. Peace was ever the way of the Suhm-yi, peace at all cost: a code of conduct I left behind in the Inner Isles when I came to seek you out. I came, found and freed you; but if I'd walked in the old ways, it were a short walk, be sure! You speak of our hearts: mine is full of you, and also full of sin. I desired and took revenge. And I have taken the lives of men. In this Primal Land, I have learned dishonourable ways, at times reverting to a primal savagery. Aye, and truth to tell, it did not disgust me . . ."

She smiled again, but sadly. "Husband, I was stolen from the Inner Isles as a child. I never knew the old laws, the old ways. But I've known the wiles of Gorgos, and I've read in the minds of men all of their black secrets. Oh, there *are* good men, but others are putrid in their cores; and it was my lot to discover them for my morbid master." She had stopped smiling and even shuddered a little. "Dishonour? I hardly think you know the meaning of the word, not even now. And as for evil, you are an innocent!"

"Still, there *is* evil in Theem'hdra," he insisted. "And so I must warn you: I'll not be still if we're threatened. And if it should ever come to that, I beg you look away. I'd not have you look upon me with blood on my hands."

"You forget," she said, "how I've already seen you smeared in blood of men, *and* slime of Gorgos! You and Tarra Khash both—and I was not disgusted. I felt only relief: that I was free of fear and foulness, and that a mate had come to find me when I had thought all hope fled. We've both suffered taints, Amyr, but that's behind us now. In the jewel isles we'll build anew, and temper the laws we pass down to our children with knowledge of the world outside the Crater Sea. That way they'll be ready, if men should come again defiling and destroying . . ."

"So be it," he said, and without looking back gave the merest nod of his comb-crested head.

Now, approaching more closely the dark silhouette lit in one window with a warm, welcoming glow, Amyr saw that the place was a castle or fortress—a manse, anyway, but large, sprawling and high-walled. Well provisioned refuge, doubtless, for whoever dwelled within; and Amyr began to feel the weight and responsibility of his and Ulli's journey pressing down on him.

Coming from Inner Isles to Klühn, he'd travelled alone and fast, unhindered and driven on by the urgency of his mission. But now he had a future, where before there'd been none; and now, too, he had Ulli to consider, and he knew that the perils of the Primal Land were many. Three-quarters of the return trek still lying ahead, much of it through badlands—and Ulli Eys more precious to Amyr than life itself, to be guarded and guided each step of the way.

For that reason he'd chosen the route which would seem least populated: out of Klühn and across the rugged Great Eastern Peaks, through the southern bulge of Sheb's Desert and over the Mountains of Lohmi, then follow the fringe of Ell's wasteland to the Great Circle Range, beyond which lay the Crater Sea and jewelled Inner Isles. Least populated, perhaps, but for what reason? And where populated, by what?

Lamias, allegedly, in Sheb, where one such was said to have her castle—perhaps that very lair which loomed ahead! Thieves and vagabonds, too, in ruined Chlangi the shunned city, some sixty or seventy miles south. And this only the beginning! The Mountains of Lohmi were home to small but fierce tribes of degenerate, barbarous mountainmen; and in the Desert of Ell, where lay a forbidden city of antique mystery, there dwelled demons and ill-natured djinn.

Aye, numberless miles and dangers ahead, and already Amyr feeling his strength waning, sapped by furnace sun and drawn from his muscles by sands that sank underfoot, making every step an effort of will. And only a quarter of the way covered, with the worst of it still to come.

The night's chill had freshened Amyr's Suhm-yi awareness; suddenly he felt his silvery skin prickling, a weird sensation of eyes watching, perhaps as a spider watches the fly fresh trapped in its web. "Ulli," he said, without speaking. And:

"I know," she likewise answered.

Between the castle and the travellers a jumble of weathered rock protruded slanting from the sands. Amyr led his beast with its precious burden into the heart of the outcrop's shadow . . .

IN ORBIQUITA'S CASTLE, Teh Atht sat in his cousin's Room of Runes and gazed into her shewstone, which must surely be unique in that it was the petrified eye of a Roc! The stone had no voice, and its view was quite vertiginous—bird's-eye, no less!—but the pictures had startling clarity and depth. Ideal for Orbiquita who, in winged guise, was well acquainted with views from aerial angle; less so for Teh

Atht, who'd prefer a picture scried at sea-level. Still and all, he supposed he must count himself lucky that he'd found this most secret chamber (hidden as it had been behind a pivoting slab of stone), let alone the lamia-ensorcelled orb of some sadly defunct aviasaur.

Of course, he could go out onto the tiny balcony and spy out the land from there, but it was a spooky light in the desert at night and not to be trusted; likewise the wizard's eyes weren't what they used to be. By now the Suhm-yi couple had doubtless seen Teh Atht's lantern blazing forth from the window of a room on this same floor, and he must hope they'd be attracted to it. One small lamp in habitation huge as this must signal a single habitant; and this Suhm-yi male, who'd helped slay Gorgos and bring down his temple, would hardly be the sort to turn aside or flee from one lone dweller.

Indeed, the friendly light should lure these weary travellers, and they'd find Teh Atht the perfect host when they came knocking on his door. So thought the wizard; and but for the fact that he *was* a wizard (with all the habits of that species, including scrying), so it might have worked out. But—

—Teh Atht frowned and peered closer at the shewstone, and wondered what was wrong here. Male, female and beast, all three had passed into the shadow of that fang of rock there, and by now should have reappeared on the other side. So what was holding them up? Could it be they were making camp there, with the castle a mere stone's throw away, and welcoming lantern blazing for all to see?

He drew the picture closer; which is to say, he soared down upon the crag from on high, fighting back the vertigo he felt welling inside as the scene in the stone rushed up to meet his gaze. Now he was in the shadow of the slanting

rock, poised directly over the girl-creature where she sat
silent and tranquil and waiting upon the back of her yak.
But waiting for what? Then, scanning the shadowed area all
about, Teh Atht gave an odd little twitch when he saw that
Ulli Eys was quite alone!

He caused his view to retreat from her, gazed down on
the desert between fang of rock and castle, saw—nothing!
And where was the Suhm-yi male now? And what was he
up to?

At that precise moment Amyr Arn's spatulate four-
fingered hands came up one at a time over the carved parapet wall, where like a great slender gecko he clung to the
vertical stonework. His crested head followed, a silver shimmer against the dark of the night, and his golden eyes took
in at a glance the scene in the secret room: a candle's glow
silhouetting the seated form of a rune-cloaked wizard where
he hunched over his shewstone, his back to the intruder.
Then, silent as a shadow, Amyr was up onto the balcony, inside the room, closing the distance between himself and his
target. And in his hand a gleam of silver brighter far than
the shimmer of his own un-human flesh.

"Where *is* he?" Teh Atht mutteringly demanded of Orbiquita's crystal. "Show him to me at once!"

"Why scry?" whispered Amyr from behind, in Teh Atht's
very ear. "Save your eyesight, wizard. Spy on me no more
from afar, but only turn your head!"

Teh Atht gave a gasp, began to do just that—and froze!
Cold steel touched the soft umber leather of his throat, and
a four-fingered hand of iron gripped his shoulder. "I . . ." He
gulped, aware that death stood only a breath away. And
again: "I . . ."

"Utter no runes, wizard," warned Amyr Arn, "no crafty

spells. Ah, for your first sorcerous syllable will likewise be your last!"

The biter bit! thought Teh Atht. *And how's this for wizardry!* But out loud and hurriedly, he husked: "I know this looks bad, my young friend, but believe me I acted in all innocence. Old habits die hard, that's all, and the shewstone is merely a tool of my trade."

"Clever words won't sway me," said Amyr, "nor lies deceive. Your hourglass is tipped and the sands are running. Speak swift, 'ere they run out."

Teh Atht at once commenced to babble, each word coming fast on the heels of the last. As he spoke Amyr looked behind the words, used the mentalist art of the Suhm-yi to penetrate the wizard's mind and read what was written there. In the old times that were unthinkable, but the old mores no longer applied. He saw the wizard's quest clearly delineated—his search for immortality—and read names a-plenty in connection with that quest. Among those names were his own, his darling Ulli's, that of Tarra Khash, and—and also the name of the mercifully exanimate Gorgos!

"Hold!" said Amyr then. "What? And is that what you are? Blood of Gorgos, his sorcerous kin, corrupted by him? You know of him, for I've read it in your mind. Aye, and you know something of a certain Hrossak, too, who has been my one friend among men. Now cease your babbling and answer only my specific questions.

"First, why have you lain in wait for us here? What was your plan for us?"

"I can show you much better than tell you," said Teh Atht. He carefully stood up; and Amyr's knife slipping easily from his throat to his breast, where it poised just under his heart, so light it might not be there at all.

"Lead on," said Amyr.

They went to the room where the lantern hung on a hook under the arch of a wide balcony, sending its rays out into the still desert. Here a table was set for three, all laden with meats and fruits, water and wines, cheeses and honey. Of hopper and flitter no sign, for Teh Atht had sent them below stairs to find a place of their own.

"This was my plan for you," said the wizard with a wave of his arm. "To welcome you here in the castle of my cousin Orbiquita—herself absent, I'm happy to relate—and to satisfy your needs. Here you can eat, drink, bathe, rest your weary bodies from the rigours of the sands, and all in safety absolute. And for payment, why I'd merely follow the customs of civilized folk in this Primal Land and beg of you . . . a story?"

"A story?" Amyr lowered silver shutters on his eyes, until they were golden slits. "What sort of story?"

Teh Atht shrugged innocently. "Perhaps the story of your wanderings," he said, feigning only a polite and routine interest, as required by etiquette. "Or maybe a tale of Tarra Khash the Hrossak: how you met him and became his friend, and how with his help you brought down Gorgos' Temple of Secret Gods in Klühn. Or perhaps something of his past, if you know it—for example: how and where he came by that fancy jewelled scimitar of his?"

Now Amyr's knife tickled a little where suddenly, however gently, its point pressed through the silk of the wizard's cloak and rested on his pale flesh. And now: "You're either very brave or very foolish," said Amyr, the chimes of his voice more lead than silver. "I told you Tarra Khash is my friend. And should I betray him?"

Teh Atht smiled and shook his head. "I'm neither brave

nor foolish," he said. "And you are not a killer; not natural born, anyway. Oh, I know you've looked at me with your mentalist's eyes, and I know you've found no harm in me. But I've looked at you, too, through the eyes of a wizard. Your caution isn't so much for yourself as for your lady, which I can understand well enow. But betray Tarra Khash? To me? In what way? I merely seek to save his life, and thought you'd like to help me. Indeed, I *know* you will! So put away the knife."

For a moment their eyes met: the wizard's faded and almost colourless, Amyr's golden as burnished coins. Then the Suhm-yi male nodded, sheathed his knife in the scabbard at his belt, said: "But don't think you can lie to me, Teh Atht. I can read right through your words to the very thoughts that form them. There's more to this than the saving of Tarra's life. You seek immortality, and he's the key. Now tell me: what is it threatens him?"

"First your lady," said the wizard. "Bring her in from the desert. There's food here and wine; I take it you eat like ordinary men? And I need no spells to tell me how weary you are. Now let's start again, on friendlier footing—the way I planned it in the first place, however badly it were fumbled. Agreed?"

Amyr nodded again, if a trifle slowly, and called out to Ulli in his mind, *Wife, come to the castle. You'll find us waiting below. I think all's well, but be alert for danger.*

Then he followed Teh Atht downstairs to the huge hall, all tidied now and seeming more gaunt and vast than ever, where the wizard called upon hopper and flitter to show themselves. They came and were introduced. "My familiars," said Teh Atht. "Incapable of harm, however ugly. You may hear them at their work, but they'll stay out of sight so as not to alarm your lady. There, and now I have no more secrets."

Out into the courtyard they went, and the wizard opened the great outer door on Ulli where she waited. Without pause she urged her yak inside, where Amyr helped her dismount and presented her to Teh Atht. "Delighted," said the wizard, truly awed by Ulli's alien beauty. "But let's go indoors at once; the air grows chill out here, and there's all you'll need of comforts laid out within . . ."

They entered, climbed to the prepared room, dined well on the food Teh Atht's familiars had set out for them. And as they ate so the wizard told Amyr all he had learned of the travails of Tarra Khash. Then at last the travellers were done with eating and their host with talking, and now it was Amyr's turn. He stood up, paced a while, said:

"Teh Atht, you came here on a flying carpet. So you said."

"The very carpet where now you stand." The wizard nodded. "A little worn, but airworthy still."

Amyr paused and looked down at the carpet—a fairly unremarkable rug, uniformly fawn except in its corners where four black, oddly curving esoteric symbols were woven into the material—then continued pacing. And in a little while:

"Teh Atht, when first I . . . I *came upon* you," Amyr went on, attempting something of diplomacy, "you were scrying our slow progress in a crystal ball—doubtless ensuring that no harm befell us along the way. I assume that crystal to be Orbiquita's shewstone?"

"Of course, for this is her castle." Teh Atht shrugged. He looked back and forth, between Suhm-yi man and maid, then sighed. "Have I not made myself understood? Scrying is the *way* of wizards!"

Amyr nodded thoughtfully, continued pacing. "Flying

carpets, shewstones—black magick! 'The ways of wizards.' *Hmmm!"* he mused. "And Tarra Khash, our one friend among men, captive of the slavetaker of just such a foul sorcerer, eh?"

Fearing himself ranked alongside Black Yoppaloth of the Yhemnis, now Teh Atht waxed a little indignant. "I thought I'd already made myself perfectly clear," he said. "We're not *all* cut of the same cloth!"

"Oh?" Amyr turned and stared hard at the wizard through penetrating golden eyes. "No, perhaps you're not," he finally allowed, "but whichever, I suspect you're all of a very intricate and mazy weave." He nodded again, but more sharply, decisively. "Very well, I would see Tarra's predicament for myself—in the shewstone!"

They all three went to Orbiquita's secret chamber behind the pivoting slab which was its door, and there the wizard activated the petrified Roc's eye. Knowing almost exactly where to look, it took only seconds for Teh Atht to locate his target; and then, all three heads together—the wizard's and those of his silvery, un-human guests alike—their rapt eyes saw . . .

. . . TARRA KHASH LAY sleeping under the moon and stars. He was curled in the leathery elbow of his big hauler, snoring gently into the corrugations of that hugely folded reptilian limb. His bed, while somewhat musky and subject to sudden, shuddery convulsions, was at least middling warm. Blood did course in those great veins, however sluggishly; and that was important, for this close to the Eastern Ocean the night breezes tended to blow cold. Tarra's new jacket had kept him warm for a while, but then the big lizard had scratched himself with a blunt claw, and the jacket, caught on a scale, had been snatched away. Now the Hrossak lay exposed to starlight and breezes both, silken shirt ragged on his back, shivering a little as the temperature fell. The cold might wake him up, but unlikely; today had been a hard one for all concerned, and Tarra no exception. He was weary in every limb and would probably sleep through a volcanic eruption.

Standing close by, just now returned from his solitary stroll in the dunes, Cush Gemal looked down on him and his black eyes shone in the darkness. Behind him, keeping a respectful distance, a pair of Yhemni watchmen waited on their master's command. Nor was it long in coming:

"Fetch a blanket," Gemal ordered, but quietly for all the depths of his tone. "Drape it over him—but don't waken him. He needs his sleep as much as any man. And so do I . . ." He turned away, but over his shoulder reminded: "Keep well your watch this night." Then he strode away toward his black tent—and paused.

He looked up, jerking his head sharply, and his black eyes grew huge. "What?" he said, almost in a whisper. And again, sharp as ice now: *"What!"*

"Master, what is it?" his blacks ran toward him, their hands fluttering in sudden alarm . . .

. . . IN ORBIQUITA'S SECRET chamber, Teh Atht knew only too well what "it" was. He commanded the shewstone, "Be still!" And throwing up his hands he turned his face away. At the same time he lurched against his guests, buffeting them aside. And as the picture in the shewstone dwindled and faded into mist, so he sighed long and loud. A close thing, that. Another moment and the eyes of Cush Gemal might well have seen right through the space between, out of eye of Roc and *into* those of the three who had watched! To Amyr and Ulli, by way of explanation and apology both, he said: "He sensed us!"

"What?" Amyr was astonished. "Is it possible?"

"For a great wizard, aye," Teh Atht nodded, his face chalk now in place of its usual faded umber.

"But he's only a slaver, in Black Yoppaloth's employ!" Amyr was plainly puzzled.

Teh Atht nodded slowly, gave the matter some consideration. "That he is," he finally muttered, "and under his protection, too. It becomes obvious: Yoppaloth has spelled him, given him a guardian aura. Only penetrate it—which with our combined and concentrated gazing we did—and Gemal knows it! Ah, but his master, Shad's sorcerer, is cautious to a fault! He would keep *all* of his works secret, even the business of his hirelings; and the closer we draw to the appointed hour, the more effective his protections become."

"The appointed hour?" This time it was Ulli's tinkling voice that questioned.

"The hour of his renewal, when like the phoenix he'll rise up again restored! That's what this is all about: somewhere in this mystery lies the secret of Yoppaloth's immortality . . ."

They went back to the room where they had dined, found the table standing empty of every last trace of their meal, and Teh Atht bade his guests be comfortable on a low, cushioned couch. Amyr declined, but paced the floor as before. "Now here's the thing," he said in a while. "I do believe you will help Tarra Khash if and when you can, and *if* he needs it, if only to appease your dreadful cousin. But as for saving his life—why, it hardly seems threatened! Indeed, this curious slaver Cush Gemal appears to have taken to him. So what is it you're really up to, Teh Atht? Is it perhaps that you've caught a whiff of Yoppaloth's immortality, and that now you fear to lose it?"

Teh Atht appeared hurt. Then: "Very shrewd," he said, unsmiling. "But why ask, when you can read it all in my mind?"

"That is not our way," said Ulli at once. "Before, Amyr read your thoughts to protect me. Now that you've proclaimed yourself a friend, he may no longer intrude. We are all private people, Teh Atht, and our minds inviolate."

Amyr frowned. Ulli had it right, of course, but on this occasion he wished that she had not.

"Madam," said the wizard, "your candour in this matter fills me with a great relief." He gravely nodded his approval. "But still I fear your husband distrusts me."

Amyr's golden eyes narrowed a little. "Is that so strange?" he said. "After all, we already know of this lusting of yours after immortality, which seems to me unnatural. It is nature's way that things are born to die; without death there can be no purpose in living; what man would grasp at each new day, if days were interminable? And yet you insist upon this immortality."

"Am I lectured?" Teh Atht cried, apparently amazed. "I am what I am, and I cannot change it, I'm a wizard, and the world full of wonders which I can never hope to grasp. Not in one short span. Can't you see? I have runes to unriddle, mysteries to plumb, all the secrets of space and time to unravel—and neither time nor space to even begin! I'm a quester—no, a *hunter*—after knowledge, Amyr Arn; but as any hunter will tell you, it's the chase that counts, not the kill! This thing is a puzzle of a thousand pieces, and one by one I track them down and fit them in until the picture is complete."

"I see," said Amyr, nodding. "So one by one you're grad-ually fitting together all the pieces of this great puzzle, are you? And who can say but that as I tell you my pieces, they, too, will fit in place, so that the puzzle more rapidly nears completion."

"But that's it exactly!" cried Teh Atht. "And Tarra Khash would seem to be a key piece, as you correctly deduced from just one small peep into my mind. Which is, of course—entirely in keeping with my altruistic nature, and not to mention Orbiquita's vile threats—the reason I'll keep Tarra Khash from harm. If I can."

Amyr stopped pacing, faced the wizard squarely. "And if the puzzle completes itself *before* Tarra is safe . . . what then? Immortality is immortality: an infinite extension of life. What weight would a lamia's threats carry then, Teh Atht, to one who cannot die? And of what value the life of a mere man to a mage immortal, eh?"

"Eh?" Teh Atht repeated him, blinking rapidly. "What are you saying?"

"Who will there be," Amyr pressed home his point, "in the hour of your triumph, to ensure you don't desert the Hrossak's cause and leave him to whichever fate awaits him?"

Teh Atht puffed himself up. "A wizard's word is his word!" he said.

"And do you give me your word? That if I tell you what I know of him, and of his sword, you'll see him master once more of his own destiny?"

"I'll do my best," said Teh Atht.

"That isn't good enough," Amyr shook his head. "On those terms I'll tell you nothing."

"But what do you expect me to do?" the other protested. "Fly in there on my carpet, physically snatch him away?"

"Why not?" Amyr stared hard at him. "Indeed, that seems to me the most direct and logical course. Then, out of gratitude, he'd probably answer all of your questions himself."

"Logic?" Teh Atht's brow took on a darker shade. "I'll have you know, Amyr Arn, that the blood of Mylakhrion himself flows in these veins—and you talk to me of logic? You've seen how this Cush Gemal is protected by Black Yoppaloth's magick. What? He even knows when he is spied upon! And yet you'd have me swoop down in broad daylight—"

"At night," Amyr corrected him.

"—swoop down anyway, and steal the Hrossak away? What is that for logic? Madness! Black Yoppaloth would work vile magicks against me, and against you, too—as he worked them upon a time on the person of Exior K'mool. Last of the Suhm-yi, are you? Let me tell you that when the Mage of Shadarabar was done with you, there'd *be* no more Suhm-yi! None at all!"

"Very well," said Amyr, "if you fear this Yoppaloth so, then show me how to fly your carpet and I'll bring Tarra out of there."

"What?" The wizard seemed aghast. "Are you mad? You, control my carpet? Impossible! Long ago I laid upon its weave irreversible runes so that it might never be stolen. It would fly you into the sun, or maroon you on the moon, or drown you in ocean deeps; aye, and then fly home to me. And even if such a plan were feasible—which it is not—still the necromancer Yoppaloth would trace the source of this . . . this *invasion,* back to me. No, there is honour among wizards, Amyr Arn. Codes of conduct exist for us, too, just as they do for the Suhm-yi. I may not be seen to interfere with the legitimate works of another."

Amyr nodded. "You may spy upon him—so long as he remains in ignorance of it—but you may not openly work against him." His silvery tone was scathing. "And did you say 'legitimate'?" Now he raised scaled, glinting eyebrows in caustic inquiry. "The legitimate works of another?"

"All works of wizardry may be termed legitimate," Teh Atht blurted, "except where they work against another wizard."

Amyr snorted and cried: "Enough! Your words have the shape of a maze: we might tramp for hours and get nowhere. Do what you will, but expect no help from me. We thank you for your hospitality, and now we'll be on our way." He took Ulli's hand and she stood up.

Flabbergasted, Teh Atht could say nothing. He considered various runes, then un-considered them. None of them seemed of much use here. Curious Concretion wouldn't solve the problem but only stiffen Amyr's tongue to stone; his brain, too, so that its secrets could not be stolen. Hypnotism? What? Against a quicksilver mind like this? And as for any sort of threatening move in the female's direction . . .

"Wait!" Ulli Eys held up her tapering, delicately spatulate hands. And to Amyr: "Husband, if you refuse Teh Atht your assistance, then it seems to me that Tarra Khash likewise goes without. Is there no middle road?"

Amyr looked at Teh Atht; the wizard in turn gazed at him; Ulli looked from one to the other and back. And after a while Amyr nodded his crested head. "Fly us to Inner Isles—now, tonight—and on the way I'll tell you all I know of Tarra Khash and his jewelled scimitar, which be sure amounts to a great deal."

"Done!" cried Teh Atht at once. "But, why didn't you say

so before? Why, that were the simplest of all solutions! Safety for yourself and the lady, and missing pieces of puzzle for me: who can say fairer than that?"

"Hold!" said Amyr. "Hear me out, for I'm not finished. Then, when my wife is safe, fly me to the Eastern Ocean's strand, there to wait on Tarra's arrival with the slaver caravan."

"But—" Teh Atht began to protest, for he knew there was scarcely time for all of this flying in a single night, and that in any case it went against his plans. But then he saw the stubborn set of Suhm-yi jaw, the glint that brooked no denial in alien, golden eyes. And he shrugged. "Very well," he said, "but at ocean's rim, there I leave you to your own devices."

"Good enough," Amyr replied. "And if worst comes to worst, be certain your name shall not be mentioned."

"So be it," said Teh Atht. "And likewise, if I can later be of assistance . . ."

As for Ulli: she cried a little inside, but her husband was Suhm-yi and his was a debt of honour. He owed Tarra Khash, and this would be payment in full.

Then, without more ado, the white wizard of Klühn ushered his passengers aboard the carpet and bade them sit together toward the rear, and he took up a position in front and crossed his arms on his chest. He uttered a rune and the burdened carpet rose up, indented a little where they sat; and windows crashed open at the levitator's approach; and out into the night they drifted, their destination the dreaming jewel isles of the Suhm-yi . . .

AWAY ACROSS DESERTS and plains and peaks, almost as far east as south, Tarra Khash lay snug in the crook of a saurian elbow, with a blanket draped over him to keep out the chill. Overhead, the stars turned slowly in their titan wheel, Gleeth the moon god waxed a little more full, and clouds were haloed silver where they drifted inland from the sea. At least, most of the clouds were silver.

But one of them was black and seemed to pulse and throb like some strange angry squid! Aye, and it had positioned itself in the sky so as to shut out the moon's gleamy glare from Cush Gemal's tent. Loomar Nindiss, unable to sleep for thoughts of his sister lying chained in the hull of the boat on the platform of the lead wagon, had watched this strange black cloud swell and pulsate as it sped in from the east— and he'd also seen it slow down until it stood on high, stationary over Gemal's tent.

Then, only moments ago, the chief of the slavers had thrust aside the flap at tent's door, stuck out his lacquered topknot and ebony head and beckoned to his black night watch where that pair prowled the outer perimeter. They had flown to him at once, their robes turning them to fluttering rags of movement in moon and starlight; but as they'd approached Gemal more closely, so they had slowed until they barely crept forward. At the last, edging fearfully into the shade of the tent, then they had seemed simply to disappear, jerked inside and out of sight.

After that . . .

. . . The black cloud turned green at its rim, sent down emerald coruscations like curtains of shimmering rain to engulf Gemal's travelling pavilion. Then a wind sprang up, at first low and moaning, which gathered up sand-devils and sent them nodding and cavorting, to and fro in the central space. Grit was blown in Loomar's eyes and he blinked them, and after dabbing away cleansing tears looked again.

Ghost-fires danced in the scalloped eaves of Gemal's tent, which glowed green in its heart like some poisonous gem on night's dark cushion.

Then on high, having seemingly emptied itself of morbid energies, the black cloud shrank and quit its peculiar pulsing, turned more nearly yellow and drifted off westward with its commoner cousins. The witch-lights about Gemal's tent paled to eerie lambencies that finally flickered out; the fretful wind fell to a bluster, then to a gentler, steady breeze. And the night was back to normal.

Normal?

Two less frizzies to worry about, come morning, thought Loomar. *Little wonder Gemal brought so many of them with him! And if that's the lot of Gemal's own people, what of us slaves? And in particular, what's in store for Jezza?*

It was thoughts such as these which denied him his rest . . .

VII

Teh Atht's . . . Treachery?—
Orbiquita's Defiance

ENCASED IN HIS invisible Climatic Capsule, Teh Atht's gravity-defying carpet sped high over the foothills of the Mountains of Lohmi; spied below, there flickered the fires of certain fierce tribesmen who'd inhabited that range since times immemorial. The carpet's master paid the guttering campfires scant heed, however, for Amyr Arn had commenced his story, which held far more of fascination.

"And so this gang of cut-throat barbarians were come into the Crater Sea," Amyr continued, "and landed their raft on the beach of the tiny jewel island which Lula and I had made our home.

"Lula was alone when they found her . . . to this day I cannot speak of what they did. Northern barbarians are . . . *barbaric!* At that time we had considered ourselves last of the Suhm-yi; after the Northmen were done, I *was* the last. It was not until later that I learned of the cruel fate of Ulli Eys, and set off to rescue her from Gorgos.

"Anyway, then there was Tarra Khash the Hrossak. He pursued this evil gang for his own reasons. And when he found my Lula, dead, he was . . . kind to her. He couldn't know that I watched—or how close he came to death!

"For a while I was insane, but what was done was done. Eventually Suhm-yi teaching and training took over; my anger subsided and I reverted to type; I could no more pursue and punish the evildoers than blaspheme against my gods. Indeed, to take revenge would *be* to blaspheme against those gods! So I had been instructed. But Tarra Khash was not Suhm-yi, and against him, too, had these barbarians wronged greatly. He pursued them across the Crater Sea, while I remained behind and prayed for him. In those days, you see, I had standards and a code to live up to. Ah, but I have learned much since then.

"At that time, however, I could only pray. Old Gleeth, so-called 'blind' god of the moon, answered those prayers of mine. He took his time about it, as gods are wont to do, but indeed he answered them. By then, Tarra had killed five out of six bullies in a fair fight; but the last, Kon Athar, the massive leader of that band, had broken the Hrossak's scimitar with his great broadsword. Tarra was in trouble. Wounded, trapped on a beach, he could fight no more. Only magick could save him. But where magick is concerned, old Gleeth is a powerful god indeed!

"I was far, far away from Tarra, upon the Rock of Na-dom where it rises lonely from the sea. Na-dom is a holy place, the *only* place where Suhm-yi priests might ever commune with the gods. But Gleeth sees far, gazing down 'blindly' upon the whole world, on all of Theem'hdra. He hearkened to me and saw me there upon the rock of Na-dom; ah, but at the same time he saw the sore plight of Tarra Khash.

" 'Take up your bow,' he commanded me, 'and shoot an arrow into my eye.' Madness? Perhaps. But I did as Gleeth commanded. And the eye of the moon-god blinked, swallowing up my arrow. Later I was to learn that Tarra saw that same blink of the moon's eye, which for him was salvation!

"For now Gleeth spat out the arrow, which bedded itself in Kon Athar's back even in that instant when he would deliver his final killing blow. And of course, that blow never fell. The barbarian was dead, and Tarra saved . . ."

"And so you became friends," Teh Atht spoke up without looking back, "and eventually the Hrossak told you the secret of his sword?"

"Secret? Has it a secret, then?" Amyr answered, devious as the wizard himself. "I don't know about that; only that it has a history, which were almost but not quite forgotten. If forgotten things are secrets, then perhaps you are correct. In any case, Tarra could not tell me anything for he did not know. His curved sword had come into his hands almost by accident. Or maybe not. The ways of the gods are strange and mazy. I shall get to the scimitar's 'secret,' never fear, but first let me tell you more of Tarra Khash.

"From the night of my prayers to Gleeth, the shooting of my arrow into his blinking eye, and the subsequent death of Kon Athar, I saw Tarra no more until that recent time in Klühn. Between times I had learned that I was not last of the Suhm-yi, but that Ulli Eys was captive of Gorgos in his Temple of Secret Gods. I was the last *male*, and Ulli the last female, of our people. I vowed to bring her back to Inner Isles or die in the attempt. For without her, what use to live? And so I journeyed to Klühn.

"In so-called 'sophisticate city,' there I found the Hrossak falsely accused and sentenced to death on some trumped-up charge of temple priests. I freed him, which was not difficult, but for which he considered himself in my debt. Once you have won Tarra's friendship, then it's yours for life—or for death, as the case might well have been! But prior to freeing Tarra, I had taken the trouble to learn a lot more of this Gorgos: that were necessary, if I was to enter his temple and steal Suhm-yi maid away from him.

"What I had learned was this:

"That Gorgos was in league with the blackest, most monstrous Forces of Evil, and that he would open gates out beyond the nethermost spheres to let in—"

"The Thromb!" Teh Atht finished it for him, nodding. "Yes, that much I've already learned. And yet even so— even knowing that he stood against the very gates of hell itself—still he entered with you into Gorgos' temple?"

"Who, Tarra?" Amyr's silvery voice was grave. "Aye, be sure he did. What's more, it were no longer sufficient simply to rescue Ulli, but now we must also destroy Gorgos, destroy him utterly!"

"And you succeeded," Teh Atht breathed. "Flesh and blood against . . . against *that!* And still you succeeded . . ." And then, turning his head just a little: "But surely that must have been the point where his jewelled sword entered the story, eh?"

Amyr nodded. "Aye, and now I shall tell you about that sword—for that was the other reason Tarra must enter Gorgos' temple. The priests of that place had taken his shattered stump of a sword and made it whole again. That was the reason he'd been falsely accused in the first place: so that they might steal his sword, which one of them had recognized! Ah, but pity the man, or creature, who'd steal from Tarra Khash!"

"Recognized it, you say?" Now Teh Atht turned his head

fully to look back at Amyr where he sat upon the carpet, one arm holding safe his Ulli.

"Indeed," Amyr nodded. "Even as you yourself would seem to have recognized it . . ." And he watched Teh Atht's reaction.

The wizard frowned. "Have I?" he said. "I think not. Oh, faint memories stir, but—" Then his eyes went wide, and suddenly he snapped his fingers. "Here I sit in conversation with a man of the Inner Isles, of the very Suhm-yi, and my mind so mazed in the puzzle that I can't see the twists for the turns! A sword, aye! A great curved scimitar, with jewelled hilt, ceremonial until the day a certain Hrossak gave it life by taking it in his calloused hand! Ah, but what *sort* of ceremonies had it known before that, eh? Strange ceremonies indeed! And did not the Suhm-yi in their heyday boast the finest white—or silver—wizards of all? That they did. I've read of it in runebooks older than my ancestor Mylakhrion himself!" He slapped his thigh. "A sword, aye! Why, *it's one of the three Suhm-yi Swords of Power!*"

"And there you have it," Amyr Arn slowly nodded.

"What?" Teh Atht half-turned his body, the better to see who he was talking to, and the carpet at once began to fly in a vast circle. Its flight-path was controlled by the directional attitude of its master. "But I disagree, for there I *don't* have it! I know that the Hrossak's sword is one of the three leg-ended Suhm-yi Swords of Power, but not how it was lost from Inner Isles, or how it came into his possession. I know that it's now the property of one Cush Gemal, slaver in the employ of Black Yoppaloth, but not how—" He sat himself bolt upright and his jaw fell open.

"Not how?" Amyr prompted him.

"Not how it will benefit Black Yoppaloth!" Teh Atht

blurted out. "What? That mighty necromancer of jungled Shadarabar? Why, he'll know the sword in a trice, the moment he claps eyes on it! And with its mystical, magickal properties, it will make him master of all Theem'hdra!"

"Good!" said Amyr vigorously.

"Good? But then you *are* mad!" Teh Atht cried. "How, good?"

"Because now you have a real reason to see Tarra set free," Amyr answered, smiling. "One thing for Black Yop-paloth to be immortal, but another entirely that he's also omnipotent! And what of all you lesser wizards then, eh? Would he even tolerate your petty squabbles and runecast-ings? I doubt it."

There was no answer to that, and so Teh Atht simply groaned and said, in lowered tone: "Come, tell me the rest of it, for the more I know the more clearly I might see how to deal with this problem. *If* I can deal with it at all!"

And in a little while, when the carpet flew straight once more and passed over the yellow fringe of the Desert of Ell, so Amyr continued:

"It was Gorgos stole the swords, at the same time as he stole away the maiden Ulli Eys. She would guarantee his es-cape, for no Suhm-yi would interfere while there was slight-est danger to Ulli. Later, he used her as a mentalist, to steal the secrets of his rivals and opponents. And all against her will, she was his 'oracle' in the Temple of Secret Gods. He stole all three swords from the place of treasures on Na-dom.

"But the priests of my people cursed him: that so long as a single member of our race survived in the jewel isles of the Crater Sea, he would know no peace. His truest servants would sicken and die, his most treasured possessions would be lost or stolen. It was a very powerful curse, of course, and the first things he lost were the Swords of Power. For years he searched for them, to make them his again, but to no avail; and always the Suhm-yi curse worked against him. In the end he must have divined that he was cursed, and then it would have been a simple matter to discover the source of his torment. His answer was . . . devastation! He sent a poisoned cloud from volcano's vent to choke all Suhm-yi to death! All were killed, except myself and my young wife. Following which . . . but the rest of it you know."

"But Gorgos' troubles weren't over yet." Teh Atht nodded. "For you were left alive. Aye, and Suhm-yi curse fully realized in the end. Now tell me: what of the swords, after he had lost them?"

"When Gorgos had made himself something of a force to be reckoned with in Theem'hdra," Amyr answered, "then he sent out false priests into the land. They, too, searched for the swords. One of them was eventually found in the gut of a whale, harpooned by a whaler out of Khrissa. Gorgos acquired it for a song. A princeling of Klühn bought the second sword in auction to hang on the wall of his apartments. Later, when Gorgos was established there in his temple, the princeling disappeared without trace. Likewise his gem-studded scimitar.

"As for the third sword, that had fallen into the hands of a very fat, very offensive jeweller in Thinhla. His name was Nud Annoxin, and he dealt with Tarra Khash very badly indeed. Alas for him, he likewise sinned against Ahorra Izz—"

"Another of the steppeman's weird friends!" said Teh Atht.

"—Arachnid lord of scarlet scorpions," Amyr went on. "Tarra would have killed Nud Annoxin for what he did to him, but scorpion-god got there first. And so Nud's ceremonial scimitar became the sword of the Hrossak."

"All fits," said Teh Atht, "except for one oddly shaped piece. What use to Gorgos a broken sword?"

"None at all," replied Amyr, "not until he had it repaired! Then: it was very nearly a perfect job, but not quite. There was a certain slight imbalance. That was how Tarra knew which of the three swords was his, enabling him to snatch it back again. Which was what in the end put paid to Gorgos' evil schemes—and to Gorgos himself."

After a while the wizard asked: "How does the sword aid Tarra Khash?"

"That I've seen, not at all." Amyr shrugged. "He's no wizard, like you, Teh Atht. But he *is* a wizard swordsman! A fighter born, the Hrossak. He's probably better with it than any other man—but using it as a sword, not as a wand."

"*Hmm!*" said the other, and there followed a long silence.

Now they were flying over the Black Isle, that enigmatic rock to the east of the Crater Sea proper, then skimming the peaks of the Great Circle Range, and moments later dropping down over the moon-mirroring Crater Sea. Ahead, the scattered jewel isles of the Suhm-yi.

"Observe," said Teh Atht. "We climbed to a considerable height in order to clear the mountains back there. This was not without effort both on my part and the carpet's. Now, however, we can soar! Journey to Inner Isles is close to an end."

He leaned forward and the carpet likewise tilted. Now it seemed to poise in mid-air, then dipped forward and gathered speed, and in a great sweeping glide went whistling down to level out just above the still waters of the Crater Sea. Islands reared their low hills and night-dark foliage on every hand.

"Which will you make your home?" the wizard inquired.

"Any will do," Amyr answered. "I'll build a boat and we

can decide later. But for now, one of the smaller islands, I think. Like that one there." And he pointed.

Teh Atht flew the carpet close to the shore of the indicated islet. "Well, here's hoping all goes well with you," he said. "And who knows, we may even meet again."

"Now hold!" cried Amyr, warning chimes sounding in his head. "The deal was we'd put down Ulli safe and sound, then that you'd fly me—"

But Teh Atht wasn't listening.

He clung fast to the carpet's fringe, uttered a breathless rune of Instant Inversion. All within the Climatic Capsule was immediately upended—with the exception of gravity itself! Amyr and Ulli fell like stones—all of six or seven feet into tranquil, temperate waters. And overhead, repeating his rune and correcting carpet's orientation, Teh Atht squinted anxiously down to ensure his passengers had come to no harm. Like all island peoples, the pair could swim like fishes, and the wizard saw that already they stood upright in the shallows watching him.

"And how's *this* for a wizard's word?!" Amyr choked back his fury.

Teh Atht hovered out of reach, sadly shook his head.

"Do you think I enjoy this?" he said. "It isn't for me but for you! Last of the Suhm-yi, Amyr Arn, you and your Ulli both. An entire race of beings in your bodies, but no use one without the other. Fearless you are—but where a certain Hrossak's concerned, foolish too. Oh, I know well enow how you'd rush off to his rescue, and perhaps to your death—but what of Ulli then?"

"All of that is our concern!" Amyr cried.

"No," Teh Atht denied. "It's mine. And I'll not see myself damned to all eternity for what might well amount to genocide! So you stay here in your jewel isles, and I'll do what I can for Tarra Khash."

"Cheat!" Amyr shook a clenched fist. "Be sure your treachery will find you out. You'll do what you can for Tarra? Am I supposed to believe that? You're in this for yourself!"

Teh Atht gazed gravely down, finally nodded his agreement. "True enough," he said, "and useless to deny it. Certainly I've my own interests to look after; aye, and it's a sad fact that you'd likely get in my way. Which can't be allowed. But always remember this, Amyr Arn: I'm a white wizard, not a black magician—and there's a big difference, my friend . . ." With which, and without further ado, he bade his carpet rise up and bear him home.

. . . Home to Klühn.

RETURNING ALONG ALMOST the same aerial route, though naturally in the opposite direction, Teh Atht reflected on all he'd learned.

He now felt that he knew Tarra Khash personally; certainly he believed he recognized the Hrossak's persuasive power over people—not to mention creatures and even deities! Time alone would tell if he was right. But if he was . . . well, there was a certain magick in it, albeit of a sort beyond the range of "mundane" magicians. As for the steppeman's sword: that, too, was *very* special! Veritably a Sword of Power. One thing for sure: it must not be allowed to fall into Black Yoppaloth's hands in Shad.

Which in turn meant Teh Atht would likely have his work cut out for him. For how to stop Cush Gemal taking the sword with him across the Straits of Yhem?

With matters such as these to distract him, the wonder is

that Teh Atht spied, far below, emerging from a pass on the Klühn side of the Great Eastern Range, a pair of creatures whose freakish forms he knew at once. They were keeping up a fair pace (considering the ground they'd covered, which had taken them more than halfway home) but both were wearying now, and their flits and hops were less vigorous. Teh Atht swooped down, called them aboard the carpet.

For once they were glad to see him. Flitter clung with his claws to the tail end of the carpet, folding his wings back like a dart and gliding, while hopper simply flopped down centrally, causing something of a sag. And shortly thereafter all three of them were back in Teh Atht's apartments overlooking the Bay of Klühn.

Worn out, the wizard's familiars went to their private places and at once fell asleep; Teh Atht saw the sense in that, snatched a ten-second "night" in a state of Rapid Repose. After that, with dawn showing faintly pink on the eastern horizon, it was time for breakfast. Following which . . . business as usual.

Time now to discover what the shewstone had recorded, and to see how things stood at present. Ah, but all very softly-softly! In no wise a clever thing to scry on Cush Gemal too intently, or for too prolonged a period. No, in no wise wise at all . . .

TARRA CAME AWAKE with the strange, nagging sensation of being scrutinized both from afar and close at hand. There was a pink flush on the eastern horizon; smallest stars were fast fading; a hooded figure, furtive however familiar, leaned over him.

Someone leaning over him?

The Hrossak whipped his blanket aside and continued the motion to snatch for hilt of scimitar—where it no longer protruded above his shoulder! A hand hard as old leather clamped itself to his face and mouth, and well known voice hissed in his ear: "Be still! It's me, Stumpy!"

Tarra relaxed in the lizard's elbow and Stumpy withdrew his hand. But in another moment: "Stumpy Adz?" Tarra hoarsely whispered. "What the hell—!"

"*Shh!*" Stumpy cautioned, desperately squinting all about.

"Shh?" said Tarra. "Are you totally daft? If they catch you, they'll have your ribs for tent pegs!" He sat up, gazed all about in the deceptive false-dawn light. "How'd you get past the watch?"

"What watch?" Stumpy answered with a question of his own. "Nothing stirs round here, believe me. Now let's cut the blather and get out of here!"

Tarra slid down from his honker's elbow, but carefully, so as not to disturb the slumbering giant. "Where's your—" he checked himself, "—no, *my* camel?"

"Behind the dune over there," Stumpy was fairly dancing with anxiety. "Come on, man, let's scarper!"

Tarra shook his head, hung back, tried to get his brain going. He should hurry along with Stumpy, of course; the camel was a good big 'un and could easily carry two; and the slavers, so close to the end of their murderous trip, weren't much likely to come in pursuit. This was Tarra's big chance, probably the only chance he'd get.

But—

"Listen," he said. "Here's what I want you to do."

"What?" Stumpy couldn't believe his ears. What did the great ox think he was doing, wasting time like this? "*What?*" he said again, hopping to and fro between one foot and the other. "What I want *you* to do is come with me, now, before the camp wakes up and—"

Tarra's turn to stifle. He grabbed Stumpy's neck in one hand, clapped the other over his mouth, shook him like a rag doll. "Listen, old friend, and listen good," he grated from between clenched teeth. "I knew it was you following us, and I hoped and prayed they wouldn't get you. Well, wily old devil, they didn't. And I appreciate you coming for me like this, which is something no man in his right mind would have tried. But . . . but I *can't* come with you!"

Stumpy's one good eye popped wide open. Tarra waited until his wriggling subsided, released him. "Why not?" Stumpy breathlessly demanded then. "Why damn it to hell *not!?*"

"Because—" (Tarra wasn't quite sure himself) "—because there's a young lad here who needs a friend. Aye, and his sister, too. Innocents, both of 'em, Stumpy. Also, the frizzy boss has my sword, and I'm not going anywhere without it. And finally . . ."

Stumpy's shoulders slumped. "Finally, you've never been to Shad before, eh?" he said.

Still gritting his teeth, on impulse, Tarra hugged him, released him, said: "Now you get back across that dune, aboard that camel, and ride the hell for Hrossa! Tell 'em right across the steppes all you know—especially that there's Hrossaks been taken into slavery by Shad, which is a lie, I know, but tell 'em anyway—and ask to be taken down into Grypha. Tell the Gryphans, too, and then board a ship for Klühn. Before you know it, all this corner of Theem'h-dra will be up in arms against Shad and Shadarabar. *That's* the best thing you can do! Maybe we'll meet again if I come out of this in one piece, and if I don't—"

"You there!" came shout in throaty Yhemni tones. A frizzy stood centrally in the circle, close to where last night's fires had burned. He'd bedded down there with several others, who now were stirring and tossing aside their blankets. "What do?" His jaw had fallen open.

"Run!" Tarra hissed.

Stumpy ran.

The black slaver came stumbling, tripped on a companion and went to his knees. When he came erect again, Tarra saw he'd picked up a crossbow. Other Yhemnis were climbing to their feet; slaves groaned and stirred under their wagons; a big lizard grumbled and honked disdainfully.

Tarra took a deep breath, held it, stared after Stumpy. The old lad was halfway up a steep dune, wallowing like a stranded whale. The black with the crossbow came running, skidded to a halt beside Tarra. He stared hard at him, then lifted his weapon and aimed it at Stumpy's back where his scarecrow figure was limned against the dawn at the crest of the dune. Tarra stood with his back to his lizard where it had just this moment started awake. Its great eyes rolled to gaze at the black leaning across its foreleg, aiming his weapon.

Tarra slid two fingers under a limp scale, nipped the tender follicle there. Old Scaly reared up, sent the Yhemni marksman flying. His bolt zipped skyward, going nowhere in particular. The black got up. "Stupid . . . *lizard!*" he spat, aiming a kick at the great beast. Tarra got between, shoved him onto his rump again.

"None of that!" he growled. "What? Injure this valuable beast? Land one kick on that scaly hide and I'll have him bite you in halves!"

Stumpy was almost forgotten; the thudding of a hard-ridden camel's hooves came faintly from far away, fading;

the furious black got up and yanked out his knife, and for a moment Tarra thought the man would go for him. Then:

"What's all this?" Cush Gemal came jerkily striding, reminding Tarra of nothing so much as a spindly, two-legged black spider. "What's it mean?" Gemal demanded.

The raging black controlled himself, put away his knife, backed off. Tarra turned to the slaver chief. "We had a visitor," he said. "Some wasteland scavenger, a lone thief. I woke up, saw him sniffing about, crept up on him. Then this idiot," he jerked his thumb at the cowering black, "came shouting and shooting, scared him off! It was probably the one who's been trailing us. No harm done, though, that I can see."

Gemal flared his nostrils, narrowed his eyes at the thoroughly cowed Yhemni. He stepped closer, appraised the Hrossak keenly through eyes gleamy as wet pebbles. Tarra gazed back, apparently undismayed. Gemal couldn't know how he held his breath. Then the caravan's master turned to a pair of Northmen where they'd mounted-up on ponies. "Get after him!" he cried. "Catch him and kill him, whoever he is if you can. And if you can't . . . then meet us at the ocean loch."

As they goaded their mounts to a gallop he turned back to Tarra, and in softer tone: "Was it the way you reported it, Hrossak?"

Tarra shrugged. "Why don't you question your night watch?" he said. "They'd be the ones with the answers. And if they haven't any, then I'd want to know what they've been doing all night!"

Gemal's gaze was so penetrating, Tarra believed he might be looking right into his soul. But then those eyes blinked and the scowl lifted from the slaver's face. Finally, raising his voice, Gemal addressed the entire camp:

"Make ready at once!" he shouted. "I'll brook no more delay. We ate well last night; this morning we breakfast at ocean's rim, before making sail. And now make haste, for the sun's almost up."

With that it seemed the incident was over, and Tarra could start breathing normally again. Watching Gemal stride away in the direction of his tent, he heard—"Pst! *Pst!*" He looked, saw Loomar Nindiss' eyes staring at him from the shadows under the wagon.

"What is it?" Tarra whispered, pretending to check various chains and fastenings on the great shafts.

"That was no raider," Loomar whispered back. "You knew him." It was no way an accusation, just a statement of fact.

"Keep your voice down, lad," Tarra told him. And in another moment: "So I knew him. So what?"

"You could have run off."

"Should have," Tarra answered. "Were you the only one awake?"

"I think so. I've been awake most of the night. But listen: Cush Gemal won't be talking to the night watch, as you suggested."

"Oh?"

"No, for last night there came a black cloud that let down green fires round Gemal's tent. And I saw him call the night watch inside with him. They didn't come out again."

Tarra thought about it, offered a slight nod of his head, said, "Thanks for the information. But Loomar, let's try to be more discreet in future, eh? There are people here—and one in particular—who'd consider that you see, hear, speak and think entirely too much! You'd lose your eyes, ears, tongue, and very likely several other bits if they overheard what you just said. Aye, and so would I!"

Following which he strode away, and went to see to Old Scaly . . .

ALL OF WHICH, in his apartments in Klühn, Teh Atht the white wizard saw and heard. What he did *not* see was this:

In the lava lair of lamia Sisterhood, the Council of Five sat in extraordinary session, of which fearsome gathering Orbiquita herself was the youngest and most junior member. Unthinkable that a lamia serving out her five-year term as Mistress of the Cavern should convene such a meeting in the first place, but Orbiquita had done just that, which was what made it extraordinary.

But Chairmistress she was not; no, for that honour went to Iniquiss, oldest and by far wisest of all that monstrous brood. The other three were Hissiliss, Suquester and Scuth. Having heard Orbiquita out, now Iniquiss barked:

"*What?* And have you called us down here from our various pleasures and pursuits to listen to drivel such as this? Methinks it's simply a scheme to cut short your irksome but well-earned detention here!"

Orbiquita, entirely unmindful of Iniquiss' magnitude, snapped, "Not the case! You know well enow that in that event—and if my deception were discovered—then that my term would be doubled. I know it, too, and I'm no such fool. No, the case I have made is reliable in every instance, and my plea stands: that I be allowed a period of time in which to pattern certain events in the outer world of men. That is all."

"All? That is all?" Hissiliss hissed, belching her astonishment in brimstone gusts. "But isn't this the same Orbiquita who already took time off to go canoodling with a man—an entirely *human* man, that is?"

"Juicy news travels fast," Orbiquita growled, venting steam. "Aye, one and the same, snakeface. There *is* only one Orbiquita! But no canoodling, I promise you. I owed him a debt and repaid it."

"But you *would* canoodle," Hissiliss sulphurously insisted, "if 'twere possible?"

Orbiquita made no comment, and: *"Hah!"* Hissiliss snorted.

"Is your current request centered in this same . . . man?" Iniquiss wrinkled her plated snout.

Orbiquita offered up a snort of her own. "How can you gnaw on their bones," she said, "and yet talk about them as if they were unclean? Men *sired* us! Some of us, anyway. Yibb-only-knows what sired you four . . ."

"Insults will get you nowhere!" Suquester and Scuth, who were true sisters, shouted together.

"I'm the one insulted!" Orbiquita gave back. "Are my rank and position in the Sisterhood entirely ignored? Am I not a member of the Council of Five?"

"A member currently undergoing corrective punishment," Iniquiss reminded. "Won't this . . . this *business* keep until your term is served?"

Orbiquita shook her head vehemently and sent lava crusts flying all about. "No, it won't. By then Tarra'll likely be dead, and—"

"Tarra! Tarra!" Suquester and Scuth chorussed.

"—and you four will be to blame," Orbiquita finished.

"To blame?" Hissiliss had a habit of repeating statements for emphasis. "For the death of a man? Orbiquita, I've been the death of countless men, we all have, and never before suffered 'blame'! Would you have us eat stones?"

"This man's a wizard, right?" Iniquiss did her best to understand. "He's put an unbreakable spell on you, for his own lustful or thaumaturgical purposes. Well, if that's the case, perhaps we can—"

"It's not the case," Orbiquita groaned, finally lowering her head. "Would that's all it were. But no, it's worse than that. Far worse . . ."

For long moments the four lamias where they floated on lesser crusts around Orbiquita's central island were awed, horrified, silent until Iniquiss inquired: "Do you . . . love him?"

Orbiquita could only nod, while steaming tears rolled down her warty cheeks. The four were stunned, but not for long.

"That settles it!" said Suquester and Scuth as one. "His life's in danger, is it? Good! Let him die." Hissiliss nodded her agreement, to which Iniquiss added:

"That were surely for the best, Orbiquita. You're poisoned, sister, plain to see. Or at least, the human female within you is poisoned. And this slow poison called love—love of and for a man—is the deadliest lamia poison of all! I've seen others taken by it in my time, and every one a hopeless case. But if this Tarra were dead—"

"Do you threaten him?" Orbiquita looked up, red-eyed, flexed her claws until they sank into and scarred deep her lava island. "Do you *dare* threaten him?" She looked as if she'd fly in their faces.

"No," said Iniquiss, "we do not. Neither do we offer him our assistance—nor yours! Your request is denied." She turned to the other three. "Sisters, we go."

The four spread their leathery wings, prepared for departure. But:

"Wait," said Orbiquita, and her doomful tone froze them fast. "There remains only one way in which this problem might find resolution."

"The 'problem,' as you call it, is already resolved, Orbiquita," said Iniquiss after a while. "In this matter we cannot be swayed. Only be thankful that for all your transgressions, still we allow you to keep your seat on this council! In this way your shame—which is ours—goes no further. What? And should we bring the entire Sisterhood into disrepute?"

"I would bring the Sisterhood to the very doors of *destruction*—" Orbiquita glowered . . . then trembled in her every fibre, "—to prevent harm coming to my Tarra!"

"Shamelessly ensorcelled!" cried Hissiliss.

"Maddened by a man!" sputtered Suquester and Scuth together. "Disgusting!"

"There is a way," Orbiquita insisted. "You know my meaning. Do you drive me to it?"

Iniquiss, for all that she was old and wise and felt something of pity for Orbiquita, gave a snort of derision. "What?" she said. "Renounce the Sisterhood, and trade five thousand years and more for the short span of a fragile human female? And what is that for a threat, sister? Why, you'd no more renounce the Sisterhood than—"

"Here and now," Orbiquita cut her off, her voice more doomful yet, "I renounce the Sisterhood!"

The four were shocked almost rigid. "Think what you're doing!" Iniquiss howled then. "You may say it only one more time with impunity, and if you utter those words a *third* time—"

"I renounce the Sisterhood!" Orbiquita shrank down into herself, shuddering in every limb as she calculated the consequences of what must be done.

For a moment, aghast, the four drew back; then Hissiliss cried: "She's bluffing! Only four foolish sisters in all lamia history have ever—"

"Damn you all!" Orbiquita whispered. "Only *look* at yourselves! You are loathsome; *I* am loathsome; five thousand years of this is no future. I have found a man like no other man. You shall not keep me from him. So hear me now, when one last time I say—"

"*No!*" they all cried out together. But too late.

Orbiquita drew herself up in all her horror, threw wide her wings and cried, quite irrevocably: "*I renounce the Sisterhood!*"

Following which, there was nothing anyone could do about it . . .

VIII

Ships of Sorcery

THE SALT SEA! Oh, this was only a loch, green where it met the shoreline and brackish, a long scummy finger of water pointing inland from the vast "hand" of the true ocean, but it was salty and tidal. Coming down from yellow dunes onto a shore whose salt-crystal pools sparkled white under a blazing sun, the "caravaneer" Cush Gemal saw it lying there and shielded his jet-black eyes against its incredible blaze of blue water, stretching eastwards away and away. And he led his wagons right down to water's rim.

The wagons were lined up where the beach sloped seaward, and stones were put under their wheels to keep them from rolling. Then the big steppes-lizards were unhitched, canvasses thrown back, tailboards let down. And now the five Yhemni boats stood at last all in open view, cradled on their shallow-draft wagons where the great wheels came three-quarters up their strakes. The slavers fed themselves and then the slaves, and the latter were loosened from the respective wagons but kept in batches, chained together. And now it was time for the launching of the first boat.

This was no big deal, indeed its mechanics were rudimentary. The stones were yanked away from the lead wagon's wheels and a gang of trotting, then galloping Yhemnis guided the shafts into the shallows, wagon rumbling along behind, until only wheels stuck up and flat-bottomed boat drifted free. Then an anchor tossed overboard and the boat lying waiting, with its former vehicle now forming a platform 'twixt sand and sea.

Five times this happened, and Tarra Khash watching all: seeing slaves driven aboard the boats and chained to their oars, masts hauled into position and sails readied, four big honkers herded protesting and with no small degree of Hrossak skill aboard their boats. Now the craft they'd hauled would carry them, right across the sea to Shad. Four of the five, anyway.

The fifth boat in the water, which had been aboard Tarra's wagon, was Cush Gemal's; now he came striding in his spindly way, with a handful of blacks behind him leading bevy of stolen virgins. "Well, Hrossak," said Gemal to Tarra where he stood patting the stumpy foreleg of Old Scaly, "and now it's farewell. A pity I couldn't have known you better, but perhaps for the best in the long run. Here, this is yours. It will more than repay anything I've taken from you." He thrust a leather pouch into Tarra's hand, stood waiting while the steppeman checked its contents.

Tarra weighed three small golden ingots in his hands, glanced admiringly at a large fistful of glowing, flawless gemstones. "Repayment?" he said. "Well, it seems I haven't much to complain about on that score. After all, what have you had of me? A few days of my freedom? Others before you took far more than that. My labours? But what are muscles for if not for working? As for my camel, lost when first we met: why, the tenth part of these gemstones could buy me a whole caravan!"

"You're well satisfied, then?" Gemal smiled in his skull-like fashion.

"But then there's my sword," said Tarra, almost as if Gemal hadn't spoken. He inclined his head toward that weapon where it swung at Gemal's hip. "And the fact is, I've become somewhat attached to that. It's stood me in good stead in many a fight, and I really feel naked without it."

The smile slipped from Gemal's face. "Haven't I paid you enough? Are you bargaining with me?"

"There was a time not long ago, in your tent, when you said you liked my company *because* I bargained with you," Tarra answered. "Have you changed your mind, then?" And before Gemal could answer, he gave him back the heavy sacklet. "Keep this, Cush Gemal, for I've no need of it. Oh, I know there's plenty more where this came from, but keep that, too. Keep all of it, for it's only stolen wealth anyway. What I'd really appreciate is that curved scimitar, which is rightly mine."

Gemal kept his rising anger under rein. "What I take stays taken," he finally answered. "No deal, Tarra Khash. And anyway, the sword pleases me. There's something about it . . ." Again he held out the pouch. "Now take what I'm offering and go."

Tarra sighed, shrugged. "The sword's yours then," he said. "So maybe I can bargain for something else?"

Gemal looked puzzled. "Such as?"

"There's a young slave I've grown fond of, name of Loomar Nindiss. If you could see your way to letting him go free with me . . ."

The slaver's frown lifted at once. "One slave? That were a simple matter." He looked toward the boats. "If you'll just tell me—"

"Two slaves," Tarra cut him short. "He has a sister, Jezza."

Gemal's head snapped round and his black eyes fastened on Tarra's. "What? One of Black Yoppaloth's brides?" He looked at the girls where they stood chained in their misery, waiting to board the boat. And: "Which one is Jezza?" he called out.

Jezza hung her head, stepped forward. She was a beautiful flower, scarce opened, not yet fully in bloom. Her hair was black silk flowing onto her shoulders, her eyes blue as the sky, skin delicate as milk. Gemal looked at her for long moments, finally turned back to Tarra. "It were your death if you so much as touched one of my master's brides," he growled. "Especially that one!" And before Tarra could make further comment: "Now listen. You've twice refused my money, and all you have left is your lizard and your life. Don't bargain yourself into an early grave, Hrossak. Go now, while still you may."

Again Tarra's shrug. "Well then, since I'm broke again and you're bent on taking my young friend and his sister with you to Shad—not to mention all the rest of the people on those boats—it seems there's only one thing for it. I'll just have to come with you!"

Gemal shook his head in astonishment, then tilted his lacquered cockscomb to peer at the steppeman slantwise. "I'll never fathom you, Hrossak," he said. "But haven't I told you that Shad's no place for the likes of you? Didn't I say I felt it in my bones we'd both be sorry if ever you came to Shad? I can't see any good coming out of it; I don't even like the feel of it! No, I'll not take you."

He turned to his blacks. "Get these girls aboard," he ordered. But when he turned back . . . still Tarra stood there, his expression unaltered. "What now?" The slaver's tone had risen a notch.

"Do you remember our contest in your tent?" Tarra gazed at him unflinching. "The knife, which you reached first?"

"What of it?" Gemal was curious in spite of himself.

"I've been practising," Tarra scratched his chin, tried to control a nervous tic tugging the flesh at the corner of his eye. "Now let me try to make one last bargain with you. Or if not a bargain, perhaps a small wager?"

By now all the boats bar Gemal's were fully loaded, waiting, sails slack where they were held side on to the breeze. Only Tarra himself, Gemal and two of his Yhemnis remained on the shore. And of course Old Scaly. "You've nothing to wager with," Gemal pointed out.

"Oh, but I have," said Tarra. "You said it yourself: my lizard and my life."

Gemal laughed, but a trifle shrilly, almost desperately. "And you'd really gamble the latter? Against what?"

"Against a trip to Shad, with you, in your boat there." And again Tarra's shrug. "I always was a wanderer, Cush Gemal."

"*Madman!*" Gemal hissed. "I think you're mocking me!" He stood erect, scowling, then quickly made up his mind. "Very well, what's the bet?"

Tarra took a step closer, lifted his hands chest high, thumbs pointing in toward his body. And Gemal knew what the bet was, for he saw the Hrossak's eyes where they peered at the jewelled hilt protruding from the scabbard at his hip. "I've been practising, like I said," Tarra repeated. "And now who's fastest, Cush Gemal? Shall we see?"

Gemal's black lieutenants also stepped closer. Tarra

looked at them, then at their master. Gemal had likewise lifted his hands chest high. "My sword?" he said. "But you can't possibly win, Tarra." His voice was soft as the sand underfoot. "Why, I've only to let my hand fall, and—"

"Ready when you are," said Tarra. And in the selfsame split second Gemal made his move. His hand blurred down toward the jewelled hilt, came to rest on top of Tarra's, jerked back in shock and disbelief!

The eyes of Gemal's frizzies popped. They drew long, curved knives—but Tarra's was longer. It slithered from its scabbard in a whisper of steel, came to rest with its point tickling Gemal's windpipe. "And how's this for bargaining?" The Hrossak's turn to whisper.

Gemal's blacks backed off. The clatter from the ships had died down in a moment. All was silent, with only the slaps of sails, the occasional grunt of a honker and the *hush, hush* of wavelets on the strand to disturb the electric atmosphere.

"What do you want?" The knob of Gemal's throat bobbed only half an inch from needle tip of scimitar.

"At the moment, staying alive's my only concern," Tarra answered.

"No one will harm you, so long as I'm not harmed," Gemal husked.

Now would seem the best chance Tarra had had, possibly the best he'd get; there was nothing he couldn't demand and win. But how long would he keep it? And anyway, that hadn't been his deal. Whatever Cush Gemal had or had not done, so far he'd played fair with the Hrossak. And what if Tarra did demand Jezza and Loomar's release, and a trio of ponies to carry them out of here? By the time all was arranged and the ponies off the boats, someone would have put a bolt in him, be sure. Even now he could hear small splashes as frizzies, coming out of their stupefaction, slipped overboard of the boats to swim ashore. All of these thoughts taking but a moment to pass through Tarra's mind. Then—

He let fall the tip of the scimitar, direct into the mouth of its scabbard, then tilted the hilt and slid the weapon rattling home. Gemal's jaw fell open and his eyes disbelievingly followed the length of the curved blade as it went home in leather; then those same astonished orbs turned themselves on Tarra. "Totally insane!" he declared.

"What?" said Tarra, his face open and completely innocent. "But it was only a game, sort of. Or maybe a lesson. A lesson in trust, in faith." Gemal's very words, as he'd spoken them in his tent that time.

"You mock me!" The slaver's black eyes were round as saucers. "Do you think you can teach me anything?"

"Not you, no," Tarra told him, shaking his head. "But it might teach those men you travel with a thing or two. Take me with you to Shad and they'll see you're a man of your word, a man of honour. They'll have faith in you. But only have me killed . . . their trust dies with me. A very bad move, for a man whom so many various people seem to trust beyond all normal bounds."

For a moment the tableau held: the two staring at each other on that narrow strand, Gemal's men starting to creep forward again, and the ships on the loch silently waiting. And then the slaver chief threw back his head and laughed. And mercifully, there wasn't an ounce of malice in all his gales of laughter.

"Tarra Khash," said Gemal when at last he could, "truly I believe you're the first man—the first true *man*, mind and muscle—I've met in too many years! Very well, then, Shad it is. Aye, and we'll make room for your big lizard, too. Except—" and his eyes narrowed and grew sterner, "—don't ever tell me I didn't warn you . . ."

ALL OF THIS, through the eye of his marvellous shewstone, Teh Atht observed in private in his apartments overlooking the Bay of Klühn. And he marvelled at Tarra Khash's audacity and skill in side-stepping (what were for any other man) certain death, and he wondered at the Hrossak's penchant for flirting with that Ultimate Opponent Invincible. Invincible, to anyone not already immortal.

As for Tarra's perversity—and how else might one describe his apparent determination to crawl into the jaws of hell?— the wizard was torn two ways. On the one hand he feared for Tarra's life . . . but on the other he was mindful of his own prime objective, to discover Black Yoppaloth's most secret secret. For if indeed the steppeman should reach and penetrate jungled Shad's barbaric splendours, be sure Teh Atht would be right there with him—in mind at least, if not in the flesh.

And so the wizard sat in the room of his astrologarium, with his back to the whorl and reel and interminable turmoil of fortune's myriad stars, planets and moons, and watched (but carefully, so as not to become himself subject of some other's scrutiny) the events aboard Cush Gemal's five boats, where now they bore out through the mouth of the loch and into the Eastern Ocean, bearing very nearly south for Shad.

He saw the land recede in the wake of the boats where they ploughed the waves abreast, and the darkening of the sky as stormwinds drove clouds from the east. Ah, but these were strange clouds, bred of forces outside of Nature!

Until now the boats had gone but slowly, with only sufficient of wind to propel them as made rowing unnecessary; but as the sky darkened so the wind freshened, and it was a wind that blew against the ships, which reared up the waves and made the going rough and roaring. Then—a wonder! Even in Teh Atht's eyes—an astonishing sight!

Far overhead the storm clouds fetched a halt, colliding a while in a mighty confusion before turning and racing in a new direction—*in the direction of Shad itself!* And now, still amazed, the white mage of Klühn turned his wary gaze on the black tent of Cush Gemal where that smallest of pavilions had been erected and made fast in the very prow of his boat. And he saw the scintillant green fires which fell from the sky to flicker in its scalloped eaves and along its ridges, and drip like flaming incense from its tassels.

He glimpsed, too, the shrivelled-seeming slaver who leaned a little from his tent's door to beckon to a pair of his faithful, fearful black retainers; and how though they shivered as from some burning fever of the soul, still they could not refuse but went in unto him. Ah, and how the great winds steadied themselves and blew true on the ships of Shad from that time onward! And Teh Atht knew he was seeing magick at work here as mighty as any he could produce, and blacker than any he'd ever dare to conjure.

It was, could only be, Black Yoppaloth working through the medium of his slaver-in-chief, hastening his vessels home to him; and for what foul purpose? Had he already seen Gemal's new sword, Teh Atht wondered? Had he recognized it as a Sword of Power? For of course Yoppaloth was capable of scrying on these distant events, even as Teh Atht himself. What? He was capable of raising a *storm* in those foreign waters, to blow his ships home! And with these slaves and innocent girls, used in some unhallowed rite, and with that sword . . . would there be any limit to the undying monster's power then?

Suddenly Teh Atht knew what he must do.

He did not relish it, but he had felt the bitter winds of the outer immensities blowing on his soul, had seen his heart—perhaps the heart of Theem'hdra itself—gripped in a mighty black fist and crushed until it dripped blood. Only a vision, one of many possible futures, true, but one which could not be suffered to become reality.

A shipwreck might be the answer: send Cush Gemal and his recently won scimitar to the bottom of the Eastern Ocean! And Tarra Khash? And those strong young slaves? And all twelve of those lovely, innocent lasses? But what would their fate be, anyway, in dark and jungled Shad? Better far the salty kiss of ocean than the mouldering lips of liches, and weedy rather than weird graves. And Orbiquita, when she discovered how her Tarra had drowned? All hell to pay there, but it would pass. Aye, and feelings of guilt would pass, too, balanced against the continuing certainty and comparative serenity of Theem'hdra's future.

So be it, a wreck!

There were islands about, and more ahead: tiny, weathered crests of rock upthrusting from ocean floor, last vestiges of land-bridges which once joined Shadarabar to the mainland. Unmarked on any map, these islands, reefs and sandbars were a menace best avoided. To that end the magick winds blew Cush Gemal's five boats well to the east of the first group of islands, so that only their rocky spires were glimpsed through the spray, and the breakers crashing on their reefs. Aye, one such group safely navigated, but more coming up fast ahead.

And now Teh Atht considered a magick of his own making. For having had some little time to think about it, he believed he could emulate Black Yoppaloth's seemingly gigantic effort, however reduced in scale. Indeed it should be a fairly simple thing, though for a fact it would leave Teh Atht very much open to discovery. Still and all, however great the risk, it was more than balanced by the dire threat poised even now over the entire Primal Land.

Sympathetic magick was the answer. Primitive witchcraft. But coupled with the complexities of Teh Atht's more esoteric thaumaturgies, it should work! Quickly he stood up, strode to the weirdly mobile globe of alien plasma which was his astrologarium, rapidly calculated the co-ordinates of Cush Gemal's planet. It was, he saw, that same sphere (subject of many a previous calculation) which influenced Black Yoppaloth's affairs: a small dark moon on the rim, which even now swam into view around the bulk of a vast and cratered parent world. So Yoppaloth and his strangeling slavemaster shared similar origins and destinies, did they? All to the good: let *both* be blind a while!

Now the white wizard took from his pocket a black silk handkerchief, the while calling to his third familiar that he show himself. Out from the very plasma the liquid one appeared, spurting like a squid in miniature star-spaces. Teh Atht held out his square of silk, saying: "Take it, quickly now, and drape it over yonder moonlet."

In a moment the thing was done, and now the moon reeled blindly in a darkness other than that of its parent's shadow. "There!" said Teh Atht, satisfied. "And now perhaps they'll not sense me while I work against them." Then, uttering a brief malediction against the moon and all in its sway, he returned to his shewstone. It were time now to make a test.

Taking a bowl of water in which he'd recently freshened his face, the wizard stirred its contents to motion and set it down beside the shewstone. He took up an old quill and broke it into five small pieces, dropping them into the bowl. Five ships of Shad, all bobbing on the water in line abreast. Then, half-shuttering his eyes, Teh Atht began to breathe slow and deeply, and was soon in self-induced trance.

His eyes narrowed to slits, filmed over as if varnished, while his breathing became so slow as to almost falter. And as the scene in the shewstone expanded in the eye of his mind, until he could almost fancy himself there aboard Cush Gemal's boat, so he commenced to blow gently on the five quill ships. Now, with skilful puffs, he separated Gemal's vessel from the others, and concentrating on that one alone drove it sideways toward the rim of the bowl— except that to Teh Atht the bowl was now grown to an ocean, and its rim a treacherous sandbar jutting out from craggy islet . . .

TARRA KHASH SAW the other four ships forging away, felt a strange sideways current drawing Cush Gemal's vessel westward. Ahead a tiny island, where a long low line of waves showed breaking over a reef or sandbar. The Hrossak made rapid calculations, saw that at this rate of veer the ship would soon run aground!

He clambered round the bulk of Old Scaly where he crouched amidships and honked his distress, made his way back to the Yhemni steersman at the long-handled tiller.

"Man, your rudder's broken!" he bellowed. "We're heading straight for that hazard!"

"Not broken," the black yelled back, fighting with the tiller. "Something bad wrong!"

"Bad wrong?" Tarra lent his own strength to the unequal struggle. "You're damned right there is!" He looked ahead through wind and spray, saw that in another minute they'd hit. The slaves had seen the danger, too, and were tearing at the chains that bound them to useless oars. Tarra turned back to the steersman. "Who has the key to those chains?" he demanded.

"I have it, in belt," the frizzy shouted back, scowled at Tarra and narrowed his dark eyes. "And I keep!"

"We have to release them," the Hrossak allowed himself to stumble against the man. "Else when the boat hits, they're goners!"

"No do," the black shook his head. "Only if master say so . . ."

"Can't wait for that," Tarra yelled. He grabbed the other's belt, tore loose the large iron key which he found there, tossed it to one of the slaves where the end of the chain was padlocked to his oar. Even as he did so the boat gave a lurch; the steersman had released the tiller to snatch out a knife. A second black, knife drawn, likewise came scrambling, converging on Tarra, and others cracked whips with less than their accustomed accuracy in a vain attempt to quell the panic of the slaves.

Now terror held full sway: chains were rattling through their staples; blacks stumbled here and there, at a loss what to do next; in the front of the boat, close behind Gemal's tent, screams rang out from the helpless knot of girls as their doom roared ever closer. And suddenly—

"*Blind! Blind!*" A mad cry rose above wind and water and all the rest. "Who has done this? What curse is on me now?" Cush Gemal was there in the prow of the boat, just now emerged from his tent, one hand clapped to his eyes and the other outstretched and groping wildly in the air. He reeled to the shuddering of the sideways drifting vessel, swayed to and fro to the tune of its lurching.

Tarra Khash had his own problems. As the former steersman made a wild stab at his throat, he ducked sideways and felt the keen edge of the man's knife slice the lobe of his ear. Then he kicked his attacker in the groin and knuckled him under the nose, caving in his upper lip. The second black came from the rear, of which Tarra wasn't aware until he heard his gurgling scream. He turned, saw the frizzy go down, one hand bent behind him where he vainly strove to grasp the knife in his spine.

Tarra would know that knife anywhere: he'd once buried it in the sand beside the body of a previous owner. And there on a starboard bench, no longer chained—one arm clinging to a shipped oar for balance and the other outstretched in a life-saving, death-dealing throw—who else but Loomar Nindiss!

And then the boat hit!

"Hit" (if the word conveys a shattering and flying apart) is probably the wrong word. "Reared upon" might be better; for indeed the flat-bottomed boat reared upon the sandbar. Driven at a furious pace, it slid home on the wide reach of submerged sand and pebbles, reared on its prow like a bucking pony, teetered there for a moment before falling back with a colossal *slap* in the water. But in that moment of slithering collision and slingshot rearing—

Cush Gemal, girls, slaves, slavers and all were hurled high

in an arc of thrashing bodies, came down in a frenzy of flailing limbs into the sea beyond the sandbar—which was a great deal calmer and not nearly so deep as the thundering ocean proper. Indeed the sandbar had formed something of a lagoon or harbour, where now ejected crew and captives floundered in water only chest-deep.

As for Old Scaly: his great weight had saved the day, stopped the boat from capsizing into the lagoon. But at the moment of the collision he'd commenced sliding forward, levelled Gemal's now ragged tent, crashed through the shallow rail of the prow and plunged headlong into the sea close to the milling swimmers. Tarra Khash was miraculously fortunate: in the very rear of the boat, his trajectory had been higher, tossing him up into the sail. There he'd been cushioned in the slackening bell of canvas; had slid down the sail 'til his feet met the boom; finally, dizzily, had lowered himself to the deck.

Behind the Hrossak, roaring water and foaming spray; here beneath his unsteady feet the boat, now empty, firmly lodged in sucking sand; ahead the shallow, calm and lagoon-like waters, and jumbled rockpile of an island close at hand. Tarra's head stopped spinning and he looked at the swimmers where they were striving for the shore. He found his voice to yell: "The lizard! Cling to Old Scaly!" For the giant lizards of Hrossa were blundering good swimmers and buoyant as corks.

Then the steppeman's eyes searched out Cush Gemal—and found him lying prone on the bottom! Overboard went Tarra Khash in a shallow dive, which took him down to where Cush Gemal lay stiff as stone on a swirly bed of sand and gravel. Stiff as stone?—he *was* stone!—but pumice, not granite. And pumice floats!

As Tarra tugged, so the slaver boss came free and drifted to the surface; and the Hrossak, utterly astonished and feeling himself dreaming, propelling him ashore face-up, like some old figurehead carved of leaden driftwood.

Then gravel sucking soggily underfoot, and hands reaching to haul the steppeman up out of clinging water, and blacks gawping at their grey-carved master bobbing on his back in the shallows. But in the next moment Cush Gemal came back to life and his black eyes were flecked with a red fury.

He sprang up in the water, stepped to dry land. His blood-shot eyes scanned the sky and fixed on something no one else saw. He pointed, shouted:

"You—you dog—*you!*" And then, in an agony of frustration: "Ah!—too *late!* But *next* time, my veiled friend! Never fear, for *next* time I'll know you! Aye, and then we'll discover what magick may do, eh?" With that, green fire leaped unannounced from his pointing fingertips, hurled itself harmlessly into the sky and burst in an incendiary flash of emerald flares. Following which Cush Gemal seemed to shrivel down into himself, and without another word collapsed into the arms of Tarra Khash . . .

OUT THE CORNER of one half-shuttered eye, Teh Atht had seen a black silk square slide from a miniature moon and flutter into the path of a flaring star. Bursting into flame, the silken kerchief's yellow flash of fire had distracted him, and his long-distance spell of Curious Concretion was broken. Panic gripped him and he at once strove to come fully awake, out of his trance.

He succeeded only just in time; a moment longer and Cush Gemal would have penetrated the veil and found him out. And leaping from his seat and away from the shew-stone, he only just managed to avoid a severe singeing as the surface of that sphere sent gobbets of green fire racing round the room of the astrologarium like tiny comets.

In that same instant, too, it had dawned on Teh Atht just who he was dealing with here. Cush Gemal? Ah, so he termed himself; but in fact this could only be one man. Little wonder he shared the same star as Black Yoppaloth; indeed, he *was* Black Yoppaloth! And Klühn's master mage shuddered as he realized how close he'd come to revealing himself to that immortal monster . . .

TARRA SAT IN morbid mood on the scaly flank of his dead honker and watched the work in progress. As the magickal storm had blown itself out, so the other four ships had returned and two of them had disgorged their slaves, who now worked to free Cush Gemal's stranded vessel from the quaggy grip of the sandbar. Labouring in six inches to a foot of choppy water, they dug away at the sand under the boat's flat bottom and slowly inched the craft off the bar into shallow water. Since the sandbar was not a true reef, the harbour it formed was not completely enclosed; open-ended, a ship might easily sail away from the rocky islet—that is if it could sail at all.

Amazingly, apart from the damage to the prow's rail and upper strakes where Old Scaly had crashed through them, Gemal's ship had suffered no real wreckage. Some of the starboard strakes were sprung, but the ship was so constructed that these could be tightened back into position by using a tourniquet system of knotted ropes. The flat bottom, of ironwood, was cracked in places but not split open, and already a lone frizzy was on board, caulking the cracks with a raw jungle resin which hardened to glass on contact with water.

The vessel would soon be seaworthy again, and apart from the loss of a couple of crewmen (whose bodies, mercifully, had not been washed up) little real harm had been done. Tarra's part in freeing the slaves had apparently gone unobserved, or those who'd observed it (said disappeared crewmen) were no longer around to make accusations. The only real loss by Hrossak's lights was that of his lizard. Tarra's honker had collapsed on lumbering ashore, and in a little while died, probably from an overdose of stress. Their great hearts could stand any amount of work, but they weren't much for suffering sudden or successive shocks. Or there again, perhaps something had got broken inside when the massive beast crashed through the boat's prow.

As for Cush Gemal: for a little while his life had been in real jeopardy—from the slaves if not from anything else. On this ocean-girt rock they far outnumbered their former masters, and none of them with an ounce of feeling (other than hatred) for the man who'd taken them into captivity. As the wind had abated more yet and it dawned on the young slaves that however cold and wet, at least they were alive and unfettered, so they'd begun to mutter darkly about Cush Gemal and his few remaining retainers. With only a handful of frizzies left to guard this lot, things might have got ugly right there and then—but that was when Tarra had spotted the four unscathed ships tacking with the wind as they returned to the isle of the wreck. Aye, and he'd spotted more than just that.

Across and above the island's central ridge of rock, whereto when last seen Gemal's limp form was being carried by a pair of his numbers-depleted blacks, now the sky was dark with a wheel of revolving spray and boiling cloud; and down from this aerial cauldron dangled the narrowing funnel of a twister, whose whorl held corkscrew streamers of green fire that gave the jutting ridge of rocks a weird coruscation and forbade intrusion.

"It's my guess," Tarra had told the gawping slaves and the small knot of shivering girls, "that when next you see Cush Gemal he'll no longer be vulnerable. And see those ships there? If you did somehow manage to kill him, what then? His lads would come ashore and slaughter you, violate the girls, finally sail off home to Shad no worse for wear. Or . . . they'd simply leave us marooned here, to die in our own good time. Wherefore I say: leave well enough alone. For now, anyway." And that had been that.

And sure enough, the swaying, nodding but apparently *tethered* tornado of green fire eventually collapsed in upon itself; and as the boats landed on the shore some little time later, so Gemal came striding like a spider across the ridge and commenced shouting orders in his accustomed fashion. But no sign of the pair of frizzies who'd crossed that ridge with him. At which Tarra Khash had narrowed his eyes and nodded, and said to himself: *Well, Cush Gemal, and now I believe I know you for sure.* For the Hrossak was no more a fool than was a certain white wizard of Klühn.

And anyone standing close to the steppeman might have seen him nod again, or even heard him mutter: "Oh, indeed I do! As I believe I've known you, in my way, right from the start . . ."

IX

Powers of Light, Powers of Darkness!

INIQUISS AND HISSILISS, most senior members of the lamia Council of Five, had returned at long last to the Sisterhood's inner sanctum. There upon her lava island crouched the lamia Orbiquita, impatiently awaiting her release from all vows, when finally she might go forth into the world as a woman. Born half-lamia, half-girl child, her form had been human; a foundling, she'd been adopted by wandering nomads, following which the monster in her had rapidly taken ascendency; until, expelled by her foster-parents, the Sisterhood had taken her in. This was usually the way of it. But the human woman in her had never been totally eradicated, so that she'd always felt herself waiting like some dull star for a glorious nova to release her long-suppressed beauty. Tarra Khash had been the catalyst, and soon the transformation would be complete.

Of the fact that she *was* beautiful in her female form, Orbiquita had little doubt; she'd often enough reverted to that delicious shape in the past, using it to seduce the foolish men (of course) who formed the Sisterhood's principle source of food. Oh, they could eat other meat readily enough, but the flesh of men had a strength and a flavour to it away and beyond that of simple beasts; a taste which from now on she'd necessarily relinquish—as must she relinquish all thoughts such as these! But old habits die hard, and Orbiquita could not help but feel a little afraid of her new and incredibly fragile life in the harsh dawn world which awaited her. Not that she intended that her lamia sisters should see that fear; be sure that she did not.

"The hour of reckoning, Orbiquita," said Iniquiss, folding back her wings to seat herself in a lava niche in the great cavern's splash-stone wall.

"When we must make it plain," Hissiliss added, finding herself a comfortable scab of tephrite lying sullen in the molten reek, "just what your renounciation means to you, delineate your many losses as set against no gains whatever!"

"No gains?" Orbiquita repeated her. "Except I'll be a woman. Gains enough there—so get on with it."

"Defiant to the bitter end," Iniquiss gloomed. "So be it." And in another moment, reading from a bone-leaved runebook: "Insomuch as you have renounced the Sisterhood, word of which we have rightfully relayed to all loyal sisters, these things which I shall now read are reckoned to be your lot. Now hear me:

"You, Orbiquita, who have known unbridled power, henceforth shall suffer total loss of strength."

"Not so," Orbiquita shook her head, "for I'll have a woman's strength, and they're not such weaklings as you'd make out. Strong men fall down before them, anyway."

"Loss of *lamia* strength, she meant," Hissiliss hissed. "Soft hands and feet, you'll have, with human fingers and toes. Not the great scythes you wear now, against which no creature in all the Primal Land may stand unscathed."

"Soft fingers, soft toes?" said Orbiquita. "Soft breasts, too, soft belly and thighs. Not your loathsome limbs and warty paps! Oh, I'll manage. Your sort of magick's not the only sort, snakeface."

"You shall have neither your own former strength," Iniquiss continued, while Hissiliss fumed and smouldered, "nor that of the Sisterhood and its individual members. You will be on your own, Orbiquita, for all future time—or for all the time the future allows you."

Again Orbiquita disagreed. "Three calls for aid I'm allowed!" she cried. "Don't rob me of my rights, Iniquiss. I've read the rules, too, you know. Three times I may call on the Sisterhood for its aid, or individual members thereof, and then no more. So it's written."

"She talks of her rights!" Hissiliss jumped up and set her cake of lava tilting. "Rights? When you've renounced the Sisterhood?"

Iniquiss merely shrugged. "It *is* her right, and so it *is* written—but it's also written that her sisters have the right to refuse such calls, if they see fit. You've not made many friends in the Sisterhood, Orbiquita."

"Name me one dear sister who has!" Their subject was unrepentant.

"Just so long as we understand one another," Iniquiss told her, turning a bone page. And finding her place:

"Your lamia powers—of metamorphosis, into dragon, lizard, harpy, bat, clinging gas and seeping moisture—are all foresaken, yours no longer. In the one shape you have chosen, that of a human female, you'll remain. Aye, and you'll live out only that number of years appropriate. The thousands you might have known are already flown forever!"

"I'll know the days of a woman," answered Orbiquita, but with something less of defiance, "and her nights." But then, brightening: "And in the arms of my chosen man, they'll be long nights and sweet. Not the noisome nights of the Sisterhood."

"Your 'chosen' man?" Hissiliss' sibilant whisper was amplified by cavern acoustics. "Have you paused to consider, he may not want you?"

In her vast armoured body, Orbiquita's heart quaked. Indeed she had considered it, and she knew that certain men were fickle. But if love is blind, hers for Tarra Khash was also deaf. Not dumb, however. "Snakeface," she said, "this I vow: that when I die they'll write on my stone, 'Here lies a woman who loved and was loved.' But what will they write on your monstrous menhir? I'll tell you:

'Here lies a beast with gorgon's crown—
This stone was raised to keep her down!'

"*HISSILISS!*" INIQUISS' CUTTING voice terminated her sister's shriek of impotent rage. "You're no match for this one where sarcasm's concerned. Can you not console yourself that you'll soon be rid of her?"

"We'll *all* be rid of her!" Hissiliss cried.

"For myself, I think it a shame," said Iniquiss, which was as much of emotion as she cared to show. And to Orbiquita:

"You know of course that you must give up, along with all the powers and years you might have known, all personal possessions?"

"All save one," Orbiquita nodded. "I may keep one small thing, according to lamia law."

"Possessions!" Hissiliss seemed hardly surprised. "She has possessions, does she? Another human attribute, this garnering of goods. Obviously she was never a true lamia! What possessions does she have?"

"Several," Orbiquita answered for herself. "My castle in the Desert of Sheb, I leave to the winds and sands of times I'll not know. My Roc's eye shewstone, to whosoever finds it there. Then there's my runebook, which I bequeath to you, Iniquiss; perhaps there's that in it which might increase your knowledge, or at least amuse you. But the one thing which I shall keep is a ring, too small for lamia digits but perfect for the finger of a woman. It is of jade and gold and bears the skull and serpent crest of my ancestor Mylakhrion. This I shall keep, for it's all I have of family, of noble ancestry."

"Noble! Noble!" Hissiliss snorted.

" 'Ware, sister!" Orbiquita warned, dangerously low-voiced. "I'm still lamia for the moment, and you still have eyes!"

"Now hear this, my final statement and decree," Iniquiss' voice of authority got between them. "Orbiquita, you have renounced the Sisterhood. So be it. There is no turning back. Here you stay for however long the final metamorphosis requires. At the end, the cavern imps shall warn of your imminent death, for a merely human female could never survive in this lava heat and reek and sulphurous cavern atmosphere. At that time you'll be borne to the surface, naked and shorn of all lamia trappings and skills. Do you understand?"

"I do," said Orbiquita.

"Your lamia memories will fade, though they may briefly recur from time to time. Likewise, it is possible that on occasion, in desperate times, the lamia which must now lie forever locked within you may briefly surface. This at your own peril, for humankind abhors us and they would rid themselves of us if they could. Is this clear?"

"It is clear."

"The Primal Land is harsh," Iniquiss continued. "What merely irritated you as a lamia may easily destroy you as a girl. Snake's bite and scorpion's sting will be fatal; knives, arrows, axes and swords likewise. And in lonesome places, men may molest you. Do you recognize these hazards all?"

"I recognize these hazards," Orbiquita repeated. "But I also know that I might bask in sunlight unharmed and unafraid, and walk with a lover under the full moon and never fear Gleeth's rays."

"Then it is done," said Iniquiss. "Orbiquita, you are—or very soon will be—lamia no more!"

She closed with finality her book of bone leaves, whose sound was that of some great sepulchral door slamming, or perhaps a gong heralding a new dawn . . .

BLIND OLD GLEETH the moon-god (though why "blind" is hard to explain, for indeed when he wished to he could "see," or at least know intuitively, almost all the many, mazy doings of men) looked down blearily on the Primal Land and frowned; or perhaps it was just a cloud passing over his crescent face. Waxing steadily, his silver horns were filling out and his reflective plains and dry ocean beds were dazzling. A fairly "young" moon in that ancient time, his face was far less cratered than it would be in, say, another two hundred million years.

As for his frown: it might be caused by something he saw through sleepfilmed eyes, which displeased him; or it could be that he "heard" something drifting up to him from the surface of his parent planet, which made him irritable. Something, perhaps, like the distant, tinkling prayers of a silver-skinned priestling. What? Suhm-yi prayers? But how could that be, since the Suhm-yi were no more? Then Gleeth remembered that the Crater Sea's secret race was not extinct, not entirely, and he grudgingly roused himself up from rarely disturbed slumbers.

His crater-walled eyes sought out the Inner Isles where once the Suhm-yi dwelled, especially that rock called Na-dom, beloved of the gods. For indeed Na-dom was Holy of Holies, whose aspect alone would turn back the merely curious. No jewel isle this but a gaunt and solitary crag rearing like some sea-beast's talon from the Crater Sea, which beckoned not but merely forbade intrusion. Black as night, that needle rock, and standing well apart from more mundane islets, for which reason the gods were sometimes wont to visit there. Or at least give ear to the priests who hailed them therefrom. Even as Gleeth now gave ear. And in a little while, drifting up to him from Na-dom, this is what he heard:

"Gleeth! Old Gleeth!" cried Amyr Arn, who knew almost nothing of the priestly preparations and ceremonies requisite to reaching out and speaking to the gods. "Old god of the moon, hear me now, as once before you heard me."

And this will be Amyr Arn, said Gleeth, but to himself, so that Amyr did not hear him. *It can only be him, for he is the last. What can he want of me now?*

"Look down on me," Amyr cried, as if in answer, "and take pity."

Pity? Pity? Why should I pity you? You're alive, young, strong. Pity? Or should I pity you because you are alone, last of the Suhm-yi? Is that your meaning? Very well, then I pity you. Now go away and leave me alone. And still Gleeth spoke only to himself, so that Amyr heard nothing.

"I ask this boon of you not for myself but for a man, whom once before you helped, in time of need."

A man? Gleeth wondered what was all of this. *An unbeliever? Suhm-yi prayers for help were one thing, but a man . . . ?*

"This man *believes!*" cried Amyr Arn, for all the world as if he had heard, although he had not. "His name is Tarra Khash, who knows you for a kind, benevolent god. Gleeth, listen to me: I know you are old, and that they say you're deaf and blind, but I believe you see and hear well enow. You heard me before, when last I dared to call your name, and now I call it again."

Tarra Khash? Faint memories stir! But I'm tired and can do without all this. Weary of questions, of the very effort of thought itself, the old god of the moon began to drift back into sleep.

"I'll not give in, old moon-god," Amyr shouted his frustration from the roof of Na-dom. "I'll call upon you night after night, forever, if need be, until you answer me one way or the other."

Do you threaten, Amyr Arn? The moon sailed all serene and silent on high. *Tarra Khash? I know him, aye. A Hrossak. He sails in a boat en route for Shad. What of it?*

"Gleeth! Old Gleeth!" Amyr despaired.

Aye, you're right, Amyr Arn. Old and tired . . . A Hrossak . . . ? He sails in a boat for Shad . . . Now go away, last son of all the Suhm-yi . . . Your people worshipped me once, but they are no more . . . So leave me in peace . . . A god's no good without his worshippers . . . Old and tired . . . Tarra Khash? I know him, aye . . .

And so the old god of the moon went back to his timeless dreaming, and in a little while Amyr Arn climbed wearily down from Na-dom and paddled his canoe back across the Crater Sea to his Ulli on the island they'd now make their home. But be sure he wasn't finished yet. No, for there'd be another night tomorrow, and when the moon rose into the sky again, Amyr would be back.

AND SO GLEETH slept, and the light of his silver crescent swept down and pointed a path right across the Primal Land. Five ships of Shad sailed that silvery swath on the Eastern Ocean, where now they crossed into the Straits of Yhem; and in the stern of the fifth, keeping the tiller, there sat Tarra Khash alone with his thoughts.

Drowsy in the night, where warm winds blew now from jungled Shadarabar, Tarra's thoughts weren't much to speak of: fleeting memories of his travels and travails, his adventures and near-disasters. He saw again a woman, or rather a girl, as he'd seen her once in the badlands under Lohmi. She never had told him her name, though he'd found it out soon enough, and then almost wished he hadn't. But she'd balmed his back where ambusher's arrow had nailed him, and her soft breasts had cradled him where he rested against her. Then—she'd kissed his neck with a kiss of fire!

She'd taken his blood while he slept—a little, a splash—and unbeknown even to herself had put something back in its place, like the fever-fly who sips and imparts poisons. Hers had not been poisons of the flesh but of the spirit, reacting only with blood which was ready for them. Nor were they true poisons, but rather passions. Tarra had known women, females, before. But none like this. And since that time—that kiss, which raised twin craters on his neck, small pinches that ached a little even now—he'd had no time for other loves. Or perhaps more important, no inclination.

Love? Was that it? He snorted in the night under the blind old moon and straightened the bar of his tiller. Then

never a love more hopeless in all of time, in all the Primal
Land. For later he had seen that female who kissed him,
seen her in her true form, which was a shape out of nightmares and madness!

Some small irritation, on his leg where his pants were
torn, distracted him. Something moved there. He went to
swat, but paused when he saw what perched upon his knee.
A small scorpion, greeny-grey: the sort which lives on the
weeds and under the stones of certain tropical islands,
whose venom is invariably fatal—or very nearly so. But
Tarra Khash was immune, who'd been stung so often as a
youth that the poisons no longer worked. Indeed, as a lad
he'd been a legend on the steppes, renowned for the number of stings he'd taken, which should have killed but
merely sickened and in the end had no effect at all.

Now, in the star- and moon-cast shadow of the sail, he
peered at his small passenger and it peered back, with tiny
faceted eyes yellow as flames. Doubtless he'd picked the
creature up on the isle of the almost-shipwreck. Well, and
he had nothing against scorpions, of whatever sort. He took
it up between thumb and finger, stared at it where it made
no effort to sting him, said: "Best go where you're safe,
small friend. Find a niche for yourself between the strakes,
where it's nice and damp." And so saying he put the scorpion down behind the box of the tiller. It quickly scuttled
out of sight.

"*Hah!*" said a now familiar voice close by. "Is there nothing you're afraid of, Hrossak?" Cush Gemal (for the moment
Tarra continued to think of him under that name) stood
watching, though how he'd drawn so close, so quietly, were
a mystery.

"I'm afraid of some things," Tarra answered. "Sorcery,

maybe—and maybe people who appear in the night out of nowhere, all sudden-like and unannounced."

They stared at each other for long moments, until Gemal sensed the Hrossak's new awareness and noticed a certain light in his eyes—the light of knowledge. He nodded then, and very quietly said: "I can see that you've learned something of the truth . . ." And then, after a moment's consideration: "Very well, you shall know all of it. Accompany me." He snapped skeletally thin fingers and one of his Yhemnis came running, took the tiller and left Tarra free to follow Gemal as he made off down the ship's wide central space, between the sleeping girls where they lay chained together under their blankets, toward his repaired tent standing as before in the prow . . .

AS THEY WENT, the small greeny-grey scorpion came out from behind the tiller frame, stared silently after them with tiny flame eyes from between the steersman's spread legs. And all it had seen with those faceted eyes, and all it had heard in its scorpion fashion, were seen and heard and known in certain other places: in the deep, all but forgotten fane of the Scarlet Scorpion himself, Ahorra Izz, and also in Shad, in a certain arena of death, where stood a likeness of that same arachnid deity.

Both facets in their separate places had received the self-same message, which was this: that Tarra Khash was on his way to Shad. And from deep below the creeper-entwined crypt which was his fane, the true god Ahorra Izz now spoke across all the leagues between to lesser idol, who however awe-inspiring in his way, was nevertheless only a simulacrum of himself:

"Have ye seen?" he clacked his mentalist message. *"Tarra Khash, a Hrossak, is coming to Shad. Ye may come across him, or perhaps he shall stumble across ye. Now hear ye: this man may not be harmed by any scorpion, neither creature, graven image, nor even myself. I forbid it, for we stand in his debt."*

"Here in the arena of death," came back the answer on the winds of night, *"I hold small sway. There are many gods here, Ahorra Izz, where I am but a one. And I am but an image, with nothing of magick in me. Hewn in stone out of your likeness, I stand and stare with crystal eyes, impotent of all save the seeing of sights and the hearing of sounds."*

"And yet I say to ye," Ahorra Izz insisted, *"that if ye hear him cry out for aid, or see him in dire peril, then shall ye give assist."* And he explained his meaning.

And deep down beneath Black Yoppaloth's ziggurat palace in Shad, around the rim of the subterranean arena of death, standing in a circle formed of other earth gods and many far more blasphemous effigies, a huge scorpion carved of chalcedony heard the words of its parent god and grimly acknowledged them . . .

WAY ACROSS THE Straits of Yhem low in the sky over Theem'hdra's farthest horizon, Gleeth the moon-god rode silent and serene, but not entirely deaf or blind. He had "seen" and "heard" many things this night, and not alone the pleading of Amyr Arn of the Suhm-yi. Of the latter: even now Amyr paddled a canoe across the deathly calm waters of the Crater Sea, and beached it on that tiny island where Ulli waited on the shore to melt into his arms. And this, too, was witnessed by old Gleeth, not yet quite asleep.

Not the last? the moon-god sighed his sleepy amaze, but

kept it to himself. *What? And shall there be more Suhm-yi to worship me after all? They were ever my favourites among the world's races; but I had thought they were no more, and a god needs his subjects.*

His silver rays cut a swath across all the Primal Land—and across the Straits of Yhem, where five boats forged for Shad—even reaching Shadarabar itself. And now the old moon-god started more fully awake, for in Shad he spied that which caused him more than a little of alarm.

It was in the sky, which was his domain of immemorial right, and it was this:

A great black cloud which boiled where no cloud should be, not born of currents of upper air but rising like some diseased puffball of smoke from below, and forming a ring that spun and sucked up the mists of the jungle swamps into the night sky, compressing them there, swirling them as if spun from within, like some dark and evil whirlpool of the skies. Except it was nothing out of the heavens but some subterraneous hell. And even as Gleeth watched, so the flat plateau of the twister grew darker yet—black as the Stygian bowels at planet's core—and its rim began to glow with the green and writhing phosphorescence of things long rotted. It whirled its weird funnel over all the fabulous city of Shad, but its stalk remained constant, seeming rooted in a ziggurat palace at the wild jungle's fringe.

Then . . . out of the whirling mass were shot like stones from a giant's sling several smaller, even stranger masses, which hurtled meteoric across the skies and out over the Straits of Yhem—and there paused. And now these eerie imps of the underworld curved down and around, fashioning themselves into green-glowing winds which blew on the ships of Yoppaloth and hastened them home.

All of which the moon-god found exceedingly interesting. And he remembered Amyr Arn's pleading, and he wondered about the fate of a certain Hrossak. But . . . dawn would soon be here and the sun risen to outshine him, and there was always tomorrow night to consider these strange events and their stranger connections. Tomorrow night, aye, when he'd waxed a little more and grown stronger. It could all wait until then, he was sure . . .

DAWN.

Yes, it would soon be dawn, and still Teh Atht fretted as he paced to and fro and hither and thither through the halls and corridors of his manse in Klühn.

"How long, 'til dawn?" he asked himself for the tenth time. And answered: "An hour at least . . ." A whole hour, before he'd dare return to the room of the astrologarium, where he'd left his shewstone. Eleven hours sped by since his magick had gone so disastrously wrong and almost revealed him to Cush Gemal—or rather, to Black Yoppaloth. And in all that time no wink of sleep taken, no morsel of food passed his lips, but only this fretting and gnashing of teeth to occupy him, as he'd paced and prowled and considered his position—which was not an envious one.

Fantastic events were in the offing, and Teh Atht knew it. More, he could feel himself at the centre of whatever was coming, without yet knowing what it would be. The answer, if it could be fathomed, lay in the room of the astrologarium, in the rush and reel of all Man's astrological moons and planets and stars, but for now Teh Atht dare not return there. Worse, his shewstone remained in that same room, without which even the smallest scrying were out of the question.

But go back into that room? No, not possible, not until he could be sure that Black Yoppaloth had quit searching for him. For all he knew the shewstone remained lethally inverse, only waiting to be activated and thus reveal him to the enemy—who'd sworn to have him! Perhaps that most powerful necromancer waited even now for him, just beyond the crystal ball's opaque curtains—which he daren't under any circumstances throw open. And this was Teh Atht's predicament.

Hopper and flitter, sensing their master's distress, had spent the long, weary hours with him—the one invariably underfoot and the other always just overhead—but Teh Atht scarcely noticed them as he wandered his mazy manse, wringing his tapering hands and vainly seeking a solution to the problem. He had considered calling his third familiar, that entirely liquid one, out of the astrologarium; but what if something *else* was there in that magickally sealed room even now—something perhaps of Yoppaloth's sending—and what if that something should come out *with* the liquid one?

"Coward!" Teh Atht cried, causing hopper and flitter to start with his outburst. He threw wide his bell-cuffed arms in the corridor where he stalked, shook his fists at the stone walls. "Oh, *coward*, Teh Atht! What? And are you not a great wizard in your own right?"

Aye, but white! some inner voice whispered back. *My magicks are white, and his are black. I have scruples—some—and he has none. I tried to kill him, and if he discovers me, which he'll surely try to do, he* can *and* will *kill me!*

"Then act now!" he cried. Following which his voice at once fell to a whisper: "While yet there's time . . ."

But at night? When baneful spells were that much more likely to succeed?

Teh Atht rushed to a window facing east across the sea, gazed out. On the horizon, the first blush of dawn, or perhaps a false dawn. Day was coming, and the darkness soon to be banished. And he knew in his bones that time was narrowing down. Soon Black Yoppaloth's renewal would be at hand; soon Tarra Khash would be at greatest peril; and all *too* soon the lamia Orbiquita would require an explanation. The more he considered the intricacies, the more intricate they became.

"Hopper, flitter, to me!" he cried, turning from the window. "Enough is enough! I now return to the room of the astrologarium—and you go with me. Three brave hearts together!" Alarmed, they drew back at once, but he reached out with a simple bind-you-to-me and they were drawn close, flitter obliged to fasten to his high collar while hopper clung to his rune-inscribed robe. And so they proceeded to the room of the astrologarium.

Here it was that the white wizard had brought about the wrecking of Black Yoppaloth's boat, and his blindness; and here, too, while the astonished necromancer had been hurled into the sea, he'd cursed him with Curious Concretion to make sure he'd sink. Alas, by virtue of the fact that the last was a sending of some distance, and diluted through the medium of the shewstone, it had been weakened: instead of granite, Yoppaloth had become pumice, a softer stone by far. What's more, a man or creature fixed in a state of Curious Concretion does not breathe or even need to, and so Yoppaloth had not drowned. In a deeper ocean, as marble, say, he'd have gone to the bottom at once; and when the spell was broken, then he'd be flattened by pressure or drowned on the way back up. But that had not been the case.

The spell *had* been broken, when by chance Teh Atht had been distracted by the blazing kerchief, which same mishap had simultaneously returned Yoppaloth's sight. The attempt on the necromancer's life had not been blundered, not by any means, but was simply ill-starred. Perhaps Teh Atht should have used his astrologarium to choose a more opportune moment.

The entire episode must therefore be counted as a failed experiment, which in its failing had produced no small hazard of its own. This had been when Yoppaloth attempted to strike back, as Teh Atht had struck, through the very shewstone itself; and only the speed of the latter's retreat therefrom had saved him from a painful blistering, and probably from much worse than that.

After that, praying that in the moment of inversion the crystal ball had deactivated, Klühn's mage had quickly left the room of the astrologarium, locked and spelled shut the door; and now, nearly twelve hours later, he stood once more outside that room, key in hand and chewing his lip. On his way here he'd reinforced by will and rune a handful of personal protections to ward off what might possibly lie in wait for him within; and finally, voice trembling just a little as he unspelled the door, he inserted his key in the lock and turned it, then pushed that portal open.

Inside . . . nothing was changed that he could see at a glance; driving hopper and flitter before him, he crossed the threshold; no dire apparition sprang out upon him. Teh Atht drew a deep breath, retracted his wand, shot further quick, cursory glances all about. Then he crossed the room and approached the shewstone—but cautiously, ever ready to jump back at first sight or intimation of unusual activity. Nothing . . .

He activated the crystal, which at once spat out several bright green sparks—residuum of that earlier, more deadly display—and fell quiescent. Startled by the sudden sputtering, hopper and flitter had taken their departure, but came creeping and winging back as Teh Atht lowered his shielding hands from before his eyes. And there the shewstone reposed as before, milky-deep and vaguely aswirl, and nothing noticeably amiss. That is, nothing amiss with the crystal sphere.

But—

The astrologarium itself was far from right! The infinitely accurate soar and swing of its multi-hued nebulae and simulated stars seemed strangely out of kilter.

Teh Atht remembered the green meteorites which, hurled at him by black Yoppaloth, had erupted from the shewstone to bound and rebound all about the room, and wondered if they could have affected the balance of this miniature, man-made universe. The astrologarium had used up years without number and magicks likewise innumerable in its construction and was his pride and joy. Half dreading to discover damage, he slitted his eyes to peer deep into its lucid plasma infinities.

And as he peered, so his third and uniquely liquid familiar came flowing from the spaces between pigmy planets, expanding from mere amoeba to blob of resin, finally into half a gallon of clear, glutinous jelly as "he" or it approached the rim. Teh Atht extended a hand, upon which with a *plop* the astrologarium ejected the weird, wobbling intelligence into his palm. There that freakish familiar quickly elongated himself slugwise along the wizard's arm, clinging there like a sheath of sentient slime.

Employed mainly in the maintenance and lubrication of the astrologarium, the liquid one felt and was disturbed by any serious fluctuations therein; and quite obviously (or obvious, at least, to Teh Atht's practiced eyes) the creature *was* agitated. Concerned, he comforted his familiar creature, let him seep into a voluminous pocket of his robe, then commenced to search the finite infinity of small worlds for the cause of such perturbation. And now indeed he saw the imbalance, portent of changes *vast* in the mundane world of men!

Strange dark stars stood in alien alignment; moons and planets were shadowed in eerie eclipses; the astrologarium itself seemed to hold its breath. "The stars are . . . wrong!" the wizard gasped aloud—and at once, with his own words still ringing in his ears, staggered back from the cosmic display. Staggered, aye; for depending on one's point of view, the stars weren't wrong at all; indeed, it could be said that they were very nearly *right!*

But for whom?

X

Cush Gemal's Story

BETWEEN TIMES . . . TARRA Khash had proceeded with Cush Gemal to his black tent in the prow of a roughly repaired boat forging for Shad.

There he accepted a seat on cushions only just dry from their salt water dousing, gazed at his weird host by the light of a small green lantern.

And finally he ventured: "Perhaps I'm unwise to accept your hospitality like this. Some come in here who don't come out again. And others make small splashes in the night, when they go overboard . . ."

Cush Gemal smiled a strange sad smile, more properly a twisting of his bony features. "Would that it could be otherwise," he said. "But it cannot. I do what I must for survival. I am what I am."

"A sorcerer," said Tarra evenly, with a slow nod. "A necromancer. Indeed, Black Yoppaloth himself! You said you'd tell me all. Well, here I am, and all ears."

Black Yoppaloth nodded, drew himself up a little straighter where he sat. Then he reached across suddenly to touch Tarra's shoulder. The Hrossak felt the iciness of that touch, drew back. He shivered and said: "Cold as a fjord!"

"Colder than that," the other corrected him. "And growing colder all the time! My time approaches, do you see? You don't see? Then I'll explain. Except I would ask you, don't interrupt. Let me tell it all, and then you might understand. Agreed?"

"Some things I already understand," said Tarra. "Like how mistaken I've been to save your life: once when you lay on the bottom of the sea, where I should have left you, and once when the slaves might have killed you if I hadn't persuaded them otherwise. What I don't understand is why I did these things."

"Then hear me out and maybe you will," said the other. And this is the story he told:

"First let me tell you, I am not the original Black Yoppaloth. I am the second. Oh, I know there are certain legends which have it that there have been nine Yoppaloths, but that's a mere myth put about by Theem'hdra's lesser mages. Most of them desire to keep secret the fact of my immortality; a jealous lot, they prefer not to believe in a superior sorcerer. Rather, they do not wish to lessen their own estates in the eyes of ordinary men. But in their hearts they fear me as a mage without peer. Ah, if only they knew!

"But in fact there have been only two Yoppaloths: the first—who grew mighty toward the end of Mylakhrion's time, more than eleven hundred years ago—and the second, myself, lord and master of kingless Shadarabar for the past millennium.

"But how can this be? I am a man like other men, as you have seen. I have man's moods and passions, man's lusts—though burning less fiercely now—and all his normal appetites. In aspect I might appear less like a true wizard than even the lowliest rune-caster! Indeed, only my physical appearance—which sets me aside somewhat, but not I think too far—belies the fact that I am *entirely* ordinary. Where are my familiars, my cloak of sigils, wand of power and rune-books? What? A wizard? How so? Well, let me tell you that I am *not* a wizard—not in the common meaning of the word! And yet I am extraordinary. Would you believe it if I told you that I have been what I have been, that I am what I am, because there is no alternative?

"More than a thousand years ago, I was a blond-haired, green-eyed lad living in a village south of the Lohr River where it meets the Eastern Ocean. Ah? Astonishment in your face, Tarra Khash? Say nothing, hear me out. A lad, aye, white-skinned—far paler than your bronze hide—and green-eyed, whose mother tended a vegetable patch while her husband fished. That was my family, and twenty more like it in that little village by the sea, at the mouth of the Lohr. But all of this a thousand years ago, Tarra Khash, and Klühn itself no bigger than a small town in those days.

"I was thirteen when Yoppaloth came up from Shadarabar along the coast with his ships out of Shad. All along the way he'd butchered and raped, looted, burned and taken slaves. His ships were crammed with slaves, and *his* ship carried a handful of virgins, which he guarded most jealously."

"I've heard this tale before." Tarra could not help but interrupt.

"Then hear it again!" cried the other. "Yoppaloth came to my village in the night from where he'd anchored his ships down the coast. My mother died that night, horribly! And my father—a bull of a man, for all that he was a fisherman—roared and raved and slew like a berserker, but in the end was taken. And Yoppaloth well-satisfied to have found a fighter like him for his arena of death. I was taken, too, for I was young, and blond and green-eyed; indeed I was a handsome lad . . . and Yoppaloth was a pederast!

"And so we were shipped to Shad. On the voyage Yoppaloth took me for himself, and because life was dear I made no real protest. While I pretended to love him, I loathed him. But I learned how to control myself and how not to cry out, how to show no fear and even how to feign enjoyment of his enormities; but inside I had set myself a goal, which was this: one day, by fair means or foul, I'd kill him!

"The ships arrived in Shad; slaves were put ashore, along with twelve wondrous virgins; all were herded through the gorgeous, sweltering city into Yoppaloth's palace at the edge of a mighty jungle. In a very little while the necromancer came to trust me. I was given free run of the palace; I could do whatever I wished, go where I pleased—except the slave-quarters, which were forbidden. And that was where I most wanted to go, for my father was there.

"Out of frustration, I wandered the length and breadth of that great palace: to the topmost roof of its five ziggurat tiers towering above the jungle, and down into the many mazy levels below. And I discovered great wonders and greater horrors! I found Yoppaloth's sunken arena, guarded by giant statues of all the dark gods and beings of an hundred alien pantheons, and I saw the work in progress there. The floor of that place was of sand turned red with the powdered blood of men; ah!—but now that floor was being freshened, replaced, made clean for—

"For what? I was soon to find out!

"Yoppaloth, that great black-skinned, black-hearted beast of a sorcerer, had made a pact with the dark god Yibb-Tstll. The pact was this: that Yoppaloth would worship Yibb and make sacrifice unto him all his days, for which the payment would be immortality! Well, and he *had* worshipped him, and payment was due now. And so that hell-god had instructed Yoppaloth in his dreams what he must do, and the preparations were these: that he must bring back an hundred slaves to Shad, and a dozen young virgins, all to be used up in the arena of death.

"Now, I will not describe the ceremonies attendant unto Yoppaloth's initiation, or the orgy of blood which preceded the hour of that vile rite, but I will say this: that Yibb-Tstll was to be paid *well* for Yoppaloth's eternal life, paid in the coin of life itself, and that Yibb-Tstll is an eater of souls!

"For an hundred years the necromancer had fed that god of outer spheres on the souls of his people—usually miscreants sentenced in his courts, where there *was* only one sentence: the arena of death—but on this special occasion, the occasion of Black Yoppaloth's ascendance to immortality, the dark god's orgy would be that much more prodigious! The way of it was this:

"The slaves would be set to fight for their lives, but not against other slaves—not even against men. They were to fight monsters out of the jungles and swamps, and others out of necromantic nether-pits, against which only the strongest would survive intact of mind and limb. And to ensure they fought well, they'd be promised that in the event of ultimate victory, then that they'd have their freedom. Ah, but victory would be hard in the winning; and in any case the promise was a lie, as will be seen. Aye, for no man ever escaped with his life from Black Yoppaloth's arena of death.

"And as each brave (or not so brave) fighter died in his turn, so the monstrous god Yibb-Tstll would wake from the stone of his idol and flow forth, and take his soul. So that even in death there was no surcease of agony, no freedom from horror.

"I have said that I will not describe that—*tournament*—in its entirety; nor shall I. But I will say this: that my father was the bravest, strongest champion of all. I know for I was witness to it all. I saw him go up against beasts from the deepest jungles of Shadarabar, and monsters from Yoppaloth's necromantic nether-caves, and rise bloody but victorious over all—until the final bout. For that last grim battle was against Black Yoppaloth himself!

"Black Yoppaloth, aye! That vile creature who'd steeped himself in all the sin of this Primal Land, where sin is usually the way of it, and all the horror of his own necromantic existence, until nothing more than putrescence of mind and spirit were left in him; and at his command all the spells of dark dimensions, which at will he could call to his aid. Against evil and *power* such as that, how might a simple fisherman win, eh?

"At one end of the arena stood a dais of blood-veined onyx, above which a chimney went up through all the levels of the ziggurat above, to the orchid-scented air of Shad. Ah, that such vileness should be so perfumed! And before the dais a pit whose rim was of green and red glass, fused from the sand of the arena; aye, a pit going down as if toward hell itself, and very likely passing *into* that or those hells! Up from that pit at the appointed time, up from mazy and menacing bowels of earth undreamed, Yibb-Tstll would call the awesome energies of the Great Old Ones themselves to batten upon Black Yoppaloth and bequeath unto him the final boon—immortality. But only after he himself had dispatched the final champion of champions, and when Yibb-Tstll had taken his soul.

"And so atop that dais—that great black and red sacrificial slab—the two fought, my father and the cheating, lying monster Black Yoppaloth. Aye, and my father might have won; for he remembered his wife and how she had died, and his strength was that of ten men, even though much of his iron blood had now leaked out of him. But the foul, puffed Yoppaloth, seeing the berserker he stood against and feeling the weight of his blows, became afraid and would not fight a clean fight. He used his magick to forge chains about my father, and only when he'd bound him securely moved in for the kill. And seeing that it would soon be finished, Yibb-Tstll called forth his instrument of transfiguration, by which Yoppaloth would be made immortal.

"Up from the slippery throat of the glass pit to hell, and from what caverns of immemorial night below, swept a black, boiling cloud which had its own coherency, its own body and being. Alive with the warp and crackle of green and putrescent fires it was; and it whirled there like a small tornado, nodding over the dais where my father stood in chains of magick, clutching his bloodied, battered sword, likewise impotent, while Yoppaloth advanced upon him with a devastating weapon of his own. It was a pole like a pike, that weapon, but it was not a pike. Driven home in flesh and when its handle was twisted, then its slender head would put out razor grapples and knives *inside* the victim, making a pulp of all his organs. Twisted the other way, the scythes would retract and the head could be withdrawn, leaving a man mangled on the inside, while outside he might appear only slightly mutilated. It was Yoppaloth's favourite instrument of torture, which appealed to his perverted brain.

"Above the arena were many tiers of seats going up like

some mighty council chamber, in which were seated the puppet officials and 'important' persons of Shad, and many insignificant princelings and shamans of Shadarabar's jungle tribes. I was in the first tier, on a balcony looking down on the dais, and beside me stood a huge Yhemni guard with a long sword in his belt. As below Black Yoppaloth drove his awful pike into my father's body, so I knew I could restrain myself no longer.

"Not caring whether I lived or died, with my father's screams of torment in my ears, I drew the guard's sword and sprang up onto the balcony, and from there down upon the dais—upon the monster himself. But in the moment of time between my father's scream and the reaction it brought in me—things had happened.

"Yibb-Tstll's idol, stone no longer, had flowed forward to receive tribute of the toppling cadaver which had been my father; the swirling, whirlpool cloud of alien energies from the pit had spawned emerald lightnings which wove themselves into a mesh about the foul, fat form of Yoppaloth; the entire dais streamed with licking rivers of tomb-fire. You have seen such fires, Tarra Khash.

"But for all that had happened, that *was* happening, I knew only one thing: which was that Yoppaloth must die, here and now! What I could not know was this: that in his dying, *another* Yoppaloth would be born.

"In my wild plunge from the balcony, I had driven my sword before me; and in the last instant before I struck, then Yoppaloth sensed all was not well and looked up. He was a sorcerer, yes, but even magick takes a little time in the weaving; and dazed by the green lightnings and astonished by the intrusion, the necromancer was at my mercy. Into his gaping mouth I drove my blade, and down that throbbing gullet, until the sword jammed within him! Then my hurtling weight was on it, and the keen edge cut him open like a gutted fish! He was sheared through lip and wobbling black chins, through throat, breast and gut, and fell with me to the dais' cold stone. Aye, and that stone *was* cold, preternaturally so! I ignored the alien rime which dusted its surface, leaped up and split Yoppaloth's head through his skull, shattering his mad and corrupt brain.

"And lo, where the green fires from some subterranean hell had fastened on him, *now they enveloped me!*"

Black Yoppaloth II's voice had fallen to the merest murmur, the veriest shiver of sound. Tarra leaned forward, ears straining, to miss no single word that was spoken. And so fascinated the Hrossak, that he ignored utterly his own possible danger in that tattered black tent on a ship speeding for Shad. "The immortality of the Great Old Ones was conferred upon you instead of him!" he finally gasped.

Yoppaloth, staring at him with eyes of doom, eventually nodded. "Indeed, for after what I'd done to the necromancer no power in all Theem'hdra—neither magick nor medicine—could ever have returned him to life. But the weird green lightning webs of the pit had to expend themselves somewhere. And they did . . . in me!"

Black Yoppaloth's glittery eyes were deep and cold as the black borehole of which he'd spoken, of which he now once more spoke:

"The cold blackened me," he said. "That coldness of the pit, evil exhalation of alien gods. It blackened my skin and my eyes and my soul, which may never more be purified. I *am* immortal! Unless by some unknown means a man or wizard slay me, or some accident unforeseen, I *shall* live forever. But no disease may ravage me, be sure, and time alone shall not prevail.

"In my first hundred years I aged to a man, since when I've stayed as you see me now; except I've suffered . . . certain alterations. But while cities of stone have crumbled and been rebuilded, and mummies withered in their sarcophagi, and men have come and gone in their many thousands, I have lived on, *must* live on—if Yibb-Tstll is not to walk free forever in the world of men!

"Did I say that the necromancer I destroyed was a cheat and a liar? And if *he* was these things, how then the immemorially evil Old Ones? How then Yibb-Tstll?

"Do you know the legend of the Old Ones, Tarra Khash? I shall tell it:

"Even before this Primal Land was born of a vast volcano—that mighty cone which houses the Inner Isles—and before ever men came to the world, there were Others here seeped down from worlds of antique horror. They came with the Cthulhu spawn, which built their cities in steaming fens before ever the first lungfish crawled out from the sea upon the land. Yibb-Tstll was one of them, Tsathoggua the toad-thing another, Yogg-Sothoth of the shimmering globes a third, and Ithaqua the Wind-Walker, who is worshipped in Yaht-Haal to this very day, a fourth. And yet these are only a handful. They were legion, these beings, a veritable army, and they fastened on the inchoate worlds of our sun, and on the worlds of other stars farther afield.

"Authors of incredible sin, they had come here to escape the wrath of others mightier still, who followed them and bound them with awesome magicks, and prisoned them in places beyond Man's five senses to perceive. Indeed, Man was merely one of nature's lesser visions, a faint possibility, when all these things transpired. But while the aeons wore on and men came to be, still the prisoned Old Ones waited out their time in dark forgotten corners, sunken sepulchres and alien spheres. The Hounds of Tindalos were trapped in time itself, and the Thromb throbbed in cauldrons of gravity in the hearts of collapsed stars. But down all the ages the Old Ones had retained their dark instinct for evil and certain immundane skills. One such skill which was theirs was mentalism, which now they turned upon the untutored, innocent, sleeping minds of men.

"Thus have the cults of Cthulhu and his minion creatures risen, and thus are they kept alive by his unspeakable dreaming! And always the Old Ones, who are themselves immortal, strive to return; which one day, when the stars are right, be sure they will. Even now Ithaqua strides in partial freedom, mercifully confined to those frozen lands north of the Great Ice Barrier, where men may not live, and to the routes of the winds that blow between the worlds; and Cthulhu lies in his sunken house, which went down in the year of the red moon under the sea. Ghatanothoa is worshipped still in Eyphra, and men have made unto themselves idols in the hideous shapes of Tsathoggua and Yibb-Tstll, one of which glooms even now in my arena of death in Shad. Mine now, aye, as is this undying nightmare which fools crave and call 'immortality'!

"Now how may men, even sorcerers supreme, have dealings with beings such as these and go unscathed? The answer is simple: they may not! Mylakhrion, that mightiest of mages, sought Cthulhu's secrets and perished. A race of lizard-kings dwelled upon a time in the land of Lohmi; they, too, worshipped the Great Kraken, and where are they now?

Gone, extinct! And Yoppaloth? That first Yoppaloth, whom I slew, would he have fared any better? Could he have done any better than the second Yoppaloth, myself, in the thousand years gone by since that time I killed him? No, for he was a coward and mad, and I think he would have let the Old Ones in—while I have done all in my power to keep them out!

"Ah, I see in your eyes that I've lost you. What, and have I rambled so? But you are a man I can talk to, Tarra Khash; and talk I must, for these things have burdened my sorry soul long enough. Let me then say on:

"In the moment when I slew Yoppaloth—as the pit-spawned emerald fires withdrew from me and the cloud itself fled back down into the gibbering dark—then the dead sorcerer's people would have killed me. Oh, they were glad he was dead and no mistake, for now they saw that their own miserable existences were safe, as they'd never been when he lived; but now that he *was* dead it would be good to show how brave they were, grand sport to come down upon me in the arena and slay me. Indeed, they would have done it—if not for a weird intervention!

"The dark god Yibb-Tstll had spent an hundred years grooming Yoppaloth for the part he was to play in a great resurgence of Old Ones' power. Most of a millennium yet to go before the necromancer would be—or would have been—ready. And should the god admit defeat and return once more to stone, and begin his search for dark receptacle again? And what of the alien infusions I had received from unthinkable pits of Cthonian horror at Earth's core? Should they, too, be wasted? I had destroyed Yoppaloth utterly, but in so doing had shown that my own instinct for destruction—even as a boy—was as great, greater than his.

"Moreover, within the limits I have mentioned, I was now immortal; unless I, too, was somehow slain or fall victim to some shattering cataclysm, I might live forever—or until They were ready!

"Yibb-Tstll 'saved' me—as I reckoned it then. Have you ever seen a likeness of him, Tarra Khash? Even an idol made in his image? Better for you if you never know that dubious privilege. And certainly the *real thing* is far worse! But he saved me and let it be known in several ways that he approved of me. First, when they shook their spears and knives at me, he came to me; and he opened his billowing cloak to let out his gaunts of night, which he set about me as my guardians, to let the men of Shad see that I was their new mage and master, not to be harmed, indeed inviolate. Then, even before those watching thousands, he hunched over the riven carcass of the dead Yoppaloth and took his soul—took it in that singular way of his, with terrible 'hands' more loathsome than any weapon of Yoppaloth's devise—and having done so tossed it, aye, and the corpse of my poor father, too, into that pit itself. And finally Yibb opened his cloak again to embrace me as his newly chosen one, following which I fell upon the dais altar as one seared and dead. But I was not dead, merely depleted. And after that they could not kill me, for he had declared me their master. Master of Shad and Shadarabar, aye, but prisoner, too. For no way I could escape from that jungled isle, where now I had become Yibb's instrument in the world of men.

"In days I was well again, and days became weeks, weeks months; so time passed . . . I found myself heir to Yoppaloth's palace, his slaves; heir to his power, within limits; heir, too, to much more than these things. A man may not be touched by the aura of the inner immensities and remain unchanged. I had been changed. Where were my green eyes, blond hair and pale skin now? Gone! I was black, and not merely in aspect. Evil was in me, and it was growing there.

"Yibb-Tstll—or his avatar, locked for the main in its stone idol in the arena of death, just as the god himself is locked in alien voids outside this universe—was wont to visit me in the night, in my deepest dreams, to remind me of my debt. For like it or not, I had also inherited the first Yoppaloth's pact: I had immortality, and Yibb-Tstll must have his worship, his sacrifices. Sacrifices, Tarra Khash—an annual offering of souls—and mine the hand of death which now must point out the victims. Ah, but I did that readily enough!

"They were the ones who'd stood up in their stone tier seats, in their pomp and barbaric splendour, to applaud Yoppaloth's terrible tournament; the ones who'd roared their heathen approval when he'd thrust that nightmarish pike of his into my father's side and twisted the handle. And I remembered each and every one of them—each tribal chief or piddling shaman, every personage of estate in Shad—the lot! And by twos and threes as the years slowly passed, so they met their fates in the arena of death. Not slaughter on such a scale as I'd seen that first time, no, but terrible for all that. To see a man taken *alive* by Yibb-Tstll, and have his soul torn out of him, is . . . terrible! It is still terrible even now, ten thousand souls later.

"And so I kept down any would-be rivals, enemies, by feeding their souls to Yibb; and so his evil grew in me, a cancer spreading through my entire being.

"I became a man with a man's needs, took wives and tired of them—or allowed them to grow too close to me—then offered them to my god. Of children there were none.

If a woman carried my child, she went to Yibb. My cruelties, all inspired by the monster-god himself, became enormous. Now I could understand why the first Yoppaloth's acts and appetites had been so gross; for at day's end and before sleeping, I would lie awake and feel the same fate which took him reaching to engulf me. It was my imagination—or was it?

"Whichever, it could not be allowed: I was immortal and would *not* be slain, neither by any man, nor by magick or any unthinkable accident. And so I must protect myself . . . But how?

"I was no magician, no sorcerer or necromancer. I *had been* a mere youth when taken to Shad. I knew nothing save those vile things Yibb-Tstll had shown me and instilled in me. But the one thing I did have in abundance was time. And given time even an ignorant man may do—may learn—almost anything.

"Magick was the answer. I was already becoming legendary to the Yhemni, and the legend grew as they aged and died and I lived on. They saw me now as a great necromancer, but I was not! And so, since I had now resigned myself to Shad and Shadarabar (where else could I go in Theem'hdra and be accepted?) I determined to *become* that legend, to indulge myself in the first Yoppaloth's legacy and learn all the mazy alchemical and necromantic secrets he'd left behind him. And who could say, perhaps I'd also discover a way to break Yibb's hold on me, leave Shad forever and cleanse myself, and thus make at least partial return to the innocence of yore.

"Such were my thoughts during periods of high spirits, when on occasion I was given to believe I might rise above the pits I'd already fathomed and others which plunged deeper yet. But when my darker side held sway and I heard Yibb's call in the night, then I'd sneer at my own childish whimsies. Nevertheless, I set about to discover all I could of the former Yoppaloth's magicks and mysteries, the full extent of his esoteric and necromantic knowledge.

"In nether dungeons hewn from the bedrock beneath his palace, he had kept creatures of unbelievable hideousness, hybrid things spawned of madness, which he'd used in his annual tournaments. Since some of these—*anomalies*—were at least part-human and intelligent, I determined to question them as to their genesis: I determined to know how Yoppaloth had created them. The most advanced of these beings, able to converse, told me that the wizard had simply followed Yibb-Tstll's instructions in this regard, for he himself had not the magickal skills to produce such miscegenies.

"I found it passing suspicious to discover Yoppaloth lacking in such matters, but put this out of mind and proceeded next to explore his laboratory. Here another revelation: such devices as he'd owned were meagre things, in no way complicated but rather crude and unbecoming of a mage of alleged magnitude. Where were his shewstones, his dire familiars, his potions and poisons and other persuasions? Where were his books and, more essentially, his runebooks? No library at all that I had discovered; no tractates, codices, scrolls or inscribed tablets, nor any incunabula whatever! Nothing! A wizard? Even a middling magician? From where I stood, Black Yoppaloth the First had not even owned a wand!

"And so I arrived at an hitherto unthinkable conclusion: he'd been no mage at all but had relied entirely upon his mentor, Yibb-Tstll, for whatever he'd required in the way of morbid magicks. In this I was somewhat mistaken, but not utterly . . .

"Eventually I came across Yoppaloth's most secret place, a locked tower room, which I broke open to discover its purpose. And now at last I could see for myself how the monster god had used and misused—and planned to *further* misuse—his priestling. For *here* were his magicks—but all of them limited to a single purpose, all channelled along the same sad route. Yoppaloth's 'magick' was that of the ultimate coward: each charm, each rune, all powers and potencies, were without exception designed *for his own protection!*

"Here were deflective devices, to turn aside the perilous spells and caustic conjurations of others; and here likenesses of Yoppaloth in precious metals, upon which certain mordancies might spend themselves in place of their true target. Here were antidotes for every known and some unknown poisons, runes against the Red Rot and Purple Pestilence (which might easily fret to nothing even a man supposedly immortal!) and assorted activates to counter and work against the senders of other thaumaturgical terrors.

"And the fantastic truth which all of these things revealed to me was this: that Black Yoppaloth's every living moment had been one of abject fear, indeed a palsy of fright! So that all that remained was to discover *what* he had so feared, and *why*."

Tarra Khash could keep silent no longer. "And did you discover those things?"

"Aye," the other nodded, as the light from the green lantern burned lower, "I did. It was all written there in the pact itself! There in that secret room, kept locked an hundred years except when Yoppaloth cowered there. And this is what he'd set his seal upon:

"That he would serve Yibb-Tstll, and through him the Old Ones, until the time of their return, which was to be a period of one thousand years. In that time, for his pains, Black Yoppaloth would be Lord of Shad and Shadarabar and master over all therein, but afterwards he would become the undisputed Master of all Theem'hdra, mighty above all men. Indeed, all man's works would be his, everything, and none to stay his hand. All the wealth of the cities would be his, and even the cities themselves, and the entire world would belong to Yoppaloth—so long as he served the Old Ones, did their bidding and made sacrifices unto them.

"Until that time, he would feed Yibb-Tstll on the souls of many men and make him strong; periodically, he would make small sacrifices to the god, and annually would glut him with souls. And each hundred years he would prepare for Yibb and the Old Ones a special feast, preceded by an unthinkable orgy of blood spilled in detestable combat; and the games would be of his devising, cruel almost beyond imagination, for which the Old Ones, though they could not be there in the flesh, would bless him and look upon him as their one true priest in the world of men.

"And that was the pact against which Black Yoppaloth, great fat fool, had set his seal, to which he'd sworn, upon which oath he'd pledged his soul! And how could he lose? Cruel by nature, the pact guaranteed an excess of cruelty lasting a thousand years, and then lasting an eternity; greedy, an entire world had been promised him to rule, mighty above all men. And yet, even signing, even pledging his soul to this calamitous compact, Yoppaloth felt a tremor in his limbs, a sudden shaft in his heart. So that for the first time he felt—afraid! But that had been only the beginning of the fear.

"Now, in his dreams, he heard the booming laughter of the Old Ones and felt them near as never before; and so he determined to reassure himself, by calling up Yibb-Tstll to come to him and tell him how it would be when in fact the Old Ones came and made him Master of the World. And the monster-god had declared that it *would be* as promised, exactly so, and had shown him the future he'd set his seal to. The future, aye, but in no wise the future as Yoppaloth had pictured it! For this is what Yibb-Tstll showed him:

"A future world where men were no more—a world *cleared off* of the entire human race—where Man's cities lay crumbling in vast red blighted deserts. And rising in the distance, the twisted spires and turrets of cities vast and grey and terrible, mighty windowless mausoleums, and mad, cyclopean statuaries whose very angles defied Yoppaloth's eye to fathom their true shapes and perspectives. The cities of the Old Ones! And so he saw the world over which he'd one day rule, and finally he *understood* the words of the pact.

" 'Mighty over all men'—because there would *be* no other men! 'Ruler of all Man's cities and works'—crumbling piles shattered by the Old Ones' coming, or simply fallen into the decay of ages, untended in a world without human tenants. But . . . if Yibb and the Old Ones would destroy the entire human race, then how might Yoppaloth make sacrifice unto them? Must he sacrifice the beasts of the fields? And was this how he'd spend his immortality, in the never-ending service of creatures from black pits of earth, far stars and darkling spheres?

"At which point Yoppaloth, who to this juncture had been half-mad, went completely insane! For he knew now that he was doomed. Beasts for sacrifice? But he had seen no beasts in that future world—there had been no beasts! *Nothing* had lived there, save the Old Ones themselves in their terrible cities, and puffed Shoggoths in foul black lakes. And if they had left nothing that he might sacrifice to them, then the pact would be broken and his own soul forfeit. Aye, and Yoppaloth had *seen* how Yibb-Tstll took the souls of men and knew only too well how monstrous would be his fate.

"His only hope was this: that if he served Them *exceedingly* well in the thousand years before their coming, then that they'd leave some small part of Theem'hdra for him, and stock it with men and beasts, so that he might continue to serve them. And so, Tarra Khash, this was Yoppaloth's lot up to the moment when I killed him . . ."

And now Black Yoppaloth II fell silent, and in the near-darkness as the lantern burned lower still, only the gleam of his black eyes and certain greenly illumined highlights of his skeletal features could be seen . . .

HYPNOTIZED BY HIS ominous host's story, and by the circumstances of its telling, Tarra Khash was silent for long moments; then, with an effort of will, he dragged himself back to the here and now. "And so you inherited his curse," he finally said. "Which seems to me a very difficult thing to understand."

"How so?" The other glanced at him.

Tarra shrugged. "He'd spent the best part of an hundred years gathering protections for his life—indeed he *was* protected by Yibb and the Old Ones themselves—and yet you succeeded in killing him."

"Good!" said the other. "That was a mystery which puzzled me, too, when first I gave it thought. Especially having found the necromancer's secret tower room and read his story. But while I have *called* him a necromancer, wizard, mage and such, in truth he was none of these things. I reason it like this:

"That in the moment of supramundane influx—when that whirlwind from subterranean regions would have transferred to Yoppaloth strength to resist the ages, which I received in his stead—then that all his protective devices were cancelled. The magick of the Old Ones was greater than his and put all such petty spells and simples aside, which left him open not only to Their device but also to my sword."

Tarra nodded. "Since when you've accumulated magicks of your own, such as the powers you call on to give you strength, which you draw like a vampire from your victims. Also the bolt you hurled at some unseen foe, back there on the island where all very nearly came unstuck."

Yoppaloth shook his head, gave a wry laugh. "I am protected," he answered, "right enough—and certainly I've done what I can to protect myself—but as for any other form of magick . . . I have none! Do you not see? Even in a thousand years, I have learned nothing of the true thaumaturgies. The Old Ones, through Yibb-Tstll, have kept all such knowledge from me. What? And do you think they'd let me dabble, and perhaps discover a means to rid myself—and the world—of their curse?"

"But I have *seen* you hurl a bolt of green fire, which expended itself in the sky!" Tarra insisted.

"I was *warned* that someone spied upon me," the other patiently explained, "and was delivered of just enough power to deal with the incursion. I tell you, I have no magick—not of my own making! Even the winds which blow me home to Shad, they are not of my calling. They are *sent*, by powers whose sway over me is great and greater than any puppet-master's over his puppets . . ."

Tarra shook his head in wonder. "Then your fix is exactly the same as that of the first Yoppaloth," he said.

"No, it is worse than that of the first Yoppaloth," the other gloomed, "for he had worried over his fate for only one century, while I have worried over mine for ten. It drove him mad in a very little while, and as for me . . . Well, in any case, that fate is now upon me."

"Upon you?" Things were only just beginning to connect up in the Hrossak's mind. He frowned—then gasped: "A thousand years—the compact nears completion!"

Black Yoppaloth nodded. "Indeed," he said. "It matures tomorrow night, in Shad, in the arena of death!"

"Turn back the boats!" Tarra cried at once. "Flee! There's no alternative, for you've seen what the Old Ones intend for this world."

The other laughed a harsh, grinding laugh. "I've fled more times than I can number," he answered. "Always they bring me back."

"Then kill yourself!" The words slipped out before Tarra could stop them.

"Oh?" The other's gaze was bleak upon him. "And would you be so brave? Yes, I dare say you would. Well, I have tried—and failed—and then been punished. Do you forget? I'm immortal."

"Unless some man kill you!" Tarra barely breathed the words; but this time at least, he let them come out of his own will.

Their eyes met in the near-darkness. "But how?" Black Yoppaloth whispered. "It can't be done, until tomorrow night. And even then only at the exact moment, that single instant of time."

Tarra felt the muscles bunching of their own accord in his

arms, felt his fingers crooking, his body trembling as he fought against its leaning towards his host. Immortal Black Yoppaloth might well be, but there were certain things a man must find out for himself. At which moment, the guttering lantern went out . . .

Tarra forced himself to relax, heard Black Yoppaloth's frosty voice in the sudden, smoky darkness:

"You see, Tarra Khash? Protected!" Then fingers of ice took Tarra's shoulder, drew him to his feet, thrust him from the tent. He stood blinded by moonlight, gazed back into utter darkness. "I knew you'd be tempted," came that cold, cold voice from within. "And didn't I tell you not to come to Shad? Didn't I warn you? Well, and now we're almost there, and so another warning:

"No man will harm you in Shad, Tarra, so long as you stay well clear of my palace. That's my word. Even if you come there, they'll not harm you—but be advised in this matter, do not come."

"Because in that case *you* would harm me?"

Silence answered the Hrossak's question.

"But what good will it do to stay away?" Tarra pressed. "The world is doomed anyway."

"So it would seem," the cold voice agreed, "but would you risk a thousand-year nightmare for yourself—or immediate physical destruction and eternal torment for your living soul—when it can all be ended for the world in a single moment?"

Tarra gritted his teeth, slowly turned away; but from behind:

"Tell me just one thing, Hrossak. That first time in my tent, the trial with the knife: did you let me win?"

"I don't know," Tarra answered truthfully. "Maybe I

could have moved faster. But I knew that if I won I lost: if I tried to kill you, then that you or your Yhemnis would surely kill me."

"*Hmm!*" the other mused.

"And you?" Tarra's turn to question. "At ocean's rim, the trial with the sword? Oh, I know I moved faster that time than ever before in my entire life—but did you let *me* win?"

After a moment: "Perhaps," said Yoppaloth. "It was that or kill you, which I had no desire to do. And of course I knew that you couldn't kill me. So—maybe Shad was always your destiny after all. We can only wait and see."

Then there was nothing but silence and the soft slap of waves against the hull, and in a little while Tarra moved away . . .

XI

Various Magicks!

A NEW DAWN came to Theem'hdra, turned to a new day, which in time lengthened toward evening. Perhaps the last evening.

As the sun surrendered to Cthon's nets and dipped down under the rim of the world, so Orbiquita was borne safely to the surface of the desert. Changing even as her ex-sisters carried her up from the brimstone reek of their secret place, the excommunicated lamia lost all of her loathsomeness and metamorphosed into that delicious human female form she had always loved best; so that by the time the blowhole opened to a smoking pit, her delicate lungs were burning and her eyes streaming from the sulphurous heat and stench. Lamia memory was fading, too, but not so much that she'd forgotten her rights.

"To Teh Atht," she gasped, choking out the words as they dumped her unceremoniously onto the side of a dune which was already cooling in its own shade. "Take me to my cousin, in his manse in Klühn."

Iniquiss was with them and listened awhile to their grumbling, but finally she gave the request her approval.

"Aye, take her to that puny sorcerer relative of hers, if that's what she wants," she said. And to Orbiquita: "Two more requests, my girl, and then you're on your own."

As a cloud they flew her over the Mountains of Lohmi, the plains and scrublands, the Great Eastern Range and the River Lohr, then dipped down out of a sky already sprinkled with stars toward the softly litten aerie which was Teh Atht's manse. And all accomplished at a great, whirring speed, so that Orbiquita—a mere girl now—was breathless from the headlong rush of it and dizzy in the spiral of the final descent to her cousin's place, built on the craggy stub of a promontory in the rounded bite of the Bay of Klühn.

There, all day, the wizard had worriedly paced the crystal-paved flags of his rooms, finally going up to a tower workshop he no longer used and out onto its balcony. And there, too, he now saw against the stars and dark blue sky a darker knot of figures falling, and wondered at this weird aerial phenomenon. But not for long.

"Lamias!" he breathed as their shapes became more apparent, and he at once threw up a Keep-Ye-Out, which might have worked with one lamia but not with an entire flock. They dropped right through the spell, their wings beating their hot, foul stink into Teh Atht's face as they deposited Orbiquita upon his balcony.

"What?" he cried, falling back from them, toward the archway leading to the descending stone stairwell. "What? Lamias—with whom I've nothing of disagreement—invading my house and at such a time? Or is it merely portent of the hastening calamity? Are you, then, the chosen harbingers of a world's doom?"

"Our visit is portent of nothing, wizard," Iniquiss breathed brimstone upon him, pushed Orbiquita into the protection of his uplifted arms. "Except this poor creature desired to be brought here, to the manse of her cousin!"

"Her cous—?" Teh Atht began to repeat the Great Lamia's words, until his jaw fell open and stopped him. He looked at the lovely naked girl in his arms, then at her vile ex-sisters where they lifted off on leathery membrane wings. "Orbiquita?"

She by now was recovered from her momentary nausea, and she clutched at him in seeming desperation. "Does he live?" she begged, in an urgent but entirely human voice, indeed with the voice of a sweet girl. And then of course Teh Atht knew for a certainty that this was Orbiquita.

"Tarra Khash?" he said, quite needlessly.

"Of course, Tarra Khash," she answered, with that creeping into her voice to hint of what she'd recently been. "Only say that he lives, cousin, for if not I'll call down Iniquiss and her brood and beg of them my second boon, which will involve yourself most direly . . ."

By now the lamia flock was risen far up into the night, but still Teh Atht peered nervously after them and held the girl close. And when at last they were diminished to black specks against the stars, then he answered: "Aye, he lives, cousin—for now. We *all* live—for now! But what's this? Have you broken your vows, put the Sisterhood behind you? For a man? Incredible!"

She nodded, shivered, and he at once took her inside and down into warm apartments where he found clothes for her. Then he led her to the room of the astrologarium and showed her the flux and flow of its plasm, explaining to her the awesome meaning which he read in the doomful rush and reel of moons, planets, comets and stars. Following which, when his words had sunk in, he said:

"And so you see, Orbiquita, how all of your trials are come to naught. Your Tarra is doomed, as are we all—as is the world!"

She had been patient, but now demanded: "Show him to me."

"Have I not explained?" Teh Atht threw wide his hands. "I *dare not* use my shewstone! For all I know Black Yoppaloth is waiting for me even now on the other side of the scrying. And in any case, this is only a small—"

"But the merest glimpse!" she pleaded, cutting his protests short. "A glimpse—of Tarra alone and not this necromancer you so greatly fear."

Fear Shad's monstrous mage? Yes, Teh Atht had to admit that he did. But the contradiction was clear: what use to fear anyone or anything when the sands of time were running out for all Theem'hdra, a process due to terminate in ultimate chaos, death and destruction this very night? Teh Atht hesitated a moment longer, then strode to his shewstone.

Activating the orb, he commanded: "Seek out the Hrossak and let me see him—for an instant only!" Then he shielded his eyes and advised Orbiquita to do the same.

The crystal ball's screen opened, then closed at once. But not before the maiden and mage had seen Tarra seated by lantern's gleam on the flat, walled roof of a tavern, where an obese, worried-looking Yhemni proprietor served him booze before shuffling back to a low bar. Other than these two, however, tradesman and customer, the place had seemed very empty and lonely.

"There!" said Teh Atht, nodding. "In Shad, as I foretold.

Alive and well, it would seem. Meanwhile the evening turns to night, and there are far more important things to—"

He paused and his eyes grew very round. And in that moment all became clear to him, the pieces of the puzzle falling into place and locking there, so that the white mage of Klühn could see all at a glance. Before . . . everything had seemed coincidental, but now at last the final connection was made.

The astrologarium had told him that the world was to end, that tonight the stars would stand in strange conjunction, when the Ultimate Forces of Evil would stride forth to claim their sovereignty. This much he had known, but not the mechanics of the thing. Now he knew all, knew *how* they would breach those dimensional gates which so long had held them at bay. Black Yoppaloth was in their service, and held the keys to their immemorial prisons. Tonight, in his arena of death, the necromancer was going to let them out, and let them *in* to the comparatively sane and ordered world of men! And nothing, no one, no man strong enough to stand in Yoppaloth's way. Unless . . . Tarra Khash?

Out of darkness, light at the end of a tunnel. But a very faint light, holding little of promise as yet. Still, a little hope is better than no hope at all.

Teh Atht turned from the contemplation of his now quiescent shewstone, said: "Orbiqu—?"

She was no longer there!

From above came a faint whirring of wings, the harsh tones of barely female voices in seeming argument, a hot waft of sulphur and hell's own vapours. Teh Atht, for all that he was old and tired, ran from the room of the astrologarium and took the stone stairs three at a time. Lurching out onto the topmost balcony, he saw that he was too late, saw the lamia flock distantly limned against the sky where the indigo horizon met the black of space.

Orbiquita's second boon had been granted: to be with the man she loved on this one last night of all nights! By the light of the stars, and of Gleeth, whose rim now showed rising over the mountains, the creatures she had called her sisters winged her south for Shadarabar!

ON THE ROOF of Na-dom, Amyr Arn turned the bleak bronze discs of his eyes toward Gleeth, whose rim was up over the edge of the world. Bronze those eyes of his, aye, where they should be golden, and bleak, too, his frame of mind. Suhm-yi senses, which numbered in excess of Man's usual five, had warned him that things were far from right in the Primal Land. And not alone for Tarra Khash, though certainly he were the focus.

The stars, reflected in the Crater Sea far below, seemed somehow to peep and leer in a manner strange and ominous, and an unseasonably chill wind had blown all day from the south-east, which by rights should have been a warm breeze. And these things, plus the leaden weight of his own heart within him, told the silver-skinned Suhm-yi male that much was amiss. Worse, instincts keen as a knife had connected these omens inextricably to the plight of Tarra Khash, whom Amyr Arn loved as a brother.

And so he'd come up again to Na-dom's peak, that jagged fang beloved of the gods, to call upon Gleeth for his aid and implore the benevolent old moon-god to do whatever was in his power to do for a Hrossak in peril far away in distant Shad. And now Gleeth was rising, fat-bodied and blunt-horned, and there was something of strength in him where he cleared the rim of the horizon and sailed for the sky. Now Amyr could make his obeisances, commence his prayers and beg of Gleeth his favours. But as to whether the moongod (traditionally deaf and blind) would see or hear him, that was a different matter . . .

THE SAME MOON shone at a shallow slant down upon barbarically splendid Shad, where now the taverns and dwellings were beginning to empty as a silent populace made its teeming way through the streets toward Black Yoppaloth's palace at jungle's fringe. All of marble, copper, gold, ivory and ironwood, Shad's domes and spires, roofs and façades caught and gave back the moon's glints; likewise the white, often sharply pointed teeth of Shad's people, and their golden bangles, earrings and other trinkets—and the sweat on their shiny-black trembling faces. Aye, for their terror was also reflected, and not alone by moon and starlight. No, for another source of illumination lit Shad this night, the alien aerial beacon which called the people to Black Yoppaloth's nightmare games.

Tarra Khash saw this malevolent manifestation from across the city—this weird wheeling of a corkscrew cloud, alive with coiling green serpents of fire, whose funnel stem went down to Yoppaloth's palace as if tethered there—and tossed back his fiery Yhemni drink at a single gulp. For the hellish twister over Shad seemed full of pent power, crouching on high like some silent beast, only waiting its chance to roar out loud and spring down upon the city. The clouds at its rim rolled and boiled and seethed with that now familiar phosphorescent emerald bile, and its corkscrew coil had origin in the palace whose ziggurat tiers rose square, dark and menacing across a night-gleaming panorama of vine-clad spires, domes and turrets.

The Hrossak had seen much the same sort of display before one time in Klühn, and knew that it was not of Nature's doing. Nothing of good clean earth, air, fire and water this, but born of magicks beyond the mundane mind of man to conceive; and Tarra could not help but shudder as he called for another drink.

That time in Klühn, not so very long ago: yes, it had been much like this, and yet different. Then he'd had Amyr Arn of the Suhm-yi at his side, and a positive mission in mind, with at least a chance of success. But now? What could one man, alone in a strange heathen land, hope to achieve against this? Attempting to brave the terrors of that palace would put him in jeopardy not only of his life but his immortal soul! *If* he could find his way to the arena of death, and *if* no one stopped him along the way—what then?

Tarra cursed a conscience which would not let him be to die in peace or pieces but kept prodding his all too vivid memory. The look on Loomar's face when the ships had docked in Shad's harbour this morning and the slaves— Loomar Nindiss included, and his sister, Jezza—were led away through the leering, jeering black throng. The astonishment of Northmen and rogue Hrossaks alike as they, too, had found themselves chained and dragged cursing from the dockside toward the ziggurat palace.

And what of those poor lads and lasses now?—the slaves at least, if not the betrayed mercenaries? But Tarra Khash, he'd been set free, to go his way and live whatever remained of his or anyone else's life this day. And now that day was evening, and soon it would be blackest night. The last night . . .

Galvanized, Tarra stood up so quickly he banged his knees, clouted the table with a fist hard as horn, gritted his teeth, scowled and sat down again. What? Challenge Yoppaloth on his own ground, in his own palace and on his terms—and hope to win? And *if* he won—why, even then he'd lose!—become heir to all the horror of a thousand-year nightmare, as the Old Ones fashioned *him* in his turn as their gateway to chaos and hell on earth! So perhaps Shad's necromantic master was right: sit back and do nothing, and let the world go to blazes in one last mad catastrophic awakening of ancient evil.

But . . . the madman Yoppaloth had taken his sword, and no man had ever stolen from Tarra Khash. Not and kept what he'd taken. And if this really was the last night, well wouldn't the risk be worth it? Wouldn't *anything* be worth it? Yes, it would—but first he'd put another drink away.

"COWARD!" TEH ATHT said it out loud for what must be the tenth time; said it to himself, for there was no one else to hear him. Even hopper and flitter, sensing the doom hanging in the air, had gone off on their own to hide. As for the wizard's third familiar, the entirely liquid one: he was in the astrologarium even now, blindly smoothing the way for the world's slippery slide to hell.

And again, for the last time: "Coward!" cried Teh Atht— but coward no longer—and he strode with great purpose and determination to the table where rested his shewstone. For he'd come to the same inescapable conclusion as Tarra Khash himself: since the end was nigh, what use to hide from it? Orbiquita, no longer lamia but soft and fragile human female, had gone in search of her Hrossak, had begged her sisters to fly her direct into the jaws of death; and Amyr Arn, if he'd had his way, would have long since beaten her to it. So what was lacking in the white wizard of Klühn, who at the flick of a wrist could command more sheer power than both of these might muster in their entire lifetimes?

Nothing was lacking in him, except he'd been old and afraid. Well, he couldn't make himself young again, but fear was simply a state of mind, which the mind recognized in degrees. To have been afraid of what *might* happen to himself had been one thing, but his fear of what *would* happen if he took no action was far greater. With that resolution made, now he would see what could be done, would do what must be done.

"The Hrossak!" he cried, activating his shewstone. "Let me see him. Let me know his circumstances. Let me at least try to make amends for my failures, while still there's time."

The orb's opaque screen cleared: Tarra Khash sat as before at a wooden table on the flat, open roof of a tavern where it looked out across a square, out across Shad itself. Behind the Hrossak the sky was fantastically patterned, where green lightnings leaped and coruscated along the undersides of madly gyrating clouds. And seeing that vast aerial confusion of forces, Teh Atht knew he'd been right to seek Tarra out and attempt some sort of intervention. For certainly this was the portal which the Old Ones would use to gain entry into this sphere.

But first things first: now he must discover what Tarra had learned, if anything, of the man or monster he'd travelled with all these days and nights. Metempsychosis would be the answer, not a mode the wizard liked greatly (for fear of getting stuck in someone else's body) but he'd committed himself, and no turning back now. First he must take simple precautions—against the Yhemni taverner doing damage when he discovered himself transposed—and then he'd be on his way.

He clambered onto the table with the shewstone and spelled an Admirable Adhesion onto the floor all about, which at once turned soft and gummy. That should do the trick! Now for the transmigration, a more complicated magick far, which would take some little time in the fixing. Teh Atht concentrated, peered deep into the crystal ball, fixed the lumbering Yhemni with his eyes where he approached Tarra's table with another drink, and—

"IF YOU WANT more drink, order now." The fat black's guttural jungle tones startled Tarra back to reality, or maybe back from the alcoholic pit he'd been pursuing for much of the day. Indeed, he'd been drinking almost unabated since Black Yoppaloth had gone off with his captives and left him standing alone on the dockside; it had seemed a very logical thing to do.

Several things had seemed logical, on what was scheduled to be the world's last day. Bedding a woman or three, starting a fight, getting roaring drunk. But while Tarra made no racial discrimination, he'd known Shad's beauties wouldn't appeal to him; no woman did these days, not since he'd accepted the kiss of a certain lamia. As for brawling: Yoppaloth had decreed that no one harm him, but that didn't mean they couldn't throw him in chains! Which had left only getting drunk, something he was passably good at. But not this time; for, try as he might, and despite all the liquors which had scalded his throat and innards, he'd somehow stayed at least relatively sober.

"Order now?" he repeated the taverner. "Why, are you going somewhere?"

The other grinned a wobbly, sickly grin, showing teeth filed to fine points. "Yes I am," he nodded. "Into the jungle and find a place to hide! Until tomorrow. The jungle, aye, where there are only beasts to worry about, shelter for the thousands who have sense enough to stay away from the master's palace."

"What do you fear?" Tarra asked him.

"Death!" said the other at once. "The shrieking madness of Yoppaloth's arena! The corpses and hybrid monsters which he pits against his gladiators!"

Tarra scowled. "With your size and weight and—teeth! You, an eater of men, afraid?"

The other scowled back. "I'll eat men, when I can get 'em," he answered. "But Yoppaloth eats souls! And the slaves aren't the only ones who fight in his arena; if he runs out of captives, there's always plenty more meat amongst the onlookers."

"What's to stop me going into the palace?" Tarra questioned.

"Nothing," the Yhemni cannibal answered. "The more the better! Why, with luck you may even come out again!"

Tarra nodded. "Except he's forbidden me to go."

"He? Who? Black Yoppaloth?" The black's eyes stood out in his head. "Then you're mad to even think of it—and I'm mad to stand here talking to you!" He began to turn away. "I wish you luck, Hrossak, and—" And he paused, almost as if frozen there, half turned away.

Among all the strangeness, Tarra sensed a weird addition. Slowly the Yhemni turned back to face him; his fat black lips opened, spoke—and Tarra gasped! Gone now the man's untutored jungle slur and mode of expression, his gurgled formation of unfamiliar words. And in its place—the voice of a scholar! Oh, the *voice* was the same, but the way it was used, and what it said:

"Tarra Khash, you don't know me but I know you well enow." The huge man seated himself in a chair opposite, stared at Tarra through eyes which had lost all their sloth. "Now listen, you're a strong man and can stand any shocks I throw you, and so I'll name names and then you'll know I speak the truth. Do you understand? If so close your mouth and nod."

Tarra had been gaping. Hardly knowing why he obeyed, nevertheless he did. And the fat, black, strangely altered Yhemni taverner nodded in his turn and rapidly spoke these words:

"Stumpy Adz, Amyr Arn, Ahorra Izz, Orbiquita! There, and now you know that I know you. Now listen and I'll tell you a stranger thing: I am *not* the Yhemni taverner you take me for. Oh, I inhabit his body, for the moment, but my mind is the mind of another. Or rather, his is."

Tarra's jaw had fallen open again.

"You remember on that island where I wrecked your ship, and turned Yoppaloth to stone so that he'd sink?" The black's voice was urgent now. "Well, *do* you remember—when Cush Gemal, or more properly Black Yoppaloth, hurled a bolt of green fire into the sky? He hurled it at me! I was the wizard who scried on him that time, and did my best—or what I thought was my best—to destroy him. Close your mouth."

Tarra snapped his jaws shut again, shook his head to clear it—both of alcoholic fumes and of madly whirling thoughts. And at last he found words of his own to speak. "If you're not the man I see before me, then who are you?"

"Teh Atht," the other replied. "White wizard of Klühn. And right now *this* fellow's mind is in my body in my manse in that city. I swapped places with him, d'you see, in order to speak to you. Now listen, if we're to defeat Black Yoppaloth and keep them out who he'd let in, there are things I need to know. First off: I notice you're not wearing your sword. Does he still have it?"

Tarra nodded.

"That's bad. You know that blade's a Suhm-yi Sword of Power?"

Again Tarra's nod.

"But does Yoppaloth know it?"

"Not from my lips, no."

The black man sighed his relief. "Well, that's one point in your favour, anyway."

"In my favour?" Tarra frowned. "How do you mean?"

The other continued as if he hadn't heard him: "But it's strange that with magick such as his . . . I mean, I'd have sworn he'd immediately recognize such a sword."

"Magick?" The Hrossak was coming to grips with the situation. "Such as Yoppaloth's? *Huh!* He has no magick! Not of his own making. He's protected by the Old Ones, that's all." And again: "Huh!—that's *all*, indeed!—and by his own protections, which with their permission he's gathered over the years. But harmful magick to command? He has none. He can deflect, turn back another's spell upon the sender, use what powers the Old Ones may lend him—and that's all. They've taught him a little necromancy, too, and the making and mating of hybrid creatures for his arena, but that's the lot. And now? Why, now I fancy he's little more than a dangerous madman—a madman with the destiny of the whole world in his hands, yes—but no more a sorcerer than I am!"

Teh Atht's black host's turn to gape. And after a moment: "That might explain a great deal," he whispered. "For instance: I had expected him to seek me out when he discovered how I spied on him, but he did nothing except threaten."

"He wouldn't know where to begin," said Tarra.

"But he *did* hurl a bolt at me, which could have caused me great harm!"

"Power of the Old Ones," the Hrossak insisted. "The same green fires which twist and writhe in the maelstrom over the palace even now. Look, see for yourself." And he turned where he sat and pointed at the sky over Shad. "He uses that power occasionally, when he has to, but it depletes him mightily, and then like a vampire he draws on the strength of others to fill himself up again."

"But it's recorded that upon a time he sent onyx automatons against the wizard Exior K'mool!" Teh Atht protested.

"The Old Ones may well have," Tarra countered, "on his behalf, but not Yoppaloth himself. No, for if he has any magick at all, it's only—"

"Yes?"

"—It's only that people trust him. I mean, I know it sounds daft, but it's the truth. For all he's a crazy butcher, he commands respect, even loyalty. Damn me, *I* respect him!"

"*Ah!*" said the other, and sat back in his chair. Then he straightened up, looked directly into Tarra's eyes. "When you said he was no more a mage than you yourself, you came nearer to the truth than you knew. That magick you speak of is very special, Tarra Khash, a natural earth magick which men seldom aspire to. It explains your mutual attraction, yours and Yoppaloth's. And now I know why Ahorra Izz, Orbiquita, Amyr Arn and others I've seen or spoken to like and respect you so well. For it's a magick you share with him, do you see?"

"Me, magick?" Tarra could only snort, shake his head.

"Aye." The white wizard nodded his huge black curly head. "A magick which might yet save us all . . ."

The whirling cloud over Shad was slowly descending, lighting up the city's roofs and domes and minarets with a reflected green shimmer. Where before the city had been hushed, silent, now sounds came drifting on a wind stirred up by the lowering twister. The massed sighing of a great host of people! And then other sounds—screams! And finally the roar of a crowd's voice lifted in savage applause.

"The games in Yoppaloth's arena of death," Tarra gasped. "They've started!"

"How long will they go on, before—?" Teh Atht left the unspeakable unspoken.

"There are a lot of slaves to die first," Tarra answered.

"Then it's high time I was on my way back to my own body," said the other. "With luck I'll see you again, presently, in the arena of death."

"What?" Tarra felt the hairs rise up on the nape of his neck, but despite his dread, he understood well enough what Teh Atht meant.

The black man smiled a strange smile, and—*was changed in a moment!* Gone now Teh Atht, and the Yhemni taverner Moota Phunt returned to his rightful body. His eyes opened wide; he sprang up, fell down in a faint.

Tarra got to his feet, stood over the fallen man. He felt faint himself—both from excess of drink, and from the stink of DOOM which now hung almost tangible in the hot, jungle-perfumed air—but no time for fainting.

Time for only one thing now . . .

———

TEH ATHT WAS back in his own body, on all fours on the gummy floor of the astrologarium, to which he adhered quite admirably. He cancelled the spell, stood up and dusted himself down, called hopper and flitter to attend him, and likewise the liquid one out of his astrological plasm. One glance at that miniature universe, where its wheeling spheres moved ever closer to completion of the pattern, told the white wizard that time had very nearly run out. In a matter of hours, the stars would be right. And before that he must be back in Shad.

Then, familiars three in attendance, he donned his Primary Robe of Runes and materialized his favourite wand; and moments later he and his troupe sped out from a high balcony, making all speed for Shad aboard his fantastic flying carpet. Faster than ever before, that wonderfully woven vehicle arced skyward and raced south, and Teh Atht in the prow pointing the way with his wand, never worrying that he might burn the carpet's power right out of it, but only that he get to Shad in time.

Except . . . in time for what?

AT ABOUT THE same time as Teh Atht crossed the Lohr, Orbiquita and her ex-sister escorts were descending toward jungled Shad. Black Yoppaloth's palace, by virtue of the many lights along its five tiers and the roar of the rabble echoing up from its vaults, was at once apparent; Orbiquita directed she be delivered there, where *exactly* being determined when she spied, on the roof of the third tier, a high-walled garden with many marble archways leading into the building at its back. For there beyond these ornate archways she'd spied rooms of fine furnishings and piled cushions, where languished a dozen gorgeous girls all scrubbed clean and clad only in silks and perfumed oils. Black Yoppaloth's harem, beyond a doubt.

The garden itself was deserted, however, for all twelve of the girls were huddled together within their quarters; and so unseen the lamia flock deposited Orbiquita there, before bidding her farewell and taking once more to the night sky. Following which she was quite alone, but resolute in her pledge that if her Tarra was in bondage to Yoppaloth, then that she'd find him here somewhere.

There in the garden she quickly shed her outer garments and hid them in a bush, and, attired as scantily as the rest, entered into the harem and found her way to huddling with the other girls. And all the while she was trying to think what best to do next. A problem which was taken out of her hands at once, for at that point precisely came an amazing diversion!

A white youth, little more than a stripling, arrived at the great latticed doors to the harem, beyond which stood a huge Yhemni eunuch. The guard started up and set about the stranger at once, to chase him away, but the boy had a knife. Before the black knew what was happening, Loomar Nindiss had slit his throat, taken the key to the harem and used it to slip inside. There he tremblingly approached the cowed girls and drew out his sister, Jezza, from their midst.

No longer chained to her companions, she left them easily enough (albeit reluctantly, for they'd all become familiar as sisters to her) and went with Loomar into the garden; the others followed after—Orbiquita likewise, to see what was happening—and began begging the youth to rescue them also. Loomar, beside himself with anxiety, frustration and regret, could only shake his tousled head; all their pleading must go for naught. His own and Jezza's escape would not be easy; any attempt to steal away the rest of the girls *en masse* would be madness!

Then he'd scaled the garden wall and, uncoiling a slender rope from his waist, had drawn up Jezza after him. A moment more and the pair had disappeared from view.

As Orbiquita and the other girls trooped back into the harem, several of them began arguing that they should raise the alarm. If not, when the dead eunuch was discovered, which must be shortly, then they'd all be implicated. And Black Yoppaloth's rage would be great. At this point Orbiquita spoke up, her voice softly sibilant as she said:

"No, we had nothing to do with it, and none can say we did." She closed the doors, reached a slender hand through their latticework and turned the key in the lock, then tossed it down alongside the dead guard. "There, and now when he's found we'll not be suspected—and those two will be away and running. For the guard and his key are out there, and we are all safe in here, and the door is locked. All is as it should be, with the exception that a eunuch is dead."

"That and the fact that we number only eleven!" one of them tearfully protested.

"Strange," said Orbiquita, very quietly, "for I make the count twelve!"

Sure enough, when they checked they found she was right, and only then did they notice the stranger in their midst. They drew back a little from her then, but Orbiquita merely put a finger to her lips, turned her head a little on one side and cautioned them. "Let it be," she warned, her eyes very bright and feral. "Or believe me, you'll have more to worry about this night than Black Yoppaloth's anger."

And then, because she looked so strange and seemed so certain, they said no more . . .

ATOP NA-DOM'S FLAT summit, a fretted needle spire of rock like a finger pointed skyward. And through the stem of this tallest crag, a hole like an oval eye, through which a man might gaze into the heavens on all the stars shining down on Theem'hdra. And the hole in the rock was the Eye of Gleeth, which Amyr Arn had used aforetime, and many a priest of the Suhm-yi before him.

The moon's orbit was taking him behind that lone spire even now, and soon his silver orb would fill the hole exactly like an eye, with the dark occluded section of its surface a huge eyeball gazing toward the east and somewhat south— gazing in fact upon far Shadarabar. Amyr Arn looked in that same direction, followed the silver swath of the moon across the Crater Sea, and saw auroral lights where never those lights should be. A green, crawling, sprawling aurora—a great emerald blotch disfiguring the horizon—weird and unhealthy there in the far south-east. And:

"Gleeth!" Amyr cried in his silvery voice. "There! Now you see it for yourself. Strange dark forces are at work in the Primal Land. Even in the sky, which is your domain, they manifest themselves. Now Tarra Khash is surely at the heart of this mystery, and I fear for his life. Indeed, I fear for all Theem'hdra! And so I beseech you, Gleeth, old god of the moon, look down in favour on the Hrossak this night, and aid him if you can."

A lone cloud drifted across Gleeth's face, when for long

moments his rays were dimmed and their pathway across the Crater Sea faded to a thin gleaming. When at last the cloud passed, the moon had swung more surely into position behind the spire, so that indeed Amyr fancied he gazed upon some vast cycloptic eye set in a face of stone. But when he would have called again upon Gleeth for his assistance—

Hold! came the voice of the moon-god, in his ears or mind he knew not. *Say no more, Amyr Arn of the Suhm-yi. I have seen and understand all. They call me "blind" and "deaf," but I am neither one nor the other. I have* made *myself blind to many of Man's doings, true, for they were not fit to be seen; and certainly I have* been *deaf to many a man's exhortations, which were unworthy. But in you yourself I can find nothing ignoble, and in the Hrossak Tarra Khash only a very little. You are both singularly rare creatures. Which is as well, for these are singularly rare times.*

Now hear me: I feel in my orbit a tremor, the dreadful lure of stars and planets acting upon me in unison, and I know that calamity strides in the star spaces, bearing down upon this region of space and time. And you are right: Tarra Khash is the key, his is the single power by which a cosmic catastrophe may be avoided. I say "may," for events teeter upon a very narrow rim, be certain! The Hrossak cannot win on his own. Others know this, too, and rush to his side even now. And you? Would you also stand beside Tarra Khash on this night of nights?

"Would that I could," Amyr breathed, hardly daring to speak in case he broke the spell. "But how? His troubles lie in Shad, far away over mountains and rivers and plains. Grim peaks, great deeps, burning deserts separate us. There are days and weeks of travel lying between. Do you speak in riddles, old moon-god?"

Do you remember, Gleeth answered, *when you fired an arrow into my eye? And how I swallowed up that arrow and shot it out many miles away to kill the northern barbarian Kon Athar? This will be similar. Except it will require a deal more of faith. Faith in me, Amyr Arn. Your forefathers were the most faithful of creatures. And you?*

"Only tell me what I must do," Amyr replied.

Now quickly, said Gleeth. *You see the silver swath I cut across the Crater Sea? It leads to Shad. Only follow it.*

"But . . . how?" Amyr felt his silver skin grow cold.

Like the arrow. Run, dive, shoot yourself along my moonbeam path—to Shad!

"Hurl myself down?" Amyr's round eyes grew rounder still.

No, not down—along! And I'll set you down safe in Shad. But quickly, while yet I stand in the oval of the pierced spire.

Faith? And did Amyr have such faith? And if he had not, what then?

"Old Gleeth," he cried, "I put my faith in you!" And he ran to the rim of Na-dom and hurled himself headlong into the glare of the moon's silver path . . .

TWO MEETINGS OCCURRED almost simultaneously: the first between Tarra Khash, Loomar Nindiss and his sister, and the second between Teh Atht and the lamia Sisterhood. The first was relatively down to earth:

Tarra Khash, loping through Shad's deserted streets toward the ziggurat palace, came round the corner of a building and almost collided with a pair of fleet shadows hurrying in the opposite direction. He instinctively reached for a sword which was no longer there, then fell into a defensive crouch. And:

"Caught!" Jezza gasped. "Oh, Loomar, what now, my brother?"

Keen eyes pierced the green-glowing gloom. Came recognition!

Tarra took a deep breath. "Loomar Nindiss!" he sighed. "And Jezza. How'd you get her away?"

The youth fell into Tarra's arms, hugged him. "Tarra Khash!" he gasped, getting his wind. "I never thought I'd be so grateful to see a Hrossak!"

Tarra caught up Jezza and gave her a quick hug to reassure her, then shoved her into her brother's arms. "Quickly," he said, "tell me what's happening and how far it's gone. Also, how you got away."

"Yoppaloth set me free," said the youth. "Out of deference to you. He told me: 'Go, enjoy your freedom while you can. And thank Tarra Khash that he befriended you.' After that, I killed a harem guard, snatched Jezza, came here. But as for the rest: the tournament has begun, and men are dying in the sorcerer's arena of death. Now come with us, Tarra, and we'll flee this place. Maybe we can steal a boat, and—"

"No." Tarra shook his head. "All of this ends—tonight. Maybe for me—for you, too, and the whole world—and maybe, just maybe, not. I can't come with you. I've a date with Black Yoppaloth in his infernal arena."

"You go to the palace?" Loomar couldn't credit his own ears. "To kill Yoppaloth? Five thousand blood-crazed Yhemnis attend the games; you haven't a cat's chance in hell!"

"Cats have nine lives," said Tarra, simply. "Now go, hide yourselves in the city. If all comes to naught fleeing will do you no good anyway. If all turns out for the best—maybe I'll see you later."

"Very well," said Loomar, "but take this with you." He

gave Tarra a knife, which the Hrossak at once recognized. He snorted, said:

"Just a lad, they never did search you."

Loomar nodded. "I *was* a lad," he said, "once . . ."

Then: Tarra wasted no more time or words but turned and loped into the shadows . . .

THE SECOND MEETING, between Teh Atht and the lamia Sisterhood, happened like this:

As the white wizard followed Theem'hdra's eastern seaboard south and soared above the mouths of the salt lochs where they opened into the Eastern Ocean, so he spied Iniquiss and her brood coming in across the Straits of Yhem at a somewhat lower altitude. Knowing the lamias of old—and knowing also that they had taken Orbiquita to Tarra Khash, and that therefore they might have news of him—he turned westward, dipped down toward them and flew parallel for a while.

Iniquiss spotted him, scowled, flew closer; at which hopper, flitter and the entirely liquid one made themselves small as possible and crowded behind their master. "Ho, wizard!" she called out. "How now? And is this a chance meeting or what?"

Teh Atht inquired after Orbiquita, learned her whereabouts as last known, then quickly explained his mission. And he likewise hinted that the lamias might care to take a hand in whatever was to proceed, for *all* the world's creatures would be imperilled together if the Old Ones were allowed to return—lamias included.

Iniquiss gave what he said some little consideration; Orbiquita was owed one last request; perhaps it were not well to desert her at this eleventh (almost twelfth) hour. "Very well," she called out, above the cackle of her protesting lesser sisters, "we'll return to Shad at once. But don't let us detain you—go on ahead and save a little time."

Teh Atht required no more urging but turned his carpet south again, and in a little while crossed the Straits of Yhem . . .

AMYR ARN'S FLIGHT on Gleeth's moonbeam carrier seemed languid as liquid silver, but in fact it was accomplished with speed and no small measure of discomfort, the latter coming at journey's end. From first leap into space from the flat summit of Na-dom, his silvery hide and its contents had been disassembled, had flowed into and along Gleeth's beam, had sped over the Primal Land like a fleeting moon-shadow, finally to be reassembled from dappled silvery light close to Yoppaloth's palace in Shad—over a moat of croco-diles where the ziggurat's lower east wall faced the jungle!

Splashing down and gathering to himself his wildly whirling senses, the last Suhm-yi male saw needle-toothed snouts ploughing the scummy water in his direction, made at once for the ziggurat's slimy, water-lapped wall. No en-tirely human creature could have hoped to scale that slip-pery surface of vertical marble blocks—not in the area where it met the water—but Amyr was not human.

His spatulate fingers (one less to each hand than in hu-man beings) found crevices others would miss, and the suc-tion of his fingertips never failed him but left astonished crocs chewing on weeds where a moment earlier his slen-der body had knifed through water, and Amyr already his own height up the wall, and going for all he was worth.

Like a lizard he climbed, and into the first window he could find, and from there following the arena's swelling roar down dripping, disused, nitre-festooned stairwells and along winding corridors, until he'd passed through something of a maze to find himself in a dungeon of sorts, where an archway covered by a grid of iron bars at last blocked his way. But here the arena's noise was an uproar, and beyond the bars—

—Black Yoppaloth's arena of death! And even if there had been no bars, the sight Amyr saw then must certainly have stopped him dead in his tracks . . .

XII

To Win Is to Lose!

TARRA KHASH LOOKED down on that same mad scene of
death and destruction; *down* on it, aye, for he'd entered the
ziggurat palace at a higher level and come here by a different route. And never a man to challenge his presence in
this place, for all of the palace guards—and the majority
of Shad's citizens, too—were here to witness Yoppaloth's
monstrous games. What Tarra (and Amyr, too) saw was
this:

A circular arena, all ringed about by statues of a great
many gods, their circle being broken in only one place
where stood a square, blood-hued onyx dais. And in front of
the dais, going down to depths beyond imagination, the
glass-throated pit of which Yoppaloth II had spoken, out of
which and up through the chimney above, passed the
writhing tail of the greenly illumined twister.

Tarra's gaze took in the arena in its entirety: it must be
forty-five to fifty paces across wall to wall, like a mighty pit itself within walls rising up maybe twelve to fifteen feet. Set in
these walls, iron-barred archways led to nether vaults; above
them an amphitheatre or stadium, with tiers of stone-hewed

seats, going up and up, divided at intervals by aisles permitting access.

Odd, but I think I've seen all this before! Tarra told himself where he looked grimly down over the heads of the Yhemnis massed in front of him. *Last time it was in Klühn: Gorgos and his Temple of Secret Gods. And now it's here. Ah, but last time it worked out in my favour, while on this occasion . . . ?*

He let dumbfounded, horrified eyes scan the arena, whose walls above the archways were adorned with jutting, red-and yellow-flaring flambeaux. In places there were still patches of yellow sand, but mainly the sand was red and slimed. Evidence of a great slaughter lay everywhere: torn bodies, and bodies without limbs, and other remains which weren't human at all. As for the remaining combatants: a tight knot of figures was fighting even now. Fighting? In the centre of the arena, a mighty melee!

There were Northmen in it, just two of them left—and it did Tarra's Hrossak heart a power of good to see a trio of steppemen there, too, one of them being Narqui Ghenz, with whom he was somewhat familiar—and also a hulking, towheaded youth who could only be the last survivor (along with Loomar and Jezza) of all the slaves Black Yoppaloth had shipped here. Six of them left, only six, of the hundred and odd they'd once numbered; and the bulk of them strewn in bits and pieces all around the arena. Gods, what a battle it must have been!

As for the cause of the mayhem: no need to look far for that—or those!

Back to back and side by side, Northmen, Hrossaks and bull-shouldered youth stood; their weapons were huge claws and mandible pieces torn from dead opponents; more of these hybrid monstrosities—things from Yoppaloth's subterranean vats and breeding dungeons—ringed them all about. And of the latter . . . they were things out of a madman's worst nightmares!

They had human parts, some of them, human legs and thighs and occasionally heads, but for the most part they were entirely alien. Squat, lobsterish, red-eyed and slavering and huge! Or spiderlike, with many human arms. And one was slender and shaped like a mantis, half as tall again as a man, with chitin-plated hooks at the ends of its forelegs; but its head was a man's, with tusks like a wild pig curving from its chomping mouth!

Nor were these hybrids the worst, for there were others which may or may not have been men entirely, but which *were* in any case quite dead—but active nevertheless! And these were all the proof Tarra needed to show that indeed Yoppaloth's masters had taught him something of necromancy, for they'd obviously been called up from the grave! And a full dozen of these monsters and corpses encircling the knot of survivors, while as many again stood back, only waiting to take their turn should one of their blasphemous brothers fall in the fray.

Even as Tarra watched, the mantis-creature fastened its hooked hands about the neck of one of the coarse-maned Northmen and yanked him bodily from the tight central knot. He was lifted up, hurled down in the gory sand well apart from the others. Badly wounded and clasping his torn neck, he lay there for a moment, then stumbled to his feet; and Tarra fully expected that the mantis-thing or some other monster would pounce upon him and make an end of it. But that wasn't the way these games were played. No, for the beast things of the arena merely singled out and weakened the prey, whose doom was to be sealed in an entirely different manner.

Black Yoppaloth cried, *"Hold!"* And the howling of the Yhemni mob in the amphitheatre seats and aisles faded to silence in a moment. His voice was not the voice Tarra had known; like the man himself, it was bloated now; its keen edge had gone, leaving it dull and booming, more like the croak of some vast, obscene and blear-eyed frog. And now he came, down the dais steps and striding almost drunkenly toward his victim, the crippled Northman, so that Tarra would not have known this were him if not for his height, his robes, and the crimson-lacquered crest of his head.

And in his hand . . . the Suhm-yi Sword of Power—Tarra's sword—against an unarmed, half-dead Northman! The Hrossak gulped back his rage, for rage was no good here—but he saved it for later. How could he ever have imagined there was anything of nobility in this monster? Yoppaloth's personal magick? So the wizard Teh Atht had avowed; but now, to Tarra Khash, the bestiality of this creature seemed obvious. And as for Tarra's sharing this power: it was the last thing he wanted. He'd be a man and live a life, not a lie! As for this "show" in the arena: why, there wasn't even a contest in it, and it had never been intended that there should be!

All activity in the arena of death had ceased; the encircled group of human combatants could only look on, like the now breathless, bloodthirsty spectators themselves. Tarra wondered if they'd be so bloodthirsty if they knew their own lives hung in the balance this night. He guessed not, but hated them all the same. And so Yoppaloth strode to the doomed man, came up to him and showed him the scimitar's keen, curved blade. "To make the end of it easier for both of us!" And he laughed with that monstrous voice of his.

Before the other could think or even move, Yoppaloth struck *upwards* with the sword, twice, slicing into the tendons under the barbarian's arms and in his armpits. And now he was truly crippled. He cried out his agony, crumpled into a seated position on the slimy sand. Tarra gaped, astonished both by Yoppaloth's cruelty, and by the sheer *speed* he'd displayed, which far surpassed anything the Hrossak had hitherto witnessed. Aye, and Yoppaloth's accuracy, too, which had been better than hairbreadth.

And the Hrossak was still gaping when the fiend tossed down his sword to the sand, leaned forward and grasped the barbarian's head between his powerful hands. In the next moment, then Tarra understood the bloated appearance of the necromancer, for now Yoppaloth began to draw off what was left of his victim's living strength!

This must be how it had been for the Yhemnis taken in Yoppaloth's black-tasselled tent. The Northman seemed to age visibly; his skin turned to leather in the time it takes to tell; he shrivelled down into himself, becoming an old, old man. Nor was his torment finished, for as his limbs began a spastic twitching and his flopping trunk toppled from Yoppaloth's grasp—even as he commenced his journey into death—so something stirred into *life* in that terrible arena.

A green shimmer had sprung up about a certain massive stone idol, one of the many dozens whose carved figures paraded in a grotesque circle around the arena. It was the image of Yibb-Tstll the Soul-Stealer, whose stony surface suddenly took on a molten emerald appearance. Tarra already knew something of Yibb-Tstll—mainly what Yoppaloth had told him, that the demon god took souls and was one of the Old Ones—but now he fixed his eyes more firmly on the idol and observed for himself. This was the first time he'd seen an actual likeness of that Dark Deity; but as his eyes widened, so he learned why Yoppaloth had warned him that to know Yibb-Tstll was a most dubious privilege.

The statue was all of nine feet tall; of more or less manlike proportions, it had a head of sorts—a polished black node atop unevenly sloping stone shoulders—with a pair of eyes which were frozen in odd-seeming positions. One was more or less naturally placed, if a little high, but the other was down where the corner of a mouth might be found in a more normal piece of sculpture.

The sloping shoulders were cloaked, as was the body beneath; but the cloak, carved of the same basaltic stone as the god, was open in front to reveal many polished black breasts. This seemed an anomaly in itself, since the figure was supposedly male! Beneath the petrified folds of the cloak and half obscured, a cluster of night-gaunts clung tightly, almost lovingly, to the barely glimpsed body of the god. In sum, the idol was a nightmare—and much more so when suddenly it came to life!

That was Tarra's first thought, that Yibb-Tstll lived and moved in the arena of death, but then he saw he was mistaken. In fact what he saw was only a simulacrum or spirit of the Dark Deity himself, a "ghost," which now flowed *out* from the stone and separated itself from it, and, completely detached, moved like a green-glowing wraith toward Yoppaloth and the stricken, dying Northman.

As it went, so the thing took on something of solidity, until with the exception of its colour it was the twin of the statue which housed it—but one which left no tracks in the gore-spattered sand! Then, with its cloak billowing in a sickly slow-motion, it closed with Yoppaloth and their mutual victim and paused while the necromancer drew back. The spectators, crowded in the amphitheatre, had been silent, awed up to this point; now they roared their applause:

Yes! Let it be now! *Take* his soul and send him to hell, damned forever!

Greenly illumined, the monster-god stood over the Northman's shrivelled, twitching form. The god's feet, or whatever propelled him, were hidden beneath his billowing cloak; his eyes, glowing like balefires, were full of a hideous mobility; they *slid* over the surface of his head and face with a swift and apparently aimless motion, like the meandering of slugs but vastly accelerated. Then—

The demon-god reached out from beneath his billowing cloak three grey- and black-mottled things which might be arms, each terminating in a nest of seven grey worms which must serve as fingers. Two of these arms grasped the pitiful husk of the Northman and drew him upright like an empty sack; the third loathsome member spread itself wide, like some weird, seven-armed squid, and the tips of its digits entered eyes, ears, nostrils, mouth! Then they slid home to fill those orifices entirely, and the barbarian's face and head were enveloped in the slime-filmed web of that awful "hand."

Yibb-Tstll took nothing physical (there was little left to take), but what he *did* take made all of the preceding torture merely a prelude. He took the very soul! The Northman's shell collapsed entirely, and as the Dark Deity withdrew his slimed "fingers" from his head, so there sounded a shriek whose origin could only be hell—the hell of the barbarian's knowing that he'd be tormented for all eternity!

In the next moment the horror of the vacillating eyes let

what it held upright collapse, withdrew its ropy arms back inside the cloak, flowed back to its idol sanctuary and melted into the stone. The green glow remained, flickering over the basalt like liquid cancer . . .

And the "games" recommenced.

Again the defenders, only five of them now, found themselves under attack from their inhuman, hybrid, and corpse adversaries; and almost at once the young Hrossak Narqui Ghenz was taken. *"No!"* Tarra cried out, as a spiderlike monstrosity dragged Narqui screaming from the knot of survivors. Tarra's cry was lost in the renewed uproar of the crowd, and when he would start forward down the steps of an aisle he found his way blocked by their milling black bodies where they scrambled to seek better viewing positions. Ignoring him as he fought his way through their crush, they had eyes only for the scene in the arena.

The spider-thing had pierced Narqui's body with poisoned fangs; he stood, swaying, one hand to his bleeding wounds, mouth open half in shock, half paralysed by venom. And Yoppaloth bearing down on him, carrying a weapon as before. But this time he'd left the scimitar with the gem-studded hilt behind atop the onyx dais; the weapon he held was similar to a pike, but it was not a pike; Tarra Khash knew *exactly* what it was.

Reaching the low balcony wall which ringed the deep arena and contained the first tier of stone seats, Tarra was in time to witness Yoppaloth's thrust. Again he cried out: "No!" But too late. The slender head of that dreadful weapon drove home in Narqui's side. This time, however, Tarra's cry had been heard loud and clear, for the spectators had once more fallen silent. It was heard by all who watched, and also by Black Yoppaloth himself. All eyes turned to Tarra Khash. But his own fierce gaze burned only on the face of Yoppaloth.

Narqui Ghenz had fallen to his knees, his hands grasping the shaft of Yoppaloth's weapon where it pierced him. He turned his eyes pleadingly on his tormentor, but Yoppaloth was gazing up at Tarra Khash. "So," he said, "you've come. And didn't I warn you to stay away, Hrossak?"

As his words echoed in that unholy place, so swords shrilled as they flickered from scabbards, and a moment later guards came plunging from the rear of the amphitheatre, hurling Yhemni citizens aside where they blocked the aisles. The first of these overeager bullies reached Tarra, found himself kneed in the groin as the steppeman ducked under his arc of steel. A second later and Tarra had wrested the sword from him, used its hilt to club him unconscious. Child's play—but other guards were closing with him.

"*Stop!*" Yoppaloth commanded. And to Tarra: "Very well, Hrossak, since we both know why you're here—come, join us in the arena!"

Their eyes locked and Tarra knew he stared at a man bereft, a man bought and paid for in madness by the Old Ones! And yet he held the lunatic's gaze, until the necromancer found it a mighty effort of will to break the spell. And Tarra thought, *perhaps there's magick in me after all!*

But then Yoppaloth threw back his crimson-crested head and laughed, and he shouted: "Come on, what are you waiting for? What's another steppeman more or less?" And with that he twisted the metal hand grip of his terrible pike.

Tarra heard Narqui's shriek of unbearable agony and it was like a fire that burned him. Something snapped in his head and bled fury like acid into his brain. Yoppaloth laughed again and turned his back on the Hrossak where he reeled in horror and outrage on the high balcony; he withdrew his weapon from Narqui's body, grasped the mangled man's head and commenced to draw off his remaining strength; and Yibb-Tstll, too, once more came flowing from his idol to claim his tribute of a soul.

Up above the arena, someone tried to take Tarra's sword away from him. Almost without thinking, he butted the man in the face, jumped up onto the wall; and taking the sword in his teeth, he leaped down to the sandy floor. He landed, rolled, came upright with the sword in his hand. It was high time a Hrossak showed what he could do!

Meanwhile . . .

Amyr Arn had found and carefully released the catches which held the iron grille in place across the arched entrance to the arena; now, seeing Tarra leap down amongst the beast-creatures, he put his shoulder to the bars and shoved. The gate crashed down in the sand, and before the dust could settle Amyr had bounded into view.

The arena and amphitheatre were well lit by many dozens of flambeaux, but the light they cast, while ample, was ruddy and yellow, reflecting like molten gold from the silver sheen of Amyr's Suhm-yi skin. Naked except for a loin-cloth, he might well have been one of Yoppaloth's creatures, but the undisputed Lord of Shad and Shadarabar knew that he was not.

"What?" cried Yoppaloth where he'd returned to his dais. "And is Shad full of trespassers this night? Well, we'll not worry how this one got here; no, for it's a fact he'll not be leaving!"

Tarra had started after Yoppaloth, but a wall of hybrids and corpses had turned him aside, driving him toward the four original combatants. Not that he went unprotesting: a spider-thing with a man's face perished on the point of his sword, likewise a pair of corpses where he left them headless, twice-dead on the sand; but the rest of them were too many for him, and finally he joined the bloodied, weary knot of survivors. By then, too, he'd spotted Amyr Arn, and at first had been unable to accept the evidence of his own eyes. Then Amyr (a mentalist, and familiar with the Hrossak's mind) had sent:

Ask about it later, bronze one, if there's to be a later. Right now we've a fight on our hands! And he came weaving his way through the arena's many monstrosities, to join the beleaguered group in the centre.

Tarra had time only to give Amyr Loomar Nindiss' knife before the surrounding hybrids and tomb-spawn closed their ranks again. And then all was mayhem.

In the fighting, Tarra saw that Yibb-Tstll had taken Narqui's soul. He vowed revenge. He'd not rest until Yoppaloth and the monster-god who was his mentor and tormentor were stopped, or until he himself was dead—which at the moment looked like being his fate anyway. No way the six of them could hold out against odds such as these. Then:

"Wait!" cried Yoppaloth, and again the arena fell quiet as the vat-things drew back a little. From his dais, Yoppaloth called out: "The time draws nigh—my time, the world's time, the Hour of the Coming—and still the contest draws on. Events have been delayed. Ah, but I know a way to speed things up! Hrossak, do you remember how your pure heart quailed at the waterhole, when the Northmen would have taken my brides and used them? I couldn't allow it, you'll recall—for they weren't 'my' brides at all but Yibb's! Innocents, virgins in mind and body: such souls are the tenderest tidbits to one such as Yibb-Tstll."

He turned his bloated face up to the amphitheatre's crush. "Guards, now bring on the girls—and we'll witness how a heroic Hrossak reacts to that!"

At least Jezza's away, Tarra thought, though what good it would do her or her brother in the long run he couldn't say. But he saw the terrible logic of Yoppaloth's twisted mind: no way Tarra and his handful could hope to protect a bevy of helpless girls in this pit of monsters; all of their time was consumed in simply keeping themselves alive! On the other hand, Yoppaloth knew Tarra, and knew he'd be obliged to try.

The girls were quickly brought on stage, led from their "harem" quarters down into the bowels of the ziggurat and then deeper still, finally jostled into the arena through one of the barred, floor-level hatchways, and the grille fastened in place again behind them.

In the interim another Hrossak had been taken, nipped off at the knees by a lobsterish nightmare and dragged away screaming for Yibb and Yoppaloth's delight; and in that same interval of time the twirl of morbid green light rising into the arena from the throat of the polished glass pit had contracted and drawn down its whirling mushroom head through the chimney, so that the brightness of the twister had acquired something of density, spinning there like a great green top or inverted cone of near-solid matter.

And this was the same phenomenon which thus far had deterred Teh Atht from making a descent of the chimney aboard his flying carpet; for try as he might, he could only get so close to that twisting green flux of awesome energy before being shoved violently away. His white magick and the unimaginably dark magick of the Great Old Ones simply did not and would not mix! So that when Iniquiss and her brood had come on the scene and spied him across some small aerial distance, he'd still been aimlessly circling the emerald spiral of alien energy, vacillatory to the last as he pondered what to do next. At which time, obligingly, the twister's stalk had shortened, drawing its flat cap down out of sight.

But meanwhile . . .

In the arena and the amphitheatre which overlooked it: several entirely unscheduled occurrences, the first of which had devastating effect upon the Yhemni onlookers.

Now, in certain of Theem'hdra's steamy jungles and hot-house regions, in the walls of olden pyramids and crumbled ruins, there dwelled a species of yellow scorpion; likewise in the massy walls and floors of Black Yoppaloth's palace, where they'd bred mainly unsuspected for a thousand years. Shy of men and of daylight, this especially *virulent* scorpion was seldom observed, and when seen invariably avoided.

Picture then the hysteria which spread rapidly through the amphitheatre when thousands of these deadly stingers were discovered acrawl about the feet of the spectators; and not only in the amphitheatre, but also down in the pit of the arena itself, where the arachnids converged in streams upon Yoppaloth's monstrosities—but *not* upon the girls or the surviving men!

A second unforeseen event, one very likely connected with the first, was this: that the great greenstone statue of Ahorra Izz, which stood in the circle of gods close to where the virgins had been thrust into the arena, was now a-shimmer in much the same way as Yibb's with an eerie light—except that in the case of Ahorra Izz the glow was red. And where Yibb-Tstll came greedily flowing from his statue, cloak billowing and trio of tentacular arms reaching, now Ahorra Izz moved in that mechanical way of his species out from *his* likeness to block the way.

And so the two simulacra faced up to one another, neither one of them capable of harming the other, but nevertheless fixed in a weird stalemate; while behind Ahorra Izz, seeing how that arachnid intelligence protected them, the girls crowded in a close pack. All of them except one, who had gone to her knees in the sand as if in an attitude of prayer.

And this was the third event of moment, for indeed Orbiquita prayed—that she be granted the last of her three requests. "Iniquiss!" she cried. "Now hear me, if the distance between is not too great. This boon I beg of you is unheard of, I know, but still I most earnestly implore it. This one last time, for however brief a spell, give me back my lamia semblance and the lamia powers that went with it. For just a little while, pray let me be the creature I used to be!"

Following which she could only wait, to see what, if anything, transpired.

Amidst all the uproar—of Yhemni spectators where they leaped and careened, some of them even toppling into the arena after feeling the deadly stings of incensed scorpions; likewise of shrieking hybrids, by no means immune to those same stingers—hope welled up in Tarra's bronze breast. That special magick Teh Atht had told him about, *his* magick, was working for him at last. What?—and was there any other man in all the Primal Land could claim Ahorra Izz for a champion?

As the milling monstrosities in the arena fell back a little and tried to save themselves from their new, far smaller adversaries, so Tarra grasped his Suhm-yi friend's elbow and said: "Amyr, now take this sword and give me back that knife. I think the tide's turning our way. Now's my chance to come up against Yoppaloth."

"What, with only a knife?" Amyr was astonished. "And him able to strike like lightning, so swift the eyes can't follow?" He shook his head, kept on fighting. "I think not."

Tarra hadn't time for arguing. He threw down the Yhemni sword at Amyr's feet, said: "Use it or not, as you wish, but I've no need of it. My sword is on that dais, with Yoppaloth, and I've a feeling it's the one weapon in all the world that can save us."

Amyr stooped, picked up the sword, gave Tarra the knife. "I'm coming with you," he said.

"No." Tarra's answer was direct. "Stay here and help save these brave lads, if you can. They're just about all in. But what's between Yoppaloth and me requires only the two of us." And with that he was away, weaving through the beleaguered hybrids toward the onyx dais. A pair of corpses got in his way, which were fearful things to look upon but not much as fighters; he smashed them into many pieces and carried on.

And atop the huge onyx block which was Tarra's target, the first intimation of failure—or of victory?—had crossed Yoppaloth's unbalanced mind. Like a man in a dream he saw events coming to a head, and for once was powerless to stop them. In one small corner of his mind—a corner containing a last dim spark of sanity—Black Yoppaloth knew that his case was hopeless: even "winning" he would lose, for when the Old Ones came they'd have no use for him. But in the mad part of his brain, which was by far the greater part, still he thought he might hold them to their pact. Oh, he'd be a lonely immortal, for sure, in a world emptied of all earthly life; but at least he'd retain his soul. Wouldn't he?

He saw the steppeman coming at a run, saw some way behind the Hrossak a beautiful naked girl, also running, and behind her the flowing, green-glowing manifestation of Yibb-Tstll. If the monster-god couldn't get at the bulk of the girls where they sheltered behind Ahorra Izz, at least he could fasten upon this one who'd somehow become estranged from the group. But the fate of the girl was no concern of Yoppaloth's; her approach faded into insignificance compared with the approach of Tarra Khash, his face a mask of grim intent.

A pity it had come to this; there had been that about the Hrossak which appealed. Curious, but Yoppaloth had genuinely liked him! But . . . he *had* warned him not to come here. And in any case, what would be the loss of one perfectly ordinary man set against the destruction of a world full of men? Yoppaloth took up his hideous weapon, propped its handle against his sandalled right foot. And so he stood, like a guard at ease, calmly waiting for the steppeman to come to him. Which, obligingly, Tarra proceeded to do.

By now the diminished but brilliant tornado of green light flowing up from the pit's glassy throat seemed more solid than ever, striking emerald glints from Yoppaloth's black skin and lending its phosphorescent fire to his eyes. Also, a strange massed *sighing* had commenced, faint at first but rapidly increasing in volume; not the sound of human voices, no, but rather the rushing of the winds which blow in the lungs of the Earth itself, or those of the alien gods known to inhabit it.

"Almost time, Tarra Khash," said Yoppaloth as Tarra skirted the pit and skidded to a halt in the sand at the foot of the dais. "The time I've waited for and dreaded for almost a thousand years. You should have heeded my warning and stayed away; for you see, we're both in the same boat. To win we must lose! And yet—I knew you would come."

"Winning—losing—I only know you have to die!" Tarra answered. "And I only wish it wasn't so." He hurled his knife straight for the other's throat—and the necromancer stood stock still, not even attempting to move. The knife seemed to bend around him, a blur of steel which should never have missed its target, but which did by inches! And Yoppaloth laughed.

"Protected, Hrossak!" he cried. "Had you forgotten? Immortal, and protected by the magick of the Old Ones— especially now."

Tarra sprang up the steps of the dais and faced the madman only a pike's length away; and still Yoppaloth stood there, apparently unconcerned, even smiling his cold, cold smile. Cold, aye, and now Tarra could feel the bitter rime of nameless gulfs reaching up to him, working on his marrow. He had to bring this thing to a conclusion, and right now.

Yoppaloth saw his mental anguish, said: "Care to try again, steppeman? Perhaps with this?" He reached out a foot and kicked Tarra's scimitar unerringly to the other's feet. Instinctively, Tarra half-stooped for the sword, heard Yoppaloth's caution: "Except it's no game we're playing this time, Tarra Khash!" Then—

In a gleaming blur of motion, Yoppaloth hoisted his weapon, whirling it to point direct at Tarra's middle. Tarra saw the wicked knives and barbs of the thing, all lying flat and close to its pointed metal head. He knew what those terrible tools could do to his guts, grimaced at the thought— and continued the downward sweep of his arm toward familiar gem-studded hilt! But his apparently foolhardy move was a feint; not once did he take his eyes from his opponent; he saw Yoppaloth take a forward pace almost as if he moved in slow motion.

The pike came lancing at him but Tarra twisted his crouching body, grabbed the staff of his opponent's ugly weapon and turned it aside, grasped and lifted his scimitar. And the Suhm-yi sword seemed almost to come to life in his hand! Yoppaloth was within range, vulnerable as never before. So Tarra thought. He struck for the other's neck . . . and the blade of the scimitar shivered to a halt only a skin's thickness from the veins that pulsed there. It *vibrated* in Tarra's iron grip as he strove to force its razor edge into flesh—but the protections of the Old Ones were too strong, or he was too weak.

The sighing of alien spheres had risen to a howl that drowned everything else out, and the whorl of green light from the pit was so dense, so *cold*, that time itself seemed frozen atop the dais. For Tarra, anyway, if not for Yoppaloth. "Protected!" the madman shrieked. "Until the very last instant, protected! If you'd waited but a moment longer . . . but now, farewell!" And he drew back his pike and drove it point-blank at Tarra's middle.

Tarra closed his eyes, if only to deny Yoppaloth the sight of the horror written in them, and waited for the torment to begin. Already he could smell hell's brimstone breath, and—

. . . Brimstone? And that gasp of utter astonishment—Yoppaloth's? As a vicious squealing of torn metal ensued, Tarra opened his eyes—upon a fantastic scene!

A moment before: there had been the impression of a gorgeous girl standing close by, and of the nightmare god Yibb-Tstll closing on her with ropy arms extended. All seen on the periphery of Tarra's awareness, blurred and out of focus in the tension of traded blows. But now . . .

The girl was gone, disappeared, and in her place—

Lamia!

And Tarra knew *which* lamia she was. Twin scars on his neck itched furiously—even at a time like this—and a strange, fascinating pungency was in the air.

Orbiquita stood beside the dais, Yoppaloth's pike trapped in a hand like a nest of scythes. She stripped away the brightly gleaming blades and grapples, twisted the lethal head of the pike until metal screamed, then nipped it off and hurled it down on the sand—and Yoppaloth was left with only a pikestaff.

Now! came Suhm-yi mind-voice in Tarra's reeling head. *Now or never, bronze one! I feel it—whatever it is—mounting to a crescendo!*

Alone Tarra could never have struck that final blow, for his entire body ached with the cold of dark dimensions, which was freezing him solid through and through. But he was not alone. The Suhm-yi Sword of Power was with him. It sliced toward Yoppaloth's neck, sliced *into* it and cut three-quarters through!

Then Orbiquita snatched Tarra from the dais.

Behind her, wildly threshing, the simulacrum of Yibb-Tstll flowed this way and that. Cloak billowing with loathsome motion and eyes sliding in crazed orbits all about his head, his confusion was obviously boundless. He had pursued a girl and now perceived a lamia! No easy victim this, but upon the onyx dais—

Yibb-Tstll flowed swiftly toward the onyx steps. Yoppaloth would be his victim. And why not, since the so-called sorcerer had failed to keep his compact with the Old Ones?

Tarra Khash looked on, saw Yoppaloth's anguished eyes—
his sane eyes—gazing into his own. *Finish it,* those living
eyes begged him. *Don't let him have my soul!*

Yibb-Tstll was on the dais, leaning over Yoppaloth in the
veritable flood of green energy from the glassy pit. Tarra
ducked out of Orbiquita's protective grasp, aimed his stroke
true. And with that simple, merciful act the Gate Between
Spheres was closed; and in the next moment, several things
happening simultaneously, defying human senses with their
rapidity and shattering finality.

One: the ages caught up with Yoppaloth at once; as his
head leapt free, so he crumbled into smoulder, was blown
away in the blink of an eye. Not even bones remained, and
Yibb-Tstll groped namelessly in dust! Two: the singing of the
spheres went from a shriek to an equally deafening silence,
was quite simply shut off—likewise the sentient, shining,
pit-spawned twister—leaving Tarra and every other living
creature in the arena staggering. Three: Yibb-Tstll's simulacrum froze, literally turned to ice-cold stone atop the dais,
and the onyx sheen of his form became as one with the
massive slab of onyx where he stood. Four: Orbiquita took
Tarra into her arms again, except that now and for always
they were the arms of a beautiful girl. Five: the Hrossak's
bulging eyes took in at a sweep the area of the arena and
amphitheatre, and refused to accept what they saw. Lamias
flew like a flock of vile, gigantic birds, harrying the last of
the Yhemnis where they fled through the exits in a mad
rout; and in the central space, midway between sand and
vaulted ceiling, a carpet floated on air, where with his incredible retainers sat a small man in runic robes, holding out
a wand toward the dais and looking just as astonished as
Tarra Khash himself.

The wizard flew his carpet close to Tarra and Orbiquita, said: "I'm Teh Atht, and I'm old and tired. But it seems the world is safe again, Hrossak, and unless I'm mistaken we're alive, you and I."

"Am I?" said Tarra.

"We're all in your debt, steppeman," the wizard told him.

"Are you?" Tarra's eyes finally focused. "You owe me favours, do you?"

"Indeed we do!"

Tarra's knees finally gave way and he sat down in the sand. "Then do you think you could possibly explain what has happened here?" he said. "But before that—is there any chance you could first get us the hell out of this place?"

Epilogue

TARRA KHASH WAS not unmindful of his friends, even the fearsome ones. In Shad, later that night, after much had been explained and many tales told, he walked with Orbiquita through deserted streets (the Yhemnis would not come out of their jungles for long and long) and when they were alone under a clear, moonlit sky gave thanks to Gleeth for Amyr Arn's assistance. Likewise he praised Ahorra Izz for the part he and his minion scorpions had played in this thing; and finally he offered silent thanks to Iniquiss and the Sisterhood, who probably didn't hear him and wouldn't much care anyway, for they never had a lot to do with men—except when they were hungry.

He thanked Orbiquita, too, in a manner mutually agreeable, by means of which he discovered that his interest in women was not extinct after all, and she that her transition was going to be worth all its attendant trials. But that's not to be gone into here . . .

Now, as they made their way back to the encampment's fire, their arms wrapped about each other, meandering in their walk as lovers are wont to do, Tarra's mind unmazed itself a little and matters hastily discussed began to fall into place and make sense. "Curious Concretion!" he suddenly said.

"Your pardon?" Orbiquita's head was in the crook of his neck, her perfume in his nostrils. She, too, had been dreaming. "Did you say something?"

"Something your cousin, Teh Atht, said," Tarra answered. "About the end of it, back there in Yoppaloth's arena of death. In that final moment, when the Gateway was to have been forged through Yoppaloth—when I killed him before Yibb-Tstll could take his soul—the wizard put a certain spell of his, a thing called Curious Concretion, on the dais and on Yibb-Tstll's simulacrum. I'd seen it work before, this spell, but then it had been diluted by distance and other circumstances. In the arena, however, he gave it all he'd got, and he struck when I struck, which was *precisely* the right moment."

"The trouble with spells," said Orbiquita, who still retained a little lamia knowledge, though it was diminishing as she firmed more fully into her delicious human female form, "is that they eventually wear off."

Tarra shook his head. "Not this one," he said. "The Old Ones *would* have come into this world through Yoppaloth, except he was already dead. I *should* have taken his place, been obliged to complete the compact, except I was no longer on the dais. Result: Yibb-Tstll's simulacrum copped the lot. Curiously Concreted for all eternity, immortalized in onyx! Him and the dais both . . ."

They arrived back at the encampment in one of Shad's squares not far from the waterfront. Loomar Nindiss and Jezza were there, where the sole surviving Hrossak of Yoppaloth's mercenaries—a lean, handsome adventurer, much like Tarra himself—seemed to be paying the girl a deal of polite attention; also the last Northman, who just happened to be the one who'd lost his shirt that time, when Tarra had watched their gaming. Tek Mangr was his name, and he'd been busy (with the ages-accrued instinct of all Northmen) filling a sack with Yhemni loot; now he stood guard over spoils and encampment and virgin girls all. Then there was the towheaded youth, who also prowled to and fro around the campsite area with a great Yhemni sword in his hand; and also Amyr Arn, sitting silently on his own, doubtless dreaming of his Inner Isles and how he'd soon be home with Ulli Eys; and lastly Teh Atht. The wizard's familiars were also about somewhere, but he'd thought it best that they keep out of sight. In all, a pretty polyglot band.

Orbiquita spoke to Teh Atht: "Cousin, I've your promise that tomorrow you'll see these people safely back where they belong?"

Seated by the fire, he nodded. "It will keep me busy awhile; but after what all have been through—and the DOOM avoided—what's a little time? I can afford it, I think." And to Tarra: "Mind you, if I possessed that sword of yours, I'd likely end up with all the time in the world, eh?"

"What?" Tarra gave a snort of disbelief. "You know, for a wizard you're not too bright. Haven't you learned anything? The stars are immortal, maybe, and also space and time, which go inward and outward forever—but men come and go, they're born and they die, and that's the way it was meant. Would you live to see the mountains crumble, the oceans dry up, the sun itself expire? Not me."

Arm in arm, he and Orbiquita walked out of the firelight, made for the wharves. "Where are you off, Tarra?" the bearded Northman called after them.

"We'll find ourselves a boat for the night," Tarra answered.

"If we're still here in the morning we'll see you then. But if the wind's favourable and the water calm . . . good luck, anyway, to all of you."

In Tarra's mind, Amyr's fond farewell: *Long life, bronze one. Come visit me some day, in the jewel isles of the Suhm-yi.*

I will, Tarra promised, also silently.

"Hrossak!" Teh Atht had got to his feet. "About that sword . . ."

"Forget it," Tarra told him, and he touched the gem-studded hilt where it protruded over his shoulder, just to be sure it was still there. "The sword's mine. Men have died for it, and probably will again." Then the city's shadows took him and Orbiquita into their embrace.

"Then if you'll not give it to me," it was the wizard's last throw, "perhaps I could borrow it for a while?"

But the steppeman and his love had already walked into the night, and into the dawn of a new life. The Primal Land was waiting, and for all that the world was old, still it was very young, too. The last Teh Atht saw of the pair was their single dark outline merging with the greater darkness, and then they were gone.

And never a backward glance from Tarra Khash . . .